C000229000

THE DIVIDED WAY

SHEILA PILLEY

All rights reserved. No part of this publication
may be reproduced, converted or archived into
any other medium without a relevant permission
first being obtained from the publisher. Nor
should the book be circulated or resold in any
binding other than its original cover.

The Divided Way

© Sheila Pilley 2015

Cover design: © Tobi Carver, 2015

Printed & Published by:
The St Ives Printing & Publishing Company,
High Street, St Ives, Cornwall TR26 1RS, UK.

ISBN 978-0-948385-75-9

THE DIVIDED WAY

SHEILA PILLEY

St Ives Printing & Publishing

THE CHARACTERS

The historical characters and events in this book which covers the years under Henry VIII and his son, Edward VI, are authentic.

The households of Sir Geoffrey Trewarne at Trewarne Manor and his brother-in-law Robert Trenwith at Penvedn Manor are fictitious, as are some other minor characters.

TREWARNE MANOR

Sir Geoffrey Trewarne
Lady Margaret – his wife

Their children:
Bart, Rose, James and Amy

Kristy – a child of unknown origin

John Darnwell – tutor to the children

Servants at the Manor:
Digory and Jinty
Kate and Samuel
Hannah and Thomas
Agnes and Emmie
Alice and Hugh

PENVEDN MANOR

Robert Trenwith
Phillipa – his wife
Richard and other children

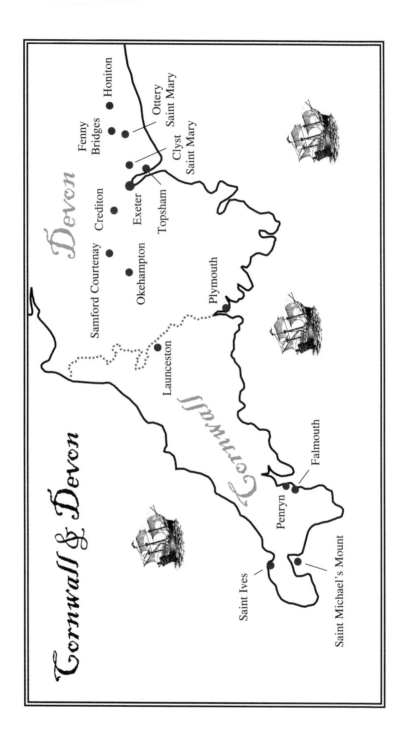

CHAPTER ONE

THE FOUR CHILDREN were hot, tired and still indignant at their sudden and unexpected ejection from the manor. They had been playing hide and seek, racing from the bright sunlight of the courtyard into the cool darkness of the great hall when their game had been suddenly interrupted by an agitated servant, pushing them from the hall into the kitchen.

"Out you go," Kate said firmly, thrusting a small loaf of bread into each hand, "and don't come back in until I call you."

"When will that be?" ten year old Bart tried to ask but a push from Kate sent him abruptly into the courtyard again where Richard, Rose and James were standing uncertainly.

"What have we done wrong?" asked James. Jinty, their old nurse who normally adored the children, hurried past them into the house but their ears only caught the end of her reply.

"Before it's time," repeated Richard in amazement, staring back at the door through which Jinty had vanished, "before it's time for what?"

Rose, a pretty, dark-haired sensitive child, was trying hard not to cry. To find she was suddenly in trouble for something she had no idea she or her brothers had done was disconcerting but she hated crying in front of boys, particularly when Richard, their cousin, was with them.

"I'm going to ask what we have done," said Bart, but he had hardly taken a step forward before Kate appeared again.

"GO AWAY!" she ordered firmly from the open doorway and this time the children fled. They ran through the courtyard, past the stables and climbed over the wall to the open ground beyond, Rose lifting her skirts as she tried awkwardly to keep up with the boys.

"Wait for me," she called and at last the boys stopped and waited for her to catch up with them. The ground beneath their feet was muddy from the previous night's rain but the strong wind which had howled over Cornwall for the past two days had now dropped and the sun was shining brightly in a clear blue sky. There was no one to stop them as they walked moodily through the woods which formed part of their father's large estate. Normally they would have been ecstatic at the opportunity to play and explore in such freedom but somehow in spite of the sunshine the morning had been spoilt and they had no idea why.

"Did you break anything?" Rose asked James. He was six years old and as the youngest in the family quite used to being blamed for anything that went wrong, but he shook his head and the others believed him.

"We were laughing and shouting quite a lot but nobody usually bothers about that," said Bart. "Father should be back from London today and generally that means that everyone is very cheerful."

"My father was in a bad mood when he rode back from Penryn last time," said Richard who was slightly older than his cousins and liked to appear more knowledgeable. "I heard him talking to Mother about the king wanting to be rid of the queen and then they noticed me and started to talk about something else."

"How can the king get rid of the queen?" asked Rose but the boys had already lost interest in that conversation and no one bothered to answer her.

* * *

They had been walking for some time and the older ones knew they had gone farther than they would normally have been allowed on their own but the humiliation of the morning had left them feeling defiant. Faintly in the distance they could hear the ringing of the church bell but neither Rose, Bart nor their cousin Richard intended to be the first one to suggest that they should go back. They could see the sun sparkling on the sea in the distance and they started to run through the bracken, jumping streams and climbing over large boulders as they drew nearer to the edge of the cliffs. Suddenly they could hear the sound of the breakers crashing against the rocks and see the spray hurling high up into the air.

"I don't think we should have come this far," said Rose nervously.

Bart instinctively caught James by his jerkin as he moved too near the edge of the cliff. Rose caught hold of the small boy's hand. The four children were beginning to forget the indignity of the morning and were captivated by the sight and sound of the sea below them, watching enthralled as great jagged rocks vanished underneath the water and emerged again, water cascading down them until they were immersed again by the next surge of the sea. A long expanse of golden sand stretched for what seemed to be miles and everything else was forgotten as they hurried along the cliff top looking for a way down.

James and Bart had been somewhere on that beach before with their father but Bart was unsure of their exact surroundings. Somewhere there had to be a path and soon Richard found it.

"I don't like it," said Rose nervously, looking down at the steep rocky path strewn with loose stones. Her long skirts were already thick with mud and torn in one place, she now realised with horror.

"I'm going," said Richard, starting to make his way down and Bart followed closely behind his cousin.

"I want to come," wailed James and the boys hesitated.

"I don't think he should," said Rose. She was beginning to panic at the sight of the treacherous looking path but James had already shot forward and was going down between the two boys.

"He'll be all right," Richard called up to her. He had been looking at the way ahead and it was easier and less frightening out of Rose's sight. "You stay there while we explore for a while."

Rose sat on a rock a short distance from the edge of the cliff while she waited for them, looking at the sea and the beautiful wild flowers which grew around her but she was too miserable to enjoy the beauty of her surroundings or the warmth of the sun. She wondered uneasily what would happen when they arrived home with their muddy clothes and ruined shoes. Richard, she knew, had caught his doublet on a bush and both Bart and James had holes in their hose. Whatever they had done that morning to upset everyone so suddenly would be nothing to the fuss their appearance would create when they returned.

*   *   *

"Rose! Rose!" came a frantic call from a long way below and the heart of the child was filled with terror as she heard Bart and Richard urgently calling her name. James must be hurt she was sure and in a dreadful panic she lifted her skirts and half fell, half scrambled down the rocky path, clinging to the side of the cliff and trying not to look at the terrifying drop below. In all her eight years Rose knew she had never felt so frightened and then suddenly she was on the firm sand, crying with relief. The three boys were all safe in front of her, but James was sobbing too and Richard and Bart were struggling hard to keep back the tears as James clung wildly to his brother.

"What is it, what's the matter?" asked Rose in terror and then she looked where Richard was pointing.

She thought at first the man was dead. He was sprawled on the sand, his waterlogged clothes half-torn from his body by the force of the sea and dried blood covering his hair and his head. His eyes were closed and something at his side suddenly moved and caused Rose to let out a frightened scream.

"It's a dog," sobbed James but the children were too terrified to go near the man and the dog was too weak to crawl to them. All four of them clung to each other as they looked at the man and the dog and then there was a faint sound which came from a bundle at the other side of the man which made them cling more frantically to each other, shaking with fear. The sound came again and this time Rose knew it was one she should recognise. The man slowly opened his eyes and saw the children. He struggled to speak and it was ten year old Bart, shaking and trying to control his sobs, who knelt down by the man.

"Jesu Christe – miserere nobis," came the half-whispered, half-choked voice and then his head fell back upon the sand and his hand fell from the bundle at his side. The dog whimpered, the baby gave another faint feeble cry and Rose was suddenly sick. When she recovered James was holding the dog, Bart had the baby and Richard was trying unsuccessfully to pull the man's body higher up the beach away from the incoming sea.

"Take the baby, Rose," said Bart when he saw she had recovered. Rose took the tiny sodden bundle from her brother's arms. Bart tried to help Richard to move the man but he was far too heavy for the two young boys and they had only moved him about a yard before there was a scream from Rose. All four children stared in horror at the sea which had been rapidly coming in until the sand between them and the pathway back up the cliff was covered in water and the waves were getting threateningly close to them.

"Leave the man," shouted Richard. "We'll have to run for it."

Bart snatched the baby from Rose who was struggling with her long skirts. Richard tried to take the dog but James clung on with all the strength he could muster.

"I want to carry him," he shouted and Richard struggled to pick up James and the dog as they waded through the water. It was almost up to Richard's waist and each wave threatened to knock him over but he struggled to the foot of the path and set James down, still clutching the whimpering dog, then turned to help the others. Bart was trying to hold the baby above the water which nearly reached his chest, almost losing his balance each time he was hit by the force of another wave. They were cold, wet, shaking with fright but at last they lay exhausted on the top of the cliff.

* * *

The children had no idea how many hours had passed since they had left home that morning. They hardly spoke as they stumbled back across the moorland. They had taken off some of their wet clothing which was dragging their tired bodies down and the sun was still hot enough to dry their shirts and Rose's petticoats. They had made an attempt to take the wet rags off the baby and wrap her in Richard's shirt which had stayed drier than the clothes of the other children because he was taller. They were fatigued and bedraggled but fear that the baby might also soon die urged them on until at last they were within sight of the manor house which they had left that morning.

They were spotted immediately by a worried Kate who had calmed down after her mistress had been safely delivered of another daughter and had spent the following hours happily tending the new arrival and vaguely worrying where the other children had gone. The sight of four filthy, very wet, half undressed figures staggering wearily across the courtyard towards her was too much on top of all the day's anxieties and Kate, who had been too busy to eat all day, collapsed in the doorway in a dead faint.

*   *   *

Sir Geoffrey Trewarne had travelled from London to Penryn by boat and had spent the previous night at an inn recovering from a very rough sea passage as he waited for the heavy rain to cease. It was at this moment that he rode into the courtyard of Trewarne Manor, accompanied by two of his men servants, to find his usually peaceful household plunged into chaos.

CHAPTER TWO

LADY MARGARET AND her new daughter were asleep. Rose and James, scrubbed in a tub by Jinty, were also in bed. The two older boys, clean and in dry clothes, stood nervously in front of Sir Geoffrey in the great hall.

A few hours previously his shock at the sight of the filthy exhausted children staggering into the courtyard had resulted in an explosion of anger directed first against his servants for their lack of care and then against the children themselves. At last Jinty, their old nurse, concerned for the cold shaking children, had hustled them away into the big warm kitchen and left Sir Geoffrey still storming at the other servants trembling before him.

It was Jinty too who waited for her master to finish his tirade before informing him that in the last few hours his household had increased by two babies and a dog. Sir Geoffrey had experienced a long difficult journey by road and sea from London but Jinty had no sympathy to waste.

"Don't ee tell m'lady nothin' now," she warned him as he prepared to visit his wife. "She don't want no more worries till she's feelin' stronger."

*   *   *

The visit to his wife as she lay in bed with their new daughter in her arms had helped to calm his fury and now as he listened to the stammered story of events from Bart and Richard, intermingled with sobs from Kate who was convinced that she had almost sent the children to their deaths, the last of his anger subsided to be replaced by an overwhelming relief that his family was safe. His first reaction had been to punish the children severely for going so far away but the sight of the white faces of the exhausted boys standing before him made him hesitate.

"Go to bed," he said eventually, not unkindly. "Remember to thank God in your prayers for your safe return. We will talk about the matter tomorrow."

It was no use searching immediately for the man the children had found on the beach. It was dark outside and the tide would probably have washed the body many miles away by now but he would send servants in the morning to search the coast.

*   *   *

As soon as daylight began to break a servant was despatched to fetch the priest from the parish church two miles away. Jinty had hovered anxiously between the two babies all night ready with a small dish of holy water to perform instant baptism if either of them looked in danger of death. She breathed a sigh of relief when she heard the clatter of horses' hooves in the courtyard and the priest dismounted and entered the manor.

In normal circumstances Sir Geoffrey's new daughter would have been taken to the church in the next day or two and held over the font for her baptism but the other child was struggling for survival and in the opinion of Kate and Jinty too sickly to move. They had no way of knowing whether she had already been baptised so after a hurried explanation to the priest Amy was baptised in her parents' bedroom and the other child in the warm kitchen where she lay in a rough cradle, made many years previously by Digory, Jinty's husband, for the birth of their only surviving son.

"What name shall I give her?" asked the priest. Kate and Jinty hesitated.

"Better ask the master," Kate suggested. Jinty scuttled off along the passage to the great hall.

"What name?" repeated Sir Geoffrey. "I have no idea."

"She's called Kristy, sir," said James, who had been awakened earlier by the sound of voices below and had come downstairs in his nightgown, followed by Rose.

"How do you know?" asked Rose. "We don't know what her name is."

"It's Kristy, I know it is. The man said so." James looked stubborn as Rose turned a shocked face towards her father.

"He didn't say so – he was nearly dead," she said in a trembling voice.

"Is Bart awake?" Sir Geoffrey asked Jinty.

Jinty hurried out of the room and a few moments later returned with Bart, still half-asleep.

"James says the man called the child Kristy," said his father. "Did you hear him say that?"

Bart looked puzzled.

"He didn't say what she was called, sir."

"He did, I heard him," cried James indignantly. "When you went over to him, I heard him say Kristy."

Bart, still hardly awake, looked baffled for a second before his face cleared.

"Christe, he said – *Jesu Christe miserere nobis* – and then he died."

There was silence in the room for a moment and then Sir Geoffrey spoke.

"We could call her Kristy until we find out who she really is."

"That's not fair." Rose was feeling rebellious and turned indignantly to face her father. "James has chosen the dog's name. He can't choose the baby's name as well."

"Oh, and what is the dog called?" asked Sir Geoffrey.

"Storm," answered his younger son firmly. "Because he was washed up after a storm."

"That's good enough," agreed Sir Geoffrey. "Now, Rose, what do you think the baby should be called? I suppose if you all found her you should be allowed to suggest a name."

Rose hesitated. Secretly she too had thought at first that the man had been saying the child's name before she realised it was a dying prayer, but James should not be allowed to have things all his own way just because he was the youngest – or had been until yesterday. A sudden slight feeling of elation passed through her as she realised that now someone else had arrived to take James' place and no longer would he be spoiled by adoring servants who could not resist his blond curls and angelic face. She could afford to be magnanimous.

"Christine," she announced at last, and all of them, including Sir Geoffrey, went back to the warm kitchen where the priest was talking to Kate. Only Richard of the child's rescuers was missing, having gone with Digory and some of the other servants in a vain search for the man's body or wreckage from his boat.

* * *

"You will stay for some refreshment?" Sir Geoffrey invited the priest when they had returned to the great hall. Mister Vincent shook his head.

"Thank you, but I have to offer Holy Mass shortly and I have a long walk back."

"No need to walk – you are welcome to keep the mare which I sent for you."

"I appreciate your offer which I shall gladly accept," answered the priest. "My own horse died a month ago and funds to replace him are low at the moment. It is difficult to cover the parish on foot – a particular problem when someone is dying."

"You should have asked one of my men to find you a horse."

"I would not presume while you were away," Mister Vincent chuckled. "I prayed instead none of my parishioners would need my presence urgently or in bad weather and God must have heard me. The summer was good until the storm two nights ago when that poor man must have been wrecked. From what I hear your children had a miraculous escape. You might so easily have lost them all."

"We were extremely fortunate. I feel uncertain now in view of the outcome as to how I should punish them for straying so far."

"Had you ever forbidden them to do so?"

"The situation had never before arisen. My own land is extensive. They must have walked at least another four miles beyond it to reach the coast. They have never been so far unaccompanied before."

"Then you can hardly punish them for something they have never been told not to do," reasoned the priest. "Had they not acted as they did the child would have drowned as well as the man and probably nothing would ever have been known of the tragedy. Do you think there were others with him?"

Sir Geoffrey shrugged his shoulders.

"I have no idea. I sent Digory with six of my tenants to search this morning as soon as it was light. My nephew, Richard, went with them to show them where they found the body."

Mister Vincent rose and the two men walked out into the sunny courtyard.

"I will ride back with you and attend Holy Mass," decided Sir Geoffrey suddenly. "I have a great deal for which to thank the Almighty. Samuel! My horse and the brown mare for Mister Vincent."

Mister Vincent stroked the neck of the beautiful horse which Samuel brought as it nuzzled its nose against him.

"She's a fine animal, Geoffrey. Thank you again for your kind gift."

"You need not come, Samuel," Sir Geoffrey addressed his servant who was holding the reins of both horses and looking enquiringly at his master. "You have plenty to do here with most of the other men out searching. I shall only be gone for an hour or two."

Samuel nodded, dropping the reins, and both men led their horses round the courtyard to the front of the manor.

"You have a beautiful home, Geoffrey," remarked the priest.

"It's almost finished now. It's eighteen years since my father first started it, God have mercy on his soul, but it has been worth the time and the money."

The two men sat on their horses looking at the grey stone manor house. The glass of the latticed windows reflected the early morning sun. The heavy oak door around which a pink creeper twined was set in the middle, mullioned bay windows either side and tall chimneys reaching to the sky.

"I shall add another wing on each side of the forecourt when I have the time and money but first, with your approval, I would like to add a private chapel. One where my own family and workers can worship God without getting soaking wet as they are walking to church every time it rains!" Sir Geoffrey laughed then added more seriously. "One in which I can thank God for all He has done for my family and for me – give thanks for my wife and for my children and where prayers may be said for our souls when we die."

Mister Vincent looked at him, wondering if the sudden seriousness in his companion's voice was an indication of any anxiety but Sir Geoffrey spurred his horse forward.

17

"Until then I must continue to come to the parish church. Beautiful as it is, I shall enjoy building one of my own."

* * *

Lady Margaret was not told of the children's adventures for several days and then only a mild version was reported to her in order not to worry her whilst recovering from childbirth. She had not known that they were missing and as they were only allowed in to see her and their new sister for very short visits at first it was not difficult to keep the story from her. She was puzzled at times however by the distant sound of a baby crying which did not come from the wooden cradle in the far corner of the bedroom.

"It's your imagination, my lady," said Jinty firmly when Lady Margaret first stirred on her pillows at the faint cry.

Jinty had been with her mistress since Lady Margaret's first baby was born, a son who had lived only two weeks. She had stayed with Sir Geoffrey and Lady Margaret from that time, helping to bring into the world Bart, Rose, James and another child who had survived only one hour. Now another new baby had arrived, six weeks earlier than expected but strong and healthy. Sir Geoffrey had given orders that his wife was not to be worried by the events of the previous week and now Lady Margaret was resting happily in the four-poster bed, delighted with her new daughter and thankful for the safe return of her husband from London.

She turned her head, smiling at Sir Geoffrey as he entered the room. He looked down at the sleeping baby for a moment then crossed over to the bed, taking his wife's hand as he sat down. Lady Margaret thought how much Bart and Rose with their dark curly hair and grey eyes were like their father.

"Tell me about London," she said after he had kissed her. "You have not told me anything of what is going on at court yet."

"I have hardly been given the opportunity! I arrived home after a dreadful journey expecting comfort and sympathy and found my household in total disorder with no one the slightest bit interested in me. That young lady in the cradle brought chaos with her early arrival."

"Tell me now," insisted Lady Margaret. "Are the king and queen well?"

A worried expression flickered momentarily in her young husband's eyes which was gone immediately but his wife had not missed it.

"Is something wrong?" she asked.

Sir Geoffrey tried to shrug off the brief moment of unease.

"It's just a passing whim of the king. He wants to divorce Queen Catherine because she has not given him an heir. Naturally the Pope will not allow it."

"I should think not." Lady Margaret was indignant. "The poor woman has given him six – or is it seven – children. Is it her fault that all but one girl died?"

"No, but the king is blaming God. He says it is God's judgement upon him for marrying his dead brother's wife and he will never have a live son and heir until he repents and gets rid of Catherine."

"Gets rid of her – and then what?"

"He has someone else in mind – a lady called Anne Boleyn. He wants the Church to annul his first marriage on the grounds that it was sinful for him to marry his sister-in-law even though her husband was dead."

"But he had a special dispensation to marry her!"

"So he did but now he wants to marry someone else. Don't worry about it, my dear. It will never happen. The king will have his way with Mistress Anne as he has done with many others and she will soon be forgotten."

He rose, his tall strong frame momentarily blocking the light entering through the window as he paused to stroke his wife's long fair hair.

"Rest well, my love. We need you to cope with problems here, not London. I have promised the children they can come in to see you for longer tomorrow. I think they have something to show you."

"I have seen the dog," answered Lady Margaret. "James told me he found him in a very bedraggled state."

"I should think that was right," agreed Sir Geoffrey gravely, though a faint smile flickered across his pleasant face. His initial shock and anger on his arrival home had gradually changed to pride in his children. His wife was now recovering well. He had a beautiful new daughter. Tomorrow he felt he could allow the children to show their mother the other new addition to their home.

*　　*　　*

"She's called Kristy," said James, climbing on to his mother's bed, struggling to hold Storm.

"Christine," corrected Rose firmly.

Behind them all stood Sir Geoffrey. Kate was holding the unknown baby in her arms and Richard and Bart were standing on the other side of the bed as they all watched Lady Margaret's face and waited anxiously for her reaction.

"Off the bed with that dog," thundered Sir Geoffrey and James hurriedly fell off, accidentally letting go of Storm as he did so. Bart caught the dog as he raced across the room. Lady Margaret was speechless and the children's faces were apprehensive as they waited for her to speak.

"We couldn't keep her a secret any longer," explained Bart. "Richard has to go home tomorrow and we thought it was only fair that he should be here when we showed her to you. After all, he did find the path down to the beach where we found the baby."

"And where we nearly all drowned," added James but luckily Storm chose that moment to protest at Bart's firm hold and barked rapidly, so that Lady Margaret did not hear. She held her arms out to Kate for the baby and turned back the blanket in which the child was wrapped. Large dark eyes framed with long lashes looked up at her from a solemn face and a tiny hand gripped her finger.

"Poor little soul," murmured Lady Margaret gently. The baby stared at her for a moment then moved her eyes round the faces crowding around the bed.

"How old do you think she is?" asked Rose eagerly. "Kate says she is older than Amy."

Lady Margaret looked closely at the child whilst Jinty, not to be left out, picked up Amy from her cradle and laid her on the bed and the two babies lay side by side.

"She's about three months old I would say, my lady," volunteered Kate. "She's a lot bigger than Mistress Amy but then, she came earlier that she should have done."

"I think you are right, Kate," agreed Lady Margaret. She looked appealingly at her husband. "Have you no idea who she is?"

Sir Geoffrey shook his head. He had caused enquiries to be made around the coast but no one had any information and no one had been reported missing. Three fishermen from St Ives had spoken of seeing wreckage of what could have been a small boat but had been unable to secure any of it without danger to their own lives.

"They might have been from anywhere – Wales, Ireland, France, Brittany. I doubt if we shall ever know. Possibly gypsies or someone hoping to escape from trouble in a small boat. They might have succeeded had it not been for the storm."

"Father says Kate and Samuel can look after her and he will give them some land and a little cottage across the courtyard," Rose said eagerly. "We shall be able to play with her and watch her grow up."

"Why can she not live in the house with us and be part of our family?" asked Bart.

"Because I have a family to support already," answered Sir Geoffrey firmly. "She will be well looked after with Kate and Samuel."

"Jinty and Digory can be her grandparents," agreed Lady Margaret soothingly. "Samuel is their son, don't forget." She wrapped the baby gently and gave her back to Kate who was beaming.

"Samuel don't know yet, but he will be right pleased," she told them all.

"Not know yet! But I thought it was all arranged!" exclaimed Sir Geoffrey.

"Oh, no, sir. He's in for a real surprise. But he'll be pleased once he's got over the shock – won't he, Mother?"

Jinty nodded vigorously in agreement. She had waited a long time for her only son and his wife to produce a baby. Now one had arrived in the family neither Samuel nor Digory would be allowed to raise any objections, no matter how loudly they tried.

CHAPTER THREE

AS IT HAPPENED both Samuel and Digory were too preoccupied with their own thoughts to raise any objections to the baby, even had they dared to protest against Sir Geoffrey's plans. Digory in particular had experienced a nasty moment when summoned to the great hall and told to listen while the boys described the route they had taken and where they had found the path to the cove. Sir Geoffrey planned to accompany the search party but Digory, loyal and hard working in many ways, had his own reasons for not wanting his master to explore too closely that particular stretch of the coastline. It was bad enough that the children now knew about it but with any luck the fright they had received there and the difficulty of the path would keep them away should they ever have the opportunity to roam again.

Digory railed indignantly at his wife and daughter-in-law for their stupidity, heaping blame upon their heads and loudly accusing them of neglect for the danger in which they had placed the children's lives by their lack of care, but both Digory and his slow but willing son knew really it was panic at the thought of the cove and its access being discovered which had upset him.

"Stupid ol' woman," Digory continued to berate Jinty. "Wher'ud we be if they childern 'ad drowned an' you lef' in charge o' they? 'Anged for murder, I dessay, murder by neglec', or at leas' lef' to rot in pris'n."

"Don't talk like that, Father," Kate beseeched him." Mother'n me had a big enough fright without you goin' on and on about it."

"'Twern't our fault that baby came early," added Jinty, glaring back at her husband, "an' on market day too wi' all they other women away at St Ives. An' who told the menfolk to clear the ground on the other side of the manor that day? If they 'ad bin workin' on the land in the other d'rekshun they would've seen the childern so don' ee be so quick to put all the blame on other people."

Digory grunted and stumped angrily out of the cottage, looking for Samuel. He found him in a corner of the stable scratching his head and looking down at a cask he had just uncovered under a load of hay.

"Cover it up, yer fool," hissed Digory. Samuel threw the straw back again just as Sir Geoffrey walked round the corner calling his servants to bring out his horse.

"Not working, Digory?" questioned Sir Geoffrey.

"Jus' checkin' the 'orses, sir," answered Digory, not batting an eyelid under his master's steady gaze. "Thought my nag was limpin' a bit yesserday but she must've recovered."

Sir Geoffrey nodded briefly and rode out of the yard. He had not inspected his estate since he had ridden to Penryn to catch a boat to London two months earlier. It was time to see what had been achieved in his absence. He swung his horse first to head for the fertile side of his land to see how his workers and tenants were progressing with their crops. It had been a good summer and even allowing for any damage the storm might have caused there should still be a good harvest that year to provide for their families and to bring a good revenue into the estate.

His land stretched as far as he could see in all directions, good rich soil in the valleys where his father had cleared and enclosed the land, pushing back the thick wild undergrowth and using the great boulders as hedges. The timber from the felled trees had been used to build the inside of the granite manor house and to make the large four-poster bed and long table with its benches where Sir Geoffrey, his family and servants sat to eat their meals. His father had been a rich man, well rewarded by Henry VII for his part in the many campaigns against the French. He had died in the same year as the old king, 1509, both men leaving sons of eighteen to enter into their respective inheritance. Almost twenty years later Trewarne Manor and its dependants flourished under a kind and generous landlord while the country sat uneasily under a powerful and increasingly tyrannical monarch.

The crops were good, his workers removed their hats respectfully as he stopped to speak to them and the grumbles he heard were ones with which he could deal without too much trouble. One of his tenants had diverted a stream for the convenience of his own family and to the detriment of others. A sharp word from Sir Geoffrey was needed before he would alter the water back to its original course. A cow had knocked over a wall carefully built by the young son of a widow and the truculent owner refused to make good the damage until ordered by his master. Two men were accused of not paying their full share of the tithe, but these were the usual problems and the same ones which would occur again and again. A straying husband had been beaten over the head and his mistress scratched and clawed by his wife but the warring parties seemed to be living in an uneasy peace now and intervention might only provoke the situation. All seemed well with his tenants and workers on this part of his land and eventually Sir Geoffrey turned his horse to the more desolate gorse-covered moors.

The wealth of his estate lay in the beautiful valley with its gently rolling hills and grassland, but Sir Geoffrey loved the wildness on top of the moors with the distant views of the sea. On clear days such as this he could see the church and castle of St Michael's Mount and the ships trading in the bay. King Henry in London was enthusiastically building up his navy and soon more boats would be seen on the horizon, laden with goods for the new trade routes. The wood from the forests in many parts of Cornwall had been taken to build the new ships. Sir Geoffrey's own brother-in-law, the father of Richard, was away at sea now in command of one of the larger new boats in the English fleet.

* * *

His horse had been carefully picking his way across the rock strewn moor, following a path trodden for hundreds of years by the inhabitants of the western tip of the country as they carried their goods by the shortest route to the market at Marazion. For some miles there had been no one else in sight and now Sir Geoffrey guided his horse off the path and down the side of the hill. At last several small stone huts were in front of him and a group of ragged children ran towards him. They looked rougher and poorer than the children of his tenants farming in the valley but their dirty faces were laughing up at him and, though thin, they did not look starved. The few sheep he had passed on the moors belonged to these families, and hens and thin pigs were scratching around near the huts.

Half a dozen dirty and ill-clad men and women came over to greet him as he dismounted, the women curtseying and the men removing their hats.

"Good day to you all," called Sir Geoffrey. "Have you had any luck with the tin since my last visit?"

"A little, sir." One of the men gestured towards the fast running stream and Sir Geoffrey walked over to it, followed by the tinners and their families. "We've worked this p'ticular place 'afore but we thought as 'ow we'd try agen after the storm."

The others crouched down again to their work, anxious to make the most of the daylight while the men were talking. They were scooping out the bottom and side of the stream with bits of wood and inspecting each shovelful carefully, washing it in the running water until they were left with the particles of tin for which they were searching. Larger stones were turned over until discarded and the make-shift shovel dipped into the stream again.

"We'd like to try a bit further'n 'afore, sir," said the man, John Daniels. "We bin examinin' the ground further over the moor and we think as 'ow it may be worth workin' with your permission."

"You may try," agreed Sir Geoffrey, "but take care you do not go beyond the edge of my land. Sir William will not appreciate it if you do."

"Godolphin land 'as got far more tin than we're likely to find, sir. 'Tis rich pickin' there but only a bare livin' for us. Still, we'll get by wi' the grace of God."

"What about your children?" asked Sir Geoffrey. "They should be going to school. Can any of them read and write yet?"

"Now why'd they want to read and write, yer lordship?" asked the man in amazement. "What good'll that do they up 'ere on the moor?"

"It would give them a chance to get off the moor one day if they wished to do so. The tin will not support you for ever, you know."

"We'll tek our chance, sir, and trust in God and Our Blessed Lady. The childern are useful 'ere breakin' the ore and 'elpin' the womenfolk wi' the animals. No sense in wastin' time on learnin' things they don't need. They can all say their prayers and that is all they need to know."

Sir Geoffrey hesitated. He hated to see these families living in such poor conditions up on the moors which could be so bleak and desolate in winter but the tinners had persistently refused his offers of land to try farming and preferred to stake their claim to the moor with him each year, trusting to God to produce the tin with their help. There was nothing else he could do for them if they would not move to the good land in the valley below.

It was time to ride home to the manor for a meal and prayers with his household. Tomorrow Richard had to return home and there was business to which he must attend in Truro. An early start must be made and he would spend the following two nights at Penvedn Manor, Richard's home, which was near enough to Truro to provide a convenient place to stay whilst on business. Digory would accompany them. His slower nag would make the journey take a little longer but it was safer than Sir Geoffrey riding back unaccompanied. It was a pity Richard's father was away at sea but Sir Geoffrey would be pleased to see his only sister once again.

* * *

Richard was reluctant to say goodbye to his aunt and cousins at Trewarne Manor after such an eventful holiday but now it was over and he would soon return to his education. There were two grammar schools in Penryn and Robert and Phillipa Trenwith had chosen the one in the parish of St Gluvias for their son's education. They were pleased with the excellent progress Richard was making there. He was fluent in both Latin and Greek, but greatly preferred speaking in Cornish which everyone spoke and understood, rather than the other languages which it seemed to him only the canons spoke unless it was the Latin of the Holy Mass. He liked the music and the other lessons when he and the other pupils sat round the room listening to the masters, most of them in holy orders, and discussing their lessons. Occasionally they would be allowed to handle some of the precious books but they were too expensive for each pupil to have his own copy, and sometimes he was distracted by a more interesting topic being discussed by the group next to him in the schoolroom.

His cousins at Trewarne attended the school in the parish church but bad weather often prevented them from journeying there and Sir Geoffrey intended to make enquiries in Truro for a possible tutor who would reside at the manor. Bart was nearly old enough to attend grammar school but Rose and James would do better with a tutor at home. It was midday when they rode up to the front of Penvedn and Sir Geoffrey and Richard dismounted as a servant came for their horses and led the tired animals, followed by Digory, to the stables.

Phillipa Trenwith ran to the door at their approach and hugged Richard and her brother, lifting up her three younger children for their noisy greeting too.

"You must be hungry," she said when at last the kissing and hugging had ceased. "We waited for dinner for you. Come and sit down and tell me the news while we eat."

The table in the hall was already prepared. Sir Geoffrey said grace and the travellers tucked in hungrily to the steaming meat pie and gravy and the vegetables brought in to them in wooden dishes. The family sat at one end of the long table, talking and listening in turn, fascinated by Richard's account of the finding of Kristy and delighted to hear of Amy's arrival. There was little news of Robert Trenwith but Phillipa was used to her husband's absence and looked forward to his visits home.

The noise and laughter from the lower end of the table was growing louder and Sir Geoffrey banged on the table with his tankard for Digory's attention.

"No more of the ale, man," he ordered. "He can drink more than anyone else I know," he added to Phillipa. "He will be singing to us all very soon if we do not stop him and then sleep for the rest of the afternoon when he is needed. I often wonder why I keep the man."

"Why do you?" asked Phillipa.

"Because he came with Jinty, I suppose, and she has been a good servant to Margaret. He's not a bad man really – he works quite well when he is sober!"

The servants removed the remains of the meal and brought in jellies and fruit which they placed on the table.

"Do you like our pewter dishes?" Phillipa asked her brother. "Robert brought them with him on his last visit home. He hopes to bring plates back with him next time."

"They are very attractive. I have seen them in London but as yet we have none ourselves. I may take some back for Margaret if I find any in Truro. You have a good cook, Phillipa."

"He does very well. Robert brings many dried fruits and spices home after each voyage so we probably have tastier meals than most."

The bowls of water and napkins were passed along. Sir Geoffrey dipped his fingers and wiped his dagger carefully before replacing it back in his belt.

"An excellent meal. Now if you will excuse me, my dear, I have to attend to various matters of business so I must take my leave. I shall be back later this evening to spend the night."

Digory jumped up when he saw his master rise and made a slightly unsteady exit to fetch the horses. Phillipa and her children watched until the two men rode out of sight, then returned to the house where Richard was made to recount his adventures all over again.

* * *

"Bring Edward to Cornwall! But why?"

"For his own safety, Geoffrey. The king is fast losing patience with the clergy and your wife's brother has been particularly outspoken against the divorce."

Sir Geoffrey stared in astonishment at Sir William Godolphin. He could hardly believe what the other man was saying and yet as Sheriff of Cornwall Sir William knew far more of events in London than anyone else.

"The king would never imprison anyone simply for disagreeing with him!"

"I fear you are too naive, Geoffrey. Henry has gone too far now to allow anyone including the clergy to stand in his way."

"He would not come. Edward has been a priest in London for years. He is a good man and does much for his parish and the poor."

"He can do as much as he likes for his parish and the poor but if he persists in speaking against the king's divorce he will find himself in great trouble. Queen Catherine has most of England on her side but few men dare to provoke King Henry. My information is that he is proposing to make radical reforms of the Church and of the clergy."

"Reforms? What sort of reforms?"

Sir William shrugged.

"I have not heard the details. Unfortunately there are enough bad clerics neglecting their duties to give the king an excuse for any changes he plans and it may be hard to stop him."

"But there is always a bad element in every branch of society, even the Church," argued Sir Geoffrey. "The majority of hard working clergy devote their lives to God and their flock. They cannot be held responsible for the others."

"Not in normal times perhaps but we are not living in normal times. The king needs to divorce the queen to marry Mistress Boleyn and the Church opposes him, therefore the king must somehow bring pressure upon Rome."

"But all England is Catholic! Most of Europe! Spain is a Catholic country. She will never allow a Spanish princess to be cast off by King Henry after all these years. Spain will declare war."

"That seems to be a chance the king is willing to take. He is obsessed with the need for a male heir and the queen has only given him the Princess Mary."

"The need for an heir or the need for Mistress Anne?"

The two men faced each other across the room, their expressions serious. Sir William spoke quietly.

"I should not have had this conversation with you, Geoffrey, but you and Margaret are my friends. Try to get your brother-in-law down here to Cornwall. He may be safe here until the trouble is over. Most Englishmen know little of what is going on across the Tamar even if they know we exist."

Sir Geoffrey was silent for a moment, thinking of the news he had heard from Phillipa a few hours ago and which at the time had not seemed too important.

"They may soon know more of Cornwall," he told the other man. "John Tregonnell from Crantock has been chosen as one of the proctors in the royal divorce."

"So I have heard but he will be only one of many." Sir William filled their glasses as the two men sat thoughtfully for a moment. "You were enquiring about a tutor, Geoffrey. I may have just the man for you if you are still in need of one."

"Yes, I am. Bart will go to grammar school soon but Rose and James would do better with a tutor of their own. Who have you in mind?"

"A distant relative of my wife. A pleasant young man, well educated but with very little money and in need of an income and a roof over his head. I could send him to you at the manor if you wish."

"Yes, indeed. His name?"

"John Darnwell. His family were from Norfolk but he has lived in Cornwall for many years and speaks Cornish well. When do you return to Trewarne?"

"On Saturday. Where is he now?"

"Staying with us at Godolphin."

"I will see him on Monday. Ask him to ride over in the morning. If he seems suitable he can stay and have dinner with us."

"You will like him," promised Sir William. "Now I am afraid I must leave. You will be at the next session of the court?"

"God willing," answered Sir Geoffrey. "I expect we shall have a full list of offences as usual. I hear there is a lot of unrest at Bodmin between the townspeople and the monastery. There is talk about a petition to the king if a satisfactory solution is not found."

"There is always trouble at Bodmin. At least it will not be our business to sort out that particular problem."

The two men left the room and walked down the stairs into the bright sunlight of the late afternoon. Their servants had been patiently waiting and leaped up to fetch the horses. Along the street a small crowd of beggars waited outside the Dominican friary for the distribution of bread and meat on which they knew they could rely at that time of day, most of them dirty and ill-clad but some pilgrims amongst them on their long journey to the abbey on The Mount. A few of them stared sullenly at Sir Geoffrey and Sir William in their richly coloured doublets and breeches and their velvet caps.

"I shall expect your nephew on Monday then," said Sir Geoffrey as their horses wended their way along the street. Sir William nodded and the two men reined for a moment to exchange final pleasantries before spurring their horses forward in different directions, followed closely by their respective servants.

* * *

It was time for the evening meal when Sir Geoffrey arrived back at his sister's home, following which the whole household assembled for prayers. It was still daylight outside and Phillipa was anxious to show her brother around the beautiful walled flower garden which she enjoyed tending herself, leaving her servants to grow the vegetables and herbs needed for the kitchen. A good number of the unusual plants in the garden of Trewarne Manor had been passed on by Phillipa whose husband always brought home new plants from his voyages for his wife's pleasure. The generally warm, mild climate of west Cornwall encouraged the plants to flourish and it was always a delight to walk in the garden at Penvedn.

"There are compensations for being a sailor's wife," smiled Sir Geoffrey, examining one of Phillipa's latest acquisitions.

"It is just as well. It can be a lonely life with a husband away sometimes for a year or more. Margaret is lucky that you travel no further than London."

"I may not do that for much longer. My estate and responsibilities in the county take up more and more of my time. It becomes increasingly difficult to be away for a month or more in London several times a year. I seriously think of ridding myself of my business interests there and concentrating on my land here."

"Would you not miss London life?"

"No, definitely not. I would gladly forego the noise and dirt of London streets for the fresh air of Cornwall. If I sold my property in London I could afford to build a chapel at Trewarne and add another wing to the manor."

They returned slowly to the house, spending the evening pleasantly in a game of cards until it was time to retire. The children were asleep and they shared a candle until they reached Phillipa's four-poster bed. Sir Geoffrey lit her bedside candle and bade his sister goodnight before continuing along the cold passage to the guest room at the end where he undressed and lay in bed, the events of the day churning over in his head until at last he fell into a sound sleep.

* * *

The following morning dawned bright and clear again. Sir Geoffrey spent most of the day dealing with his affairs in Truro and visiting old acquaintances. He found a craftsman beating pewter and purchased dishes for his table at Trewarne and a beautiful vase in Venetian glass. He had been measured for leather boots on his last visit and they were ready for him, as also were shoes for Bart and a dress ordered by Lady Margaret. He bought a silver necklace as a gift for his wife in gratitude for his new daughter and for Rose and James he bought wooden toys.

On Saturday when they were ready to depart Phillipa added two bales of silk and some plants for her sister-in-law and a good supply of spices for the kitchen at Trewarne. Digory grumbled under his breath as the horses became more and more laden but a look from Sir Geoffrey silenced him though he continued muttering to himself on the journey home.

Several times on the way they passed pilgrims walking barefoot and a Franciscan friar in a brown robe with a white cord, his head shaven in the tonsure, was standing by a wayside cross, preaching to a large group of people. Sir Geoffrey reined in his horse to listen and Digory stopped reluctantly behind his master. A sermon on occasional Sundays was quite enough for Digory. For the life of him he could not understand folks who wanted to listen to a preacher more often.

"You spoke well," Sir Geoffrey addressed the young friar when at last the crowd dispersed. "Are you from these parts?"

"From Exeter, sir, but lately from Truro."

"You have walked from Exeter?"

The young man laughed and shrugged his shoulders.

"'Tis but a short journey in God's service and in such beautiful countryside, sir."

"You are welcome to a meal and a bed tonight," offered Sir Geoffrey but the young friar shook his head.

"Thank you, but I have already been offered food and a bed by some of the poor people who were listening to me a short while ago and I have accepted. May God send His blessing upon you, sir, and your family."

Sir Geoffrey bowed his head in acknowledgement and rode on. They travelled several miles, the stillness of the afternoon broken only by the sound of the horses and occasional muttered oaths from Digory. The narrow lane became very muddy where it led through a dense wood, dark in patches where the daylight struggled to penetrate through the branches of the trees. A distant muffled sound increased rapidly into that of thundering hooves and two horsemen galloped towards them round a sharp bend disregarding the travellers in their path. The horse on which Sir Geoffrey rode reared in sudden fright and Digory's heavily laden animal lost her footing in the mud as one of the sweating horses bumped against her. Sir Geoffrey held tightly on to his reins struggling to control his startled animal but Digory was thrown, his head striking the trunk of a tree as he landed heavily.

"God in heaven, what are the fools doing!" raged Sir Geoffrey. There was a groan from Digory and quickly fastening his still trembling horse to a nearby tree Sir Geoffrey ran to help him.

"I'm all right, sir," said Digory. He sat up rubbing his head and the colourful verbal abuse which he hurled loudly after the uncaring horsemen rapidly assured his master that in spite of his nasty fall Digory was up to his usual form.

"Who were they?" asked Sir Geoffrey. "Do you know?"

"Did'n have a chance to see, sir," answered Digory ruefully. Both men looked back along the dark track but there was neither sight nor sound of the horsemen.

"It would be of no use to follow them – they could have ridden in several directions back there," Sir Geoffrey observed angrily. "Can you ride?"

"Aye, sir." Digory staggered over to his horse which now stood quietly but his dignity as well as his head had suffered in his fall. "I sed as 'ow she was too laden when we left Penvedn," he complained. "Poor thing didn' stand a chance when she was knocked like that."

"Nonsense, man, she could have carried far more. I wish to God we had caught a glimpse of those two fools, I would have had them horse-whipped."

The last of the journey to Trewarne continued in silence except for the sound of the horses' hooves. Even Digory had stopped his muttering and at last they were home again, the children and dogs running out to welcome them and Lady Margaret eager for news. The presents were received with delight, the spices carried to the large kitchen where Jinty was helping Thomas and Hannah prepare the next meal whilst the two kitchen maids fetched water and prepared vegetables. Digory made the most of his injuries, telling and retelling the tale of their attackers to anyone willing to listen.

* * *

By Sunday the blue skies had disappeared and grey clouds threatened rain as the family rode out of the courtyard to attend Holy Mass. Lady Margaret had still not completely recovered her strength after Amy's birth twelve days previously and the two babies and Jinty remained with her at the manor when the others set forth. Sir Geoffrey sat Rose in front of him on his horse and James rode in front of Bart. Digory rode behind, closely followed by Samuel sharing his nag with Kate. The other servants had set out earlier on foot and were over-taken a short distance from the church.

Sir Geoffrey led the way through the heavy door into the beautiful parish church but even the stained glass of the windows and the brightly painted murals had lost their colour with the greyness outside. The rushes on the floor rustled beneath their feet and James and Bart became absorbed in the progress of a beetle in front of the bench where the family sat. The older parishioners sat on the few stone seats along the wall whilst the younger and more able-bodied stood or knelt throughout the service. Mister Vincent sang the Mass, assisted by the young friar they had passed on the road the previous day. Sir Geoffrey enjoyed listening to Mister Vincent's occasional sermons, preached in Cornish though the Mass was in Latin. Today the good priest was telling his listeners the story of the Good Samaritan and finished by appealing for offerings for the hospital at Helston.

The Mass was over but Mister Vincent had not finished with his flock yet. The young friar had a new prayer to teach them and the congregation repeated the words after him several times until most of them could remember it, providing they practised the words again on their way home, but Digory's first words as he opened the church door to step outside were anything but a prayer when he saw the heavy rain.

"For shame on you, father – an' you just leavin' the church," exclaimed Kate.

By the time they had reached the manor they were all soaking wet and the ones running behind on foot were even more drenched and mud splattered. The fires in the great hall and the kitchen were piled high with wood to dry everyone out whilst Jinty bustled about the kitchen serving hot drinks.

"That settles it," said Sir Geoffrey to his wife. "I shall sell our property in London and make a start on our own chapel here at the manor. We will still be able to support Mister Vincent and the parish church but have Holy Mass offered here also."

* * *

Mister Vincent was consulted and permission obtained from the bishop. The houses in London which were leased out to tenants were easily sold and Sir Geoffrey consulted Ralph Stephens from Lelant who had been in charge of the building of the manor itself. The two men, often joined by Mister Vincent, held long discussions both in the great hall and out in the courtyard, deciding first where the chapel should be built and the size and shape of it. It would be too much to expect Ralph and his other workers to travel to and from Lelant each day in bad weather, so one end of the stables was cleared and filled with fresh straw where they could stay the night should the weather be too bad, taking their meals in the kitchen.

The new tutor arrived as promised by Sir William and instantly made a favourable impression on both Sir Geoffrey and Lady Margaret. John Darnwell was scarcely twenty years old but he had been well educated before his family had fallen from grace in the king's service. A quiet, pleasant young man with an active brain, he was able to interest and encourage the children with his own enthusiasm. He proved himself thorough and patient with their lessons and Rose, in particular, was fascinated by his black curly hair and very blue eyes.

Bart liked his lessons with the young man but he could hardly wait for them to finish each day to run outside to see how the men were progressing with the building of the chapel. He and James were fascinated as the men dug the ground for the foundations, though they were nearly banned from the site the day they both slipped from the glorious pile of mud and stones thrown up by the men and landed in a water-logged trench, their clothes covered in thick mud. Luckily Sir Geoffrey was not at home that day and Jinty's threats of all she would tell their father had subsided into grumbles and warnings before he returned.

CHAPTER FOUR

IT WAS EARLY on a cold, wet morning and Agnes and Emmie, the two young scullery maids, complained frequently to Jinty in the warm kitchen as she loaded their baskets with eggs and vegetables to sell at market and reeled off a list of items for them to purchase. Agnes, the older girl, grumbled more than her sister Emmie.

"A drop o' rain never hurt anybody," Jinty rebuked her sharply. "Get off with yer both 'afore I push you out."

"Ol' witch," muttered Agnes furiously as the two girls trudged out of the forecourt and along the muddy lane. "I'm going to get away from here one day, you see if I don't."

"I like workin' at the manor," objected Emmie, trailing behind. "Anyway, where else could we go?"

"London – Exeter – I've heard folks talk of lots of places. I ain't workin' for that ol' woman for ever."

"She won't be there for ever – she must be really old now," reasoned Emmie. She was smaller and prettier than her sister who had long, dark hair but Emmie's was thicker and more curly. Both girls had been born with a quiet, gentle nature but Agnes had grown hard and aggressive since the two girls had been left alone when they were very young and left to struggle to survive. Kate had found them several years previously in Helston standing dirty and forlorn amongst a group of other labourers, all hoping to be hired. It was at a time when there was work for more hands in the kitchen of the manor and Kate had taken pity on the two young girls and brought them back to Trewarne.

Agnes continued to grumble as they walked through the fields and woods carrying their heavy baskets but Emmie hardly listened. The rain had gradually stopped and a watery sun was breaking through several hours later when they reached Helston with its busy market. It was noisy and friendly, a day to be enjoyed by both girls, and Agnes stopped moaning as they chatted to acquaintants and sold their produce.

Later in the morning she went off to buy the goods Jinty had ordered leaving Emmie with the unsold vegetables and found herself being watched with interest by two dark young men who were leaning idly against the doorway of a hostelry, tankards in their hands. She had not seen them before and she returned their gaze curiously for a moment before lowering her eyes. One of them smiled slightly and half raised his tankard but Agnes pretended not to notice whilst lingering longer than necessary with the stallholder closest to them.

"You've been a long time," Emmie accused her sister when eventually she returned but Agnes said nothing and turned her back before Emmie could see the faint smile which fleetingly crossed her face. She knew without looking that the two men had mounted their horses and were riding slowly past.

"Who are they?" asked Emmie. "They keep starin' at us."

Agnes shrugged her slim shoulders, pulling her shawl around her as the two riders looked back.

"They can stare if they want," she answered carelessly but Emmie could not help noticing that her sister had an unusual glint in her eyes.

The crowd was beginning to drift away and some of the stallholders were packing up ready for a long walk home.

"We'd better go," said Emmie nervously. It would take the girls two hours to reach Trewarne and who knew what evil spirits might be lurking on the way.

For the early part of their journey they were in a small group but gradually their companions took other paths and eventually the two girls were on their own. For once it was Emmie who was talkative whilst Agnes was quiet, looking behind her occasionally, and it was during a lull in Emmie's chattering that they heard the unmistakable sound of horses approaching from behind them and Emmie saw her sister's lips twitch in a little smile.

* * *

The walls of the chapel were nearly two feet high and Mister Vincent was watching the progress of the builders with Sir Geoffrey when one of the tinners ran into the courtyard looking for the priest. The wife of a tinner had suddenly been taken ill but although Mister Vincent rode off at once, followed by the messenger on Digory's horse, he was too late and the woman was dead before his arrival.

The men from the little community came silently down from the moors to collect the empty red coffin from the back of the church and carry it back up the hill ready for the funeral. Next day a sad little procession made its way down the side of the moor to the church, the woman's husband and five of the other men taking it in turn to carry the coffin on their shoulders, stopping to rest several times on their journey at the wayside crosses where prayers were said for the soul of the dead woman. They were followed by her children, weeping as they stumbled over the rocky path, and the rest of the tinners and their families.

Some of the farming families joined onto the end of the procession and Sir Geoffrey attended the funeral service. Afterwards the coffin was carried to the graveyard at the side of the church where the corpse, wrapped in a sack, was placed into the grave dug earlier that morning. Mister Vincent sprinkled the body with holy water and read the prayers, then the empty coffin was returned to the back of the church and the grave filled in, whilst the little community comforted the dead woman's husband and children.

"What caused her death?" Sir Geoffrey asked John Daniels quietly.

The tinner shrugged wearily.

"I don' rightly know, sir. She'd bin coughin' a lot lately but then most of us do, then she seemed to get worse 'til all of a sudden she jus' died. 'Til then she didn' seem no more sick'n the rest o' we."

"You should come down off the moor, man," urged Sir Geoffrey. "You have no protection up there from the wind and the cold."

"I reck'n we do as well as mos', sir," answered the man stubbornly. "Some die a bit earlier than the fishin' and farmin' folk but then some live longer'n they. I reck'n it's all in God's 'ands, sir, and 'e teks us when 'e's ready."

"At least move your families down into a more sheltered spot," persisted Sir Geoffrey. "Build yourselves better cottages lower down near the bottom of the stream. You can have the land there and it will be nearer to the church for you as well. With any luck you should find tin there and the land should be a little less barren too."

He felt in his pocket and gave several coins to the man.

"Buy another pig and a cow at the market next week and whatever you need for food for yourselves. I shall ride up again soon to make sure that you are living in a better place."

John Daniels took the money gratefully. Sir Geoffrey mounted his horse again and the tinner prepared to rejoin the sad little group waiting for him before making their way back onto the moor. Mister Vincent was talking to them, speaking words of comfort as Sir Geoffrey rode slowly past to return to Trewarne.

* * *

"You – a churchwarden! That's a joke if ever I 'eard one. Might as well give the job to the devil 'imself," Jinty exploded, vigorously pounding at the washing. "Who put that idea into your stupid old 'ed?"

"I put it into my own 'ed, my girl, an' if ee weren't such a poor wife to a man you would think it a gud'un," said Digory indignantly. "I be as good a man as any o' they an' I aim ter tell 'em so too."

"You can't be a churchwarden," retorted Jinty. "You 'ave to be good, 'onest, 'ardworking – and you ain't any o'they. Churchwardens are s'posed to set an example to other folks and the Lord 'elp us all if we follow the example you set!"

"You oughter be 'shamed o' yourself," answered Digory, shaking his grimy fist at her. "Some men 'ave wives who respec' them but I 'ad to 'ave ee. 'Appen as 'ow you're right, after all," he added on reflection. "I'd 'ave to be all o' the things you say an' worse to deserve a woman like you."

"Stop arguing, you two," begged Kate, running into the kitchen where all the other servants were listening and enjoying the row. "Everyone can hear you out in the hall and Master is there with some visitors."

"I ain't arguin', it be 'er," ranted Digory. "You ask any o' they who started it and they won't blame me. All I sed was as 'ow I would mek a good churchwarden an' she ain't stopped naggin' since."

"You can't be a churchwarden, Father!" began Kate in amazement but Digory had had enough.

"Now don' ee start! I've 'eard enough from that other woman. We all got to decide in two weeks time on new wardens down at parish church an' all I say is as 'ow I should be one."

"But why?" asked Kate. "Why do you want to be one?"

"Eh?" Digory was not prepared for this change of attack. He scratched his head and looked round at all the faces laughing at him, waiting for his reply.

"I know why," interrupted Jinty before he could think of an answer. "'E fancies bein' in charge of all the church ale, that's why, an' all the money us raise to keep the church in good repair. If 'e gets 'is 'ands on that, the roof will fall in 'afore ever a penny is spent on it."

"An' if it does I 'ope as 'ow you be in the church when it 'appens," Digory raged back at her. "I ain't staying in 'ere any longer ter lissen ter you two wimmin, I'm goin' outside."

"And not before time," boomed Sir Geoffrey furiously. He had stormed into the kitchen, irate at all the noise issuing from there and carrying across the passage and into the hall where he was entertaining his visitors. Repeated ringing of the bell had brought no response until at last he had angrily come himself to find what all the noise was about.

"Get to your work, all of you," he ordered grimly and the servants hurriedly shot to different corners of the kitchen to continue their tasks. "If I ever hear shouting like that again I will flog you," he warned Digory, "and anyone else behaving like that in my house."

For the moment Digory was defeated and he departed moodily into the yard, determined to broach the subject again before long, but by nightfall he had other more important things upon his mind.

* * *

The manor was silent and everyone sleeping peacefully when two figures met in the courtyard, hugging the wall to avoid making shadows in the dim moonlight. They crept past the stable block and the partly built wall of the chapel, breaking into a run as they reached the open ground beyond. The four children had taken this same route on the day they were ejected from the house and now Digory and Samuel were panting as they ran past the woods, stumbling through the bracken and over the rocks. Other shadowy figures joined them from time to time, only brief words whispered now and again or a sudden muffled curse as a foot was caught in a twisted root. The pale light of the crescent moon disappeared fleetingly behind clouds which were scudding across the dark sky.

Ever since he was a boy Samuel had felt scared yet also strangely excited furtively accompanying his father through the darkness to the distant cliff top, joined by other shadowy shapes. He never quite overcame the fear of what Jinty and Kate would say if they ever found their suspicions confirmed or, far worse, the fury of Sir Geoffrey who was a justice of the peace, but Digory always scoffed at his fears and Samuel was even more afraid of the mockery of his father. Digory had received a nasty shock when the children described the way down to the isolated cove which they had found. Under his orders Samuel, following an unsuccessful search of the shore for the dead man or signs of wreckage, had covered the top of the path with extra bracken to hide it more carefully from unwelcome eyes.

The cove was some miles from the manor and now they could hear the waves below them. There were eight figures picking their way down the twisting path, cursing one another each time a stone was dislodged to clatter noisily down to the rocks below. The sea was quite calm as it made its way into the little cove and the silent men crowded round Digory as he produced the lantern, peering out into the darkness where the moon shone faintly on the water. For some time there was nothing in sight but Digory continued to signal at intervals until finally a small boat came into sight and the men ran forward splashing through the cold water to heave it on to the sand.

The cargo was unloaded swiftly and silently, the only words spoken being between Digory and the man who was in charge of the boat as the goods and money changed hands. At one point Digory seemed to be arguing with the man but the other refused to let the last goods be unloaded until he was satisfied with the amount Digory reluctantly put into his hand. The men carried the smuggled cargo into a cave amongst large rocks at the far end of the cove and at last the boat was pushed back into the water and rowed into the darkness whilst those on shore inspected their gain with the light from the lantern.

There were several casks of brandy, wine, bales of silk, silver and spices which would all have to be disposed of carefully in order not to attract suspicion but should fetch a good price in the right hands. The men would follow Digory's orders in the handling of the contraband and half the money would be paid to him, half shared out amongst themselves. It would buy extra food and clothing for their families but not too openly. They took a risk but not too often for comfort and the excitement and the pickings were well worth it.

* * *

It had been easy for Samuel to sneak quietly in and out of bed in the past. Kate was a heavy sleeper and nothing usually disturbed her once she lay down to rest but Kristy was fretful and eventually Kate woke and rose to attend to the child. At first she rocked the cradle, her mind still befuddled with sleep, but Kristy continued to cry loudly and refused to settle again. It was cold standing there with bare feet on the stone floor and at last Kate wearily lifted her out of the cradle and lay down upon her own straw mattress on the floor, Kristy cradled in her arms. It was then that she realised Samuel was missing.

At first she was only mildly aware of it, thinking sleepily that he had gone to answer a call of nature, but as the minutes passed and Kristy gradually fell asleep Kate found herself more and more awake. Vague suspicions of an interest in one of the flighty scullery maids entered her head only to be dismissed almost immediately. Samuel was slightly simple, fearful of his father but a good husband who had never given any cause for complaint. As the hours went by Kate became even more worried but the baby was warm and peaceful in her arms and at last Kate too fell asleep.

She awoke with a start as the door creaked slightly and Samuel stole quietly back into the room. She heard the slight sounds as he removed his boots, breeches and jerkin then lay carefully down on the bed so as not to disturb his wife. She would not speak to him now for fear of awakening the baby again but she would soon find out where he had been.

* * *

At first Samuel, confronted by his wife, tried to convince her she had been dreaming and that he had been on his bed all night but he was a poor liar and it did not take long for Kate to find out the truth. She had half-suspected her father-in-law of smuggling for a long time but foolishly had not thought of Samuel being involved. Kind-hearted and loving as he was, she had not thought he had the courage to take part in illegal adventures but she should have realised that Samuel was too nervous of Digory's wrath to refuse to assist his father. Not that Digory ever laid a hand on his son, probably because of what Jinty would do to him, and Digory was not a bad father but he had a loud and colourful vocabulary which rolled off Jinty's back but filled Samuel's heart with dread. Even now as Kate castigated him for being involved he was looking nervously over his shoulder at the door, half expecting Digory to walk in.

"If Sir Geoffrey finds out we shall lose our places here," argued Kate. "Isn't it better to have work and our own cottage rather than whatever smugglin' might bring in? He might take the baby off us too," she added, suddenly near to tears. "You don't want to lose Kristy, do you, Samuel?"

"'Course I don't," Samuel answered uneasily, "but if I don' go when father says I'll be in trouble with 'im. 'E's a good father but 'e ain't easy, Kate, you know that."

"I know it," Kate affirmed, "but you ain't doin' no more smugglin' – I'll see to that."

Digory was just coming back across the fields for his dinner when he was confronted by a determined Kate. He listened with rising irritation to her terms then cursed the baby who had alerted Kate to her husband's absence.

"Don't you go sayin' nothin' against her," Kate warned him. "She's the only grandchild you're ever likely to have through no fault of ours and she ain't goin' to have no father in prison for smugglin'. Either you leave Samuel out of your schemin' or I go to Sir Geoffrey."

44

She barred his way as he tried to push past her and reluctantly Digory stopped in his tracks again.

"Don' ee be a fool," he said indignantly. "Yer could 'ave some nice little extras for the baby and yoursen."

"I don't want no extras, I jus' want peace o' mind and Samuel in bed o' nights, not roamin' the cliff tops. Make your mind up, father. Leave us in peace or I go to the master – and Jinty!" she added threateningly.

Digory capitulated. He had decided long ago that women brought nothing but trouble to him. With three of them now in the family he felt life was dealing him a very unfair hand.

* * *

For several weeks the days stayed sunny and hot, enabling the workers on the land to bring in a good harvest and store onions, turnips and other vegetables ready for the winter. The women were busy salting down pork and beef and making preserves, the barefooted children grew brown in the sunshine as they helped in the fields. A tenth share of all their crops was given to Mister Vincent and the money raised by what he did not need for his simple way of life was given to support the poor and supply the hospital at Helston. A steady stream of pilgrims passed by on their way to The Mount begging food and alms, and Mister Vincent supplied them all.

The new churchwardens had been elected without any more being heard on the matter from Digory, much to Jinty's surprise, and as Feast Day drew near everyone was busy preparing for their special day. Large quantities of ale were brewed and the women baked bread and cakes, many of them bringing them to the manor kitchen where Thomas the cook placed them in the large clay oven.

Early in the morning of Feast Day flowers were strewn in the nave of the church, covering the reeds, and continuing down the path to the narrow lane. Everyone young and old arrived early for the procession outside to sing hymns and then crowd into the parish church. The fragrance of the petals crushed under so many feet filled the air as Mister Vincent offered Mass in a church overflowing with parishioners, many more squashed into the porch and others standing on the path outside. The sun streamed through the stained glass windows, its light dancing on the beautiful red, green and gold of the painted timbers inside the roof and on the statue of Christ with the Virgin Mary, given to the church by Sir Geoffrey and Lady Margaret on the occasion of their marriage fifteen years earlier.

After the solemnity of the service everyone streamed out into the grounds round the church, laughing and chattering as they caught up with the news, the men staying close to the table where the ale was served and handing over their money in payment to the churchwardens – two of the farmers who leased land from Sir Geoffrey. The cakes, bread and pickles were sold, games and races organised in an adjoining field, everyone paying money to enter, for today they were all working to raise money to help repair the nave of the church. Mister Vincent was responsible for all the repairs beyond the rood screen but the body of the church belonged to the parishioners and this was one of their regular ways of raising money for its upkeep.

Sir Geoffrey and Lady Margaret had ordered a pig to be roasted and Samuel and Digory, together with Thomas the cook, had been busy since daybreak building the fire and turning the animal on the spit. The mouthwatering smell filled the air and a constant stream of hungry parishioners paid their money and munched at the huge hunks of bread filled with delicious roast pork.

"Where are Agnes and Emmie?" Kate asked one of the other servants half way through the afternoon but no one knew or was even interested. Even Kate soon forgot them.

James almost won a race, running well ahead of the other children of the parish, only to be brought down at the last moment by an excited Storm yapping around his young master's feet. The rest of the children ran past him as he struggled up to excited cheering and booing from the onlookers. Storm, sensing his mistake, slunk off to the side of the field until James was ready to forgive him and be friends again. Rose, undecided at first whether running races was undignified or not, finally gave into temptation and hopped into third place with a little girl from the tinners' community, but the boys had an unfair advantage in every race for the girls were handicapped with their long skirts.

Sir Geoffrey and Lady Margaret strolled amongst their fellow parishioners, stopping to chat and admire the crafts on display, introducing some of their tenants to Master Darnwell, the new tutor, and talking to Mister Vincent. One of the farm workers who cultivated a strip of a field along with several others played his fiddle, stopping only when Mister Vincent began prayers at noon, and the singing, eating, drinking and dancing continued all day.

The men of the parish took turns wrestling with each other until Kate was delighted to see Samuel emerge champion, only narrowly overcoming one of the tinners. His triumphant perspiring face was a pleasure to see as he was declared winner before all the parish and the loser shook hands with him. Sir Geoffrey shook his hand too and Kate, carrying Kristy in her arms, felt she would burst with pride in her husband. Even Digory, more than a little flushed with ale, shook his son's hand vigorously and declared to all who would listen that he was proud of his son. To Samuel, these first words of praise he had ever heard from his father were music in his ears.

By early evening after a final prayer and a hymn out in the open air they began to disperse, Agnes and Emmie appearing again unnoticed as they mingled with the others from Trewarne. The churchwardens, with anyone else they could conscript, began to clear up the mess in the church grounds and when finally they counted the takings they were delighted with the results. The repair of the nave was going to be a very expensive job but Feast Day 1529 had been a happy trouble-free day in perfect weather and a good sum had been collected as a start for the fund.

* * *

For weeks the events of Feast Day were the main topic of conversation in the kitchen at Trewarne. Only Emmie seemed to be more quiet and withdrawn. Her sister Agnes grew in confidence and responded insolently when Jinty chastised her for becoming sly and flighty in her behaviour.

"You shouldn't answer back so much, Agnes," Emmie ventured.

"Why not? I'll not be here much longer and neither will you be if you got any sense. George and Percy have promised to take us both away from here, ain't they? Why, now what's the matter!" she exclaimed in exasperation as Emmie's eyes filled suddenly with tears.

"I don't like them," she answered. "I don't like what they want to do with us."

"Don' ee be so stupid, Emmie," scoffed Agnes impatiently. "All men do that – it's just their way of showin' they like us."

Emmie turned away abruptly, struggling to control her tears as she carried on preparing the vegetables. Her face burned at the memory of their recent clandestine meetings with the two men – meetings which now took place regularly at night in the nearby woods. Poor Emmie's whispered protests to her sister that she did not want to go were ignored by Agnes and Emmie was afraid to make a fuss in case they were overheard. She had grown to dread and hate the pattern of their lives – lying in bed with Agnes on their straw mattress on the floor until almost midnight when the other servants sleeping in the same room were all asleep, praying that Agnes herself would fall asleep which she never did, reluctantly dressing and slipping soundlessly out of the manor and through the dark courtyard to the edge of the wood where George and Percy, as they had told the girls to call them, sat on their horses eagerly awaiting them. The rest of the meeting, with its accompanying coarse talk and laughter from the men and giggles from Agnes lying with George only a short distance from her, was a nightmare from which Emmie wanted desperately to escape.

Sometimes in the kitchen she was aware of Kate looking at her with a concerned expression and Emmie longed to unburden herself to someone but she could not confess without involving Agnes who had tried so hard to keep the two of them together since their parents died. She could not betray her sister but Emmie in her desperation knew that neither could she carry on bearing the guilt and shame of these unpleasant meetings.

CHAPTER FIVE

SIR WILLIAM GODOLPHIN was very interested to hear of Samuel's success as a wrestler. He had recently received a letter commanding him to send two of the best Cornish wrestlers to court to wrestle before the king but Sir Geoffrey refused on Samuel's behalf. Poor Samuel was only just beginning to gain confidence in his own small world down in Cornwall – London would be no place for him.

The divorce was dragging on and King Henry was becoming increasingly impatient with Rome. Thomas Cranmer, then making a living as a tutor, put forward the suggestion that the universities of both England and Europe should be consulted for their opinion of the proposed divorce and whilst those close to the court schemed and plotted, life in Cornwall went on peacefully.

Phillipa's husband, Robert Trenwith, returned home from sea for two months whilst his ship was repaired and Christmas was celebrated by a four-day visit to Trewarne by Phillipa, Robert and their family, accompanied by some of their servants. The children had not seen each other since Richard's departure in the summer and the younger cousins had not met for nearly a year. At first they were quiet and constrained in each other's company but they were soon over their initial shyness and great interest was shown in the two babies, both brought into the great hall by Jinty and Kate to be shown off to the visitors. Amy was still very fair with wispy blonde curls and stayed shyly on her mother's lap whilst Kristy, slightly more advanced than Amy, tried to wriggle out of Kate's arms on to the floor, her dark curls and dark eyes in striking contrast to the delicate colouring of the smaller child. Both babies were played with and admired before being taken from the room.

The children drifted to the far end of the great hall away from the adults who sat by a roaring fire, talking and listening as Robert recounted his adventures at sea. Occasionally a burst of laughter would make the children look curiously at their parents but they were too interested in listening to each other and recounting their own adventures to take much notice of the adults. Samuel came in to light the candles and the flames from the fire cast a warm glow into the room. The weather was mild for Christmas time. Providing there was no sudden change, as could often happen in that part of Cornwall, they should all be able to attend Mass in the parish church next day and return home warm and dry.

Richard was describing his days at school to the children and Bart listened with interest for he would be joining Richard at grammar school after Christmas. Richard, now 14, would be there for another year and would then go on to University, either Oxford or Cambridge. His parents wanted him to study for the priesthood or law but Richard wanted to follow his father and go to sea.

"Fancy studying for years and years then going to sea!" exclaimed Rose.

"Why not? My father did. Then when I am old, if I am still alive, I can write a book and everyone will read it."

"Not many people have books," objected Rose.

"No, not yet, but they will do. Father says a lot more printing presses are being set up in Europe now and books will become cheaper and very popular. We might even have books for ourselves at school instead of just having to listen."

"Master Darnwell says the king wrote a book and the Pope gave him a new title," Rose informed him, feeling very learned.

"I know what it was too," interrupted James. "It was *Defender of the Faith.*"

"I was going to say that," said Rose in annoyance. "You shouldn't interrupt people."

James pulled a face and turned his attention back to his younger cousins and Storm, but he could not resist a parting shot at his sister.

"You only learn things because you love Master Darnwell anyway," he mocked and this time he had provoked Rose too far. Her face scarlet with embarrassment she threw herself at him and Richard had to pull them apart.

"No, I do not," hissed Rose.

"Yes, you do," taunted James, "you told me so in bed one night."

"Be quiet down there," ordered Sir Geoffrey from the other end of the great hall and Rose reluctantly had to content herself with a final kick which James adroitly dodged.

Christmas morning dawned bright and clear and the household

travelled on horseback or on foot to the parish church, returning to the manor to exchange gifts and break their fast with mulled spiced wine for the adults and cordials for the children, jumbals and little oblong pastry tarts with mincemeat to represent the child in the manger.

The great hall was noisy with talk and laughter whilst in the large kitchen the meat roasted, carefully supervised by Thomas, and vegetables simmered in large iron pots suspended over the fire. The puddings were heated and Kate spread a fine white linen tablecloth, a present brought back from his travels by Robert Trenwith, over the long table in the great hall before placing the silver salter in the centre and laying late flowers still in bloom from the garden at intervals across the table.

The visitors and their servants would make the number too great for everyone to sit down together so it had been decided by Lady Margaret that the two families, joined also on this occasion by Mister Vincent and the young tutor, would sit together in the great hall and both groups of servants would take their meal in the large kitchen. It was an innovation which both family and servants would come to prefer and continue throughout the year.

The dinner was served at three in the afternoon, much later than usual, for Mister Vincent had many sick calls to make after Holy Mass, wearing his surplice and stole, a bell round the neck of his horse tinkling to tell those in earshot that he carried the Blessed Sacrament. Some of the sick were very ill indeed and after he had administered the sacrament and said prayers with the family he left herbs and medicines to alleviate the suffering and money for food and clothing where it seemed that the families might be in need. When his sick calls were completed he rode back to the church, spending some time in quiet prayer before setting off again for the manor.

Dinner was an excellent meal, thoroughly enjoyed by all in the candlelit hall. The children loved listening to Robert Trenwith as he told stories of his voyages and the countries which he had visited. Bart, listening to his uncle, could not decide whether it would be more exciting to go to sea or to build churches and manor houses like the men from Lelant who had now nearly completed the chapel in the corner of the courtyard.

After the meal was over the children had a surprise for the adults who were sitting lazily in front of the fire. Master Darnwell had written a little nativity play for them with easily learnt parts for their cousins who had only arrived the previous day. Kate and Jinty had been coaxed into secretly making costumes and Master Darnwell himself, sitting in the shadows, was to play on a lute as the children sang. The plans of the children to use a real donkey had been firmly squashed by the tutor and an argument over which baby should represent the baby Jesus was resolved at the last moment when a screaming Kristy was hurriedly replaced in Rose's arms by Amy.

All the household was brought into the great hall to listen and watch. The children played their simple parts beautifully. Master Darnwell was unsure whether the youngest king should really have carried an excited mongrel who licked his master's face with such love and enthusiasm that James could hardly say his few words but there was laughter and some tears from the audience when the little play was finally over.

The children stayed in their costumes, sitting on the floor around the fire, as the afternoon finished with carols. Mister Vincent led them all in their evening prayers, then the servants left for their own festivities in the kitchen and the families settled down to an evening of music, guessing games, cards and charades.

The old priest accepted the offer of a bed for the night and it was nearly morning before the lamps and candles were finally put out and everyone settled down in their beds. Tomorrow, God willing and weather permitting, they would ride over the moors, entertain friends from neighbouring villages and generally enjoy Christmas until Robert, Phillipa and their children returned to Penvedn once more.

* * *

The collegiate church at Glasney in Penryn, to which Richard's grammar school was attached, had been built in 1265 following a dream, three times repeated, of Walter Bronescombe, then Bishop of Exeter. The good bishop had been lying at Canterbury on the point of death when St Thomas of Canterbury appeared to him and promised his recovery. Once he was better, St Thomas told him,

God wished him to build in the woods at Glasney a college to the praise of God and in the name of St Thomas the Martyr.

The instructions of St Thomas in the vision for the site of the building were specific – near the river at Penryn, at a spot called Polsethow, where the bishop would find a large willow tree with a swarm of bees. On his recovery the bishop journeyed to Penryn from Canterbury and found the site with tree and bees as foretold. The land there, being a mire, was completely unsuitable but he did as the vision told him and built a large church to the glory of God, consecrating the church and its churchyard two years later.

The unsuitability of the site made the cost of repairs expensive but there now stood a beautiful large church with a tower, side aisles and chapel, cloisters, refectory buildings, an infirmary and houses for the clergy, surrounded by a fortified wall beyond which the inhabitants of Penryn could flee in times of danger of attack. The clergy residing there spent their days in prayers and spiritual reading, taking part in the services, singing and praising God, ministering to the needs of their flock outside and to the care of their souls. The school had been built later and its reputation as a grammar school had spread throughout Cornwall and to the rest of the country.

* * *

Bart had heard a great deal of the school and its teachers from his cousin Richard, some of whom were in religious orders, others ordinary schoolmasters, but he was still in a state of trepidation as he rode with his father into the town of Penryn. He had not been there before and being market day he was surprised to see so many people noisily selling and buying in the narrow streets. He could glimpse the ships in the harbour through gaps between the buildings and they reined their horses several times whilst Sir Geoffrey stopped to greet and talk with old acquaintances.

The church bell was ringing to call the faithful to midday service as they rode up to the porch. Digory was left to stable the horses whilst Bart entered the church with his father. A good many of the townsfolk were present and after the service Sir Geoffrey stayed to talk to his old friend, the prior.

Provost John Gentle was delighted to see them and took them to his room, talking as they went and pointing out the statues and the carvings on the ceilings and around the doors. He insisted that they should join him for a simple meal of bread and cold meat which they ate silently whilst one of the younger clergy read to them in Latin from a beautifully bound bible. The prior, noticing Bart's fascination with the book, allowed him to handle it carefully before it was taken away.

The two men exchanged news, their voices solemn at times but careful not to say anything which might alarm the boy, and when the bell tolled again to call the prior back to prayer Sir Geoffrey and Bart knelt for his blessing before bidding him farewell. Digory was watching for them to emerge again into the street and he brought their horses, now fed and watered, ready for the short journey to the school.

This was the moment to which Bart had looked forward yet dreaded for he had never before been away from home or family. The leave-taking at the manor earlier that morning had been an ordeal for the boy, his mother trying hard not to cry, Rose and James subdued at the prospect of not having Bart with them for ten weeks until he came home again for the holidays at Easter. The ride from Trewarne, a journey of twenty miles, had been an adventure in itself, the longest distance he had ever ridden in one day, but he was too nervous now to notice how tired and aching he felt.

The servant who opened the door to them at the house attached to the school left them in a sparsely furnished but clean room with a dark wooden table and two benches, a large crucifix hanging in the centre of one wall. Before they had time to sit a priest in a long black cassock came into the room and shook hands with Sir Geoffrey before turning his attention to Bart. He smiled at the nervous boy and Bart relaxed very slightly, glancing occasionally at his father as they sat on the bench listening to the priest outlining the routine of the school.

Bart would sleep in a dormitory with thirty other boys of mixed ages. He would rise at a quarter to five, immediately upon hearing the bell, wash in the passage adjoining and attend Holy Mass at five o'clock. After breaking his fast with bread and water, lessons would begin at half past six in the morning in the schoolroom, continuing until eleven o'clock – Latin, Greek and English would be studied. After a thirty minute break for exercise in the yard the boys would assemble in chapel for spiritual readings and prayers, followed by dinner at midday – a meal of fish or meat, bread and vegetables with fruit on feast days and Sundays. After the meal, which would be eaten in silence, lessons would begin again – mathematics, music and grammar until four o'clock when more active pursuits would be followed such as hawking, archery and the practice of musical instruments. This would be followed by the evening meal and prayers, then freedom to talk to each other until half past eight when candles must be put out and there would be silence until next morning.

It was the normal routine for grammar school boys and Sir Geoffrey and Bart listened without interruption. Bad behaviour would be punished by the use of a stick but good behaviour would be rewarded by free time on feast days. Hopefully Bart would never provoke punishment.

The two men rose and Bart knew that the moment had come when his father would leave him. He hoped fervently that Richard would soon arrive but today it was only the new boys and Bart must now make his own friends. For the first time in his life he shook hands with his father, wishing he could have his usual hug but knowing that he must now leave such childhood pleasures behind him. He was eleven years old and could no longer act like a child.

* * *

Sir Geoffrey spent the night at an inn before leaving Penryn next morning to ride to Truro. He could not help thinking about Bart but the boy had to grow into a man and a good education was essential for his future. Rose and Amy would have their own tutor at home for as long as they needed him but in four years time James would take Bart's place at St Gluvias and Bart would follow Richard to Oxford. Possibly by then there would be other children but for the moment he and Margaret had four healthy children out of the six they had brought into the world and they were content.

Today he must journey to Truro in his role of justice of the peace. Sir William Godolphin would be there and also Charles Rawlaston. He liked and respected Sir William but the other man imposed heavy sentences and had little or no patience with the accused brought before him. Privately Sir Geoffrey felt that the Rawlaston sons could do with some heavy punishment from their father themselves. The two brothers had far too much money to squander. Complaints about their heavy drinking and bad conduct were regularly made in private though no one dared to bring them to court. Charles Rawlaston, who had made his fortune as a merchant trader, lived with his sons ten miles from Trewarne between Penzance and Truro. Lately on several occasions Digory had reported seeing the two young men on Trewarne land – 'up to no good' asserted Digory – but they had ridden off before he could speak to them and search as he might he could find no damage or any reason why they should be there.

The petty sessions were in progress and between them the three justices of the peace dealt with robbery, disturbances in the streets mainly caused by drunkenness, failure to pay tithes and wife beating. In the last case Sir Geoffrey felt sorry for the husband who looked an inoffensive little man with a domineering large wife so his sentence was lenient, much to the loud vocal disgust of the woman. Some of the vagrants brought before him always aroused his pity but the law of the land ordered that they should be placed in the stocks so he could do nothing but make their stay there as short as possible and have enquiries made of possible work for them when they were later released. Those brought before Sir William received similar justice but beggars unlucky enough to be brought before Charles Rawlaston were always whipped before being placed in the stocks.

* * *

"A word with you, gentlemen."

Sir Geoffrey and Sir William stopped as the other man barred their way and motioned to them to step inside a room where glasses and wine stood ready upon a table. He poured out the drinks and the other men, though reluctant to drink with him, took the proffered glasses and waited.

"A busy session today," observed Charles Rawlaston. He was a large, overweight man with a florid face, the bolstered sleeves of his shirt under his ornately embroidered doublet adding to his size. Brightly coloured hose and a velvet flat cap with a feather added to his richly clad appearance. Sir Geoffrey felt he looked vulgar and overdressed but he waited patiently to hear his business.

Charles Rawlaston did not believe in wasting time and came straight to the point.

"I intend to stand for Parliament at the next election, gentlemen. I trust I can count on your assistance."

Both Sir Geoffrey and Sir William looked surprised. They knew the man was ambitious but he owned large areas of land in Cornwall and they had not expected him to want to extend his power further afield.

"Why, man?" asked Sir William brusquely. "You have enough responsibilities looking after your estates in Cornwall. If you become involved with Parliament who will look after your interests here?"

"My sons, of course," he answered, filling his glass, and the other two men exchanged significant looks over his bent head. "Can I look to you for support, gentlemen?"

"It is impossible to say," replied Sir Geoffrey. "We have no idea yet who else will put himself forward for election or when the next Parliament will be called."

"I take it neither of you will be standing yourselves?"

"I cannot answer that." Sir William's voice was cold. He had no intention of becoming involved with politics outside Cornwall and he knew Sir Geoffrey's feelings were the same but he would not allow Charles Rawlaston to think he was in for an unopposed fight. He put down his half-emptied glass on the table, nodding curtly, and Sir Geoffrey did the same. Outside the room they strode out of the building into the cold late afternoon air.

"I cannot see Charles Rawlaston getting himself elected," said Sir William grimly.

"Can you not? If he cannot win by fair means he will not hesitate to use foul. A good many men before him have got into Parliament that way."

"Then we must stop him," vowed Sir William. "Are you riding home this evening?"

"No, it will be dark much too early. I shall stay the night with Robert and Phillipa. They would welcome you if you care to join me."

"Thank you, but I shall stay here in Truro tonight and visit some friends. Perhaps we can ride home together tomorrow. I shall leave here about two o'clock."

"I will join you," promised Sir Geoffrey, mounting his horse, and followed by Digory he set out for Penvedn again.

* * *

In London Queen Catherine and her eleven year old daughter, Princess Mary – the only legitimate heir to Henry VIII – had been banned from court for the past two years. Far worse, they were forbidden to see each other ever again in an effort to put pressure on Catherine to accept that her marriage to Henry had been invalid.

In spite of constant suggestions that the queen should take up a religious life and retire into a convent Catherine refused to believe that her marriage to Henry had been an incestuous one and the king's 'great matter', as the divorce was called, dragged on.

Cardinal Wolsey, who had practically ruled England for fifteen years with little interference from a pleasure loving Henry, failed continually in his efforts to gain the approval of the Pope to an annulment. There was every prospect of Henry being called to Rome for the case to be tried and the thought of the king's fury if he received such a summons filled Wolsey with fear for his own position. In desperation the cardinal opened a court at Blackfriars to try the king's petition but Catherine's pleas were so eloquent as she insisted that her marriage to Henry was valid that the court was adjourned for ten weeks.

Foreign affairs turned against Wolsey and were the final blow. He was dropped from royal favour and indicted for putting service to Rome before service to his king. King Henry was reluctant to ruin him completely and although the bill of attainder brought against Wolsey by his many enemies was thrown out he was made to surrender the Great Seal.

Cardinal Wolsey always maintained that Anne Boleyn and her family at court were responsible for his overthrow because of his failure to secure the divorce. In November 1530 he was arrested and conveyed to the Tower but mercifully he died on his way there at Leicester.

Thomas More reluctantly took Cardinal Wolsey's place after a promise from the king that he would never be involved in the royal divorce.

CHAPTER SIX

THE DRAMATIC EVENTS in London had little effect on Cornwall apart from many serious discussions between the clergy and gentry and interested gossip amongst the lower classes as they went on with their work. The harvest that year had been adequate though not as plentiful as the previous year but a few silent trips to the cove on dark nights had proved helpful to Digory and some of the others working the land belonging to Trewarne. The tinners had built themselves huts in a more sheltered position and the new chapel in the courtyard, now roofed and roughly plastered inside, was almost ready.

Beautiful stained glass windows had been made in Exeter and shipped down to Penryn. Digory and one of the farm labourers took the cart to collect them, the glass lying between layers of straw to protect it as the cart bumped along the rough tracks on the long journey. The trip with the cart had been useful for taking some of the last illicit cargo from the cave to be sold to an agent from up country.

Bart, who had now been at grammar school for over a year, rode back with Digory for the Easter holidays. He enjoyed the life at school, strict and severe though it was, but he could not wait to arrive back at Trewarne to see his family again and he wanted to watch as the men from Lelant installed the stained glass windows. He had watched them finish the roof and plaster inside on his previous visits home.

Rose and James ran to meet him as the cart trundled noisily into the courtyard and Bart jumped down from his nag to hug his mother. Amy and Kristy, now two years old, ran awkwardly in their long dresses, Kristy tripping but caught quickly by James who had turned to help her. Kate and Jinty appeared from the kitchen and there was much talking and laughter as the younger children pulled Bart into the great hall. They had all grown since they had last been together but Bart in particular had added several inches to his height.

Sir Geoffrey was out on his horse inspecting the timber in the woods on his estate but he would be home soon. Lady Margaret sat happily in her sitting room with her children, Amy on her lap, reflecting on her good fortune. Bart and Rose were so like their father with their dark curly hair and alert grey eyes but James and Amy had her fair colouring and blonde curls. Lady Margaret's hair was very long and hung down her back when worn loose in her private rooms but in public, like all married women of her class, it was hidden under a fashionable gabled headdress.

Bart had so much to tell them but they were all waiting eagerly for Sir Geoffrey's return so that the stained glass windows for the church could be inspected. Digory had refused resolutely to let anyone near the cart, even the builders, until his master returned. At last they heard his horse trot into the courtyard and almost before he could dismount Sir Geoffrey found himself surrounded by his family and servants, all eagerly waiting to inspect the new windows.

Samuel and Digory uncovered the glass from its bed of straw and carefully held up each piece for inspection. There were gasps of delight as the thin sunlight shone through to show up in rich, beautiful colours the child lying in the manger watched by Mary and Joseph, the boy Jesus teaching in the temple, the Crucifixion and the Ascension. The largest window which would be placed above the altar showed Christ surrounded by children. Each panel told a story immediately familiar to those present and Rose thought she had never seen anything so beautiful in the whole of her life.

Lady Margaret and Sir Geoffrey were delighted. They had ordered the windows from a craftsman in Exeter on the recommendation of Mister Vincent and they were even more beautiful than they had hoped. The men were already discussing how to put the windows in place. Digory and Samuel covered them again with the straw, breathing a sigh of relief that they had brought them to Trewarne undamaged. Each jolt of the cart on the ride from Penryn had filled Digory with foreboding but the windows were safe, glorious in their colour, ready for the men to install.

* * *

Bart was out of bed next morning as soon as the first signs of daylight began to lighten the room. He crept down the stairs quietly on his way to the courtyard. Thomas was just kindling the fire in the kitchen and soon there were others as the builders came from the stable to break their fast with bread and meat before going out to begin the day's work on the chapel. Kate came into the kitchen carrying Kristy, putting her down in a corner to play whilst she began her work and the two serving girls and Hannah came in from the room which they shared with two more of the servants. The kitchen was warm and noisy with cheerful voices but Bart could only wait impatiently for the builders to go out to the chapel.

It was two days before the windows were fitted and the work complete, the main window placed above the altar and the others arranged two on each side wall of the little church. The grey stone and the slate roof showed the windows well from outside but inside brilliant patches of colour were cast on the rough white plaster as the spring sunshine streamed through the glass. There was only one task now to complete the work and Sir Geoffrey took Bart and Master Darnwell to accompany him on his latest quest.

* * *

The ride over towards The Lizard was a long one and the three riders set out at dawn. Sir Geoffrey had decided to take Bart with him because the boy had shown such intense interest in the building of the church since it was first begun. Master Darnwell had been invited to accompany them as a token of appreciation for the excellent way in which he was educating Rose and James. Sir Geoffrey and Lady Margaret were amazed at their children's progress, even if Rose's diligence and enthusiasm for lessons was the result of her undying love for Master Darnwell, rashly and unwisely confessed to James under cover of the bed clothes – information which he enjoyed using to embarrass his sister on every occasion on which she provoked him. John Darnwell, well-educated and gifted himself, had Rose and James enthusiastically learning and speaking Latin, French and Spanish, reading books and playing musical instruments. Sir Geoffrey and his wife liked and respected the quiet young man who accepted Rose's adoration with tolerant amusement, showing equal affection to all the children. He had no family of his own with whom he was in contact, his only known relatives residing in Lincoln.

Sir Geoffrey had spoken to John Winslade, an old acquaintance living near The Lizard, mentioning his interest in the carpenters whose hands had carved the benches in the church at Mullion. Few churches at that time had such intricately carved benches, a stone ledge round the wall of the nave being the usual seating for the old and sick, the rest of the congregation standing for Mass. Sir Geoffrey had been invited to see the benches which were well-known in the area and offered hospitality and overnight accommodation at Bochym Manor. The travellers rode up to the manor soon after noon and were taken in to dinner with their host and his family, exchanging news as they sat at the long table.

Bart paid little attention to the conversation of the adults at the top end of the table though several references in low voices to the king vaguely caught his attention. He was much more interested in chatting to the younger members of the family and a quiet, pretty girl of about his own age with long straight fair hair, plaited in a way he had not seen before, took his eye repeatedly though she seldom joined in the conversation. She was Isobel, a ward of their host, a shy thirteen year old whose parents were dead and who now lived at the manor with the other children. Bart tried to talk to her as he would to Rose and Amy so that gradually she relaxed and smiled at him, dark blue eyes looking shyly at him and long fair lashes fluttering against her pink cheeks.

After dinner the men and boys rode to Mullion to inspect the carved benches. Sir Geoffrey was impressed with the craftsmanship and a servant despatched to find the carpenter. After he had completed the work at Mullion it was arranged that he should make the benches for the church at Trewarne.

* * *

Lady Margaret was tending the flowers in her garden, the children playing on the lawn, when Jinty came to tell her that Mister Vincent was not well. He had seemed reasonably fit on the previous Sunday, though age was beginning to tell on the old priest. Now Samuel had come back from market to report that a pilgrim he had met on the way who had called earlier to beg at the house next to the church had found the old man sick and hardly able to answer the door. The woman who usually cooked the priest's meal, the wife of the farm labourer who lived nearest to the church, was herself sick and had not been to the house for over a week.

"Take a horse and go to Mister Vincent," Lady Margaret ordered Samuel. "Ask Jinty to give you some food for him and come back and let me know how he is."

Samuel's description of the priest when he returned alarmed Lady Margaret and the two of them rode back together to the house. Samuel opened the door and led the way into the dark little room which was bitterly cold inside. There was no fire and no furniture apart from a roughly made table, a stool and prie-dieu. A large crucifix hung on the wall and in the next room Mister Vincent lay hardly conscious on a straw mattress upon the floor, covered by one blanket, the room clean but completely bare except for another crucifix. Lady Margaret, accustomed to the warmth and comfort of Trewarne in spite of its draughts, was shocked at the sparseness and chill of the rooms. In the kitchen there was little food other than the bread, meat and ale packed by Jinty, only a few candles and no sign of a fire in the empty grate.

Neither she nor Sir Geoffrey had ever been inside the priest's house. They had assumed that he lived in reasonable comfort on the tithes and offerings given by the parishioners but they had never thought to query his thinness or his clothes. In one corner was a small store of turnips and onions but nothing else which the sick man could be coaxed to eat when he regained consciousness. Sir Geoffrey would not be back until the next day. There was nothing she could do but send Samuel back to fetch the cart to take Mister Vincent back to the manor and pray that his sickness was nothing which could be transferred to her own family.

* * *

The room at the far end of the passage which was usually reserved
for visitors was hastily prepared as a sick room and a fire lit to
take the chill out of the damp air. Jinty brewed soup and warm
caudle but the priest remained unconscious most of the time,
breaking out in feverish sweats throughout the night. Jinty,
concerned for her mistress, tried to keep Lady Margaret from the
sick room, taking it in turns with Hannah to sit with the old man.

"How is he?" Lady Margaret asked anxiously, coming along
the passage early next morning as soon as it was light.

Jinty shook her head.

"I don' like the look of 'im at all, my lady, 'e's not regained
consciousness all night."

"I am going to send Samuel for the priest from the next
parish," decided Lady Margaret and ran along the passage to
send Samuel speeding on his way. The priest from the
neighbouring church rode quickly back with him, hurrying into
the room where Mister Vincent lay motionless upon the bed.
Some time later Jinty escorted him back down the spiral staircase
to Lady Margaret, waiting for him in the great hall.

"My medical knowledge is usually adequate but I cannot say
what is the matter," confessed the priest, a younger man than
Mister Vincent. "I have anointed him but he is barely conscious.
His body is so thin, he looks almost half-starved. I can only
imagine that he has been deliberately observing poverty as an
act of voluntary penance. Now he has caught some sickness his
body has insufficient strength to resist it."

"He is such a kind, good man," answered Lady Margaret
helplessly. Jinty had told her of the hair shirt the priest had been
found to be wearing under his clothes and she had seen for
herself the harsh conditions under which he lived. Mister
Vincent had married her to Sir Geoffrey, baptised all their
children, comforted them at the loss of the ones who died. She
could not bear to think that they were to lose such a good man
whose whole life had been spent in the love of God and the
service of his little flock.

"He would be better in hospital at Helston but he would not
stand the journey," Mister Martyn was saying. "Is Sir Geoffrey
due back today?"

"Yes, he should be here within a few hours."

Lady Margaret wished fervently that her husband was there to help her. Jinty had potions and draughts ready for the sick man but until he regained consciousness they were useless.

"There have been stories about his frugal lifestyle," Mister Martyn reflected. "One of the reasons he has no assistant priest living with him is that those who tried could not live as he did. He would not try to make them lead their lives in his way but it is difficult to eat a good meal in front of a man who is deliberately denying himself for Christ."

"There was nothing at all to give comfort in the house," fretted Lady Margaret. "He must have received money from the bishop and from fees for conducting baptisms and funerals."

Mister Martyn looked surprised.

"He never accepted a fee – did you not know? None of his flock ever had to make an offering for his services."

There was a little pause.

"Except people like us!" exclaimed Lady Margaret.

"Of course – you could afford it and to Mister Vincent that was the difference. By his own self-denial your own offerings and support were more than enough for him. He would never take from the poor."

"And the tithes?"

"Those he accepted but not for himself. Tithes are not the personal property of any priest, Lady Margaret, they are only under his administration. They have to be divided equally between the bishop, the poor, the upkeep of the chancel and any other suitable purpose – entertaining travellers and strangers, though I doubt if any ever stayed more than one night under such conditions."

Lady Margaret was silent, reflecting on how little she had known about the holy man who had been part of their spiritual lives for so many years. Mister Martyn rose and she roused herself from her thoughts, rising to bid him farewell.

"I have some sick calls to make in my own parish so I must go. I will come again tomorrow morning. In the meantime there is very little any of us can do except pray."

They walked together to the heavy front door of the manor and he paused, waiting for Samuel to bring round his horse.

"I think he is a dying man, Lady Margaret," he told her quietly, "but remember that we are all only biding our time in this world and waiting until it is God's will that we should join Him in heaven. A man who has lived his life as Mister Vincent has done will have no fear of death, only joy that he now has almost reached the goal for which we should all strive."

He mounted and bowed to her from the saddle of his horse, leaving Lady Margaret to watch him ride out of her sight before returning sadly into the manor, wishing fervently that her husband would come home.

* * *

Sir Geoffrey returned with Bart and Master Darnwell early in the evening when it was already growing dark. He greeted his wife and listened with concern to her news, then ran swiftly up the stone staircase and along the passage to the sick man's room. Jinty was bathing the priest's temples and Mister Vincent's eyes were open at last but Sir Geoffrey's heart sank when he saw how ill the old priest looked.

"He's only just come round, sir," Jinty informed him in a low voice. 'Tis the first time e's moved since Lady Margaret brought 'im back yesterday. I don' think 'e can 'ear us even now or knows where 'e is." But Jinty was mistaken. Mister Vincent turned his head slightly towards the voices in the dark room and Sir Geoffrey took the hand fluttering weakly on the coverlet.

"Do not try to talk," he said gently. "Save your strength until you are feeling stronger."

Mister Vincent's voice was weak and feeble but he struggled to speak.

"Windows," he said at last. "I did not see the windows."

* * *

Only a week earlier Sir Geoffrey had stood with the priest inside his new church, the roof and plastering complete, the oak door hinged into position, enthusiastically describing to Mister Vincent the beautiful stained glass which Digory had brought from Penryn. The priest was due to ride over the following Sunday, now only two days hence, to bless both the church and all who had helped to build it and would worship in it. Sir Geoffrey and Lady Margaret had invited everyone from the estate to be present, packed into the church and the courtyard, and then afterwards given food and drink in the great hall to celebrate the opening of their church dedicated to St Mary the Virgin. The benches would not be carved for perhaps another two years but the church would be ready for them to give praise and thanks to God.

Sir Geoffrey looked questioningly at Jinty as the priest closed his eyes again and she shook her head. Mister Vincent was dying and seemed unlikely to last the night. The gentle old priest who had cared for their souls for so long and encouraged the building of the new church for Trewarne Manor would now sadly not see it complete. He would not even see the beauty of the new windows. Sir Geoffrey carefully removed his hand from that of the sick man, turned on his heel and left the room.

* * *

A few hours later under a starlit sky a stream of figures made their way quietly across the courtyard and into the dimly lit church. Every candle and every lamp which could be found was taken into the church. Master Darnwell, Bart, Rose and James carried their lutes and violas, standing quietly near the altar steps. Lady Margaret stood next to them, lips moving in prayer, and Sir Geoffrey held up his hand in the dim light.

Upstairs in the sick room Digory and Samuel carefully lifted the bed of the dying priest and carried it across the boards to the window which opened out onto the courtyard below. Gradually the windows of the little church began to glimmer from the light of the candles and lamps which were being lit inside, until at last the whole church was silhouetted in the faint light of the moon, the two stained glass windows which faced the manor, one of the Crucifixion, the other of Christ ascending into heaven, glowing more and more with brilliant colour.

The voices of those inside rose in a hymn, accompanied by the music of Master Darnwell and the children. Mister Vincent opened his eyes, looked down at the little church and raised his hand very slowly in a blessing. His head sank down onto his chest and with a gentle sigh he relinquished his soul to his Maker.

CHAPTER SEVEN

MISTER VINCENT WAS buried in the graveyard adjoining the parish church where he had ministered for nearly thirty years. The Provost of Glasney rode from Penryn to conduct the service which was attended by other local clergymen. Everyone on the estate and many from neighbouring parishes gathered together to pray for the soul of the gentle priest. No one else had become ill and the woman who had cooked his one frugal meal a day and had been taken ill before him had fully recovered again.

The visiting clergy stayed overnight at Trewarne before returning to Penryn. Mister Martyn from the neighbouring parish offered to say Holy Mass on Sundays until a new priest was appointed and Sir Geoffrey and the churchwardens accepted gratefully.

The builders from Lelant, their task finished, returned home well pleased with their labour and the praise of the clergy. They would return in two weeks to begin work on the new wings of the manor. Bart would soon be riding back to school and life at Trewarne began to return to normal after the sadness of the past few weeks. Lady Margaret, who had begun to believe that another child was on the way, was disappointed whilst Sir Geoffrey tried tactfully not to upset his wife by making his relief too obvious. Mercifully to his mind it was the last occasion on which his wife caused him any similar apprehension.

* * *

Early in April Digory and his fellow conspirators made another silent trip to the cove in the darkness, only to be frustrated and enraged by a violent storm which sprang up next day, the worst in living memory. Gale force winds howled and enormous waves crashed against the cliffs all along the Cornish coast, flooding the cave where the brandy had been stored and washing the whole cargo back into the raging sea. Digory, who had lain awake for two nights as the foul weather continued, had to wait until Sir Geoffrey rode to Truro accompanied by Samuel before he could risk venturing to the cove. His worst fears fulfilled, loud curses filled the empty cave and for several days everyone suffered from his surliness and ill temper.

The gales and torrential rain had caused much damage to the crops which had been planted and the spirits of the farmers and labourers were low when the new priest arrived to take up residence in the parish. Sir Geoffrey, riding back from Truro, had overtaken the man and ridden the last part of the journey with him.

There were mutterings when the new incumbent began to claim all the fees which Mister Vincent had never accepted and which they had even forgotten that they should pay. Men who had taken Mister Vincent's free services for granted complained to the churchwardens when the new priest required payment after performing baptisms, weddings and funerals. Masses offered for the souls of dead relatives had been said freely by Mister Vincent but now an offering was requested when it could reasonably be afforded.

Sir Geoffrey, listening to the complaints of the irate churchwardens standing before him in the great hall, began to wish that the old priest had been a little less saintly, less eager to help his flock, most of whom in a good year could have paid the amounts due without too much hardship. The Church had always taught that men should offer back to God some of His bounty and so provide not only a reasonable living for the clergy who served them but also money for the poor and funds to build and repair churches, hospitals and schools. Mister Vincent, loved and revered as he had been by all his parishioners, had not made them fully accept their responsibilities. Now a good deal of ill-feeling was being stirred up by the new man's rightful stand.

The churchwardens were waiting for Sir Geoffrey's sympathy and support. The thought fleetingly crossed his mind that now every other member of the parish was being asked to accept their fair share of responsibility he might be better off himself but he was wealthy enough and had never resented Mister Vincent's policy of using the rich to make life easier for those not so well off. Perhaps he too was as responsible as the old priest for the present situation. He roused himself and looked at the two men patiently standing in front of him.

"Mister Douglas is right," he informed them. "All those who can afford it should pay towards the upkeep of the church and the clergy. Are you not paid for your labour? A good priest works hard for his parish and has to live, just as you do. You are allowed to keep what you have left after paying your tithe but a priest is expected to give what he has left to the poor."

"Mister Vincent never took anythin', sir," one of the men argued.

"He should have done so. Our offerings are made to God in thanks for His great mercy and blessings. Is it right that we should take all He has to offer and give nothing back in return?"

It was obvious from the resentful faces before him that they did not agree with his words and Sir Geoffrey sighed. In many parts of the country people grumbled because the clergy took too much. Mister Vincent had left a legacy of trouble because he had taken so little.

The villagers continued to grumble but Mister Douglas stood firm until gradually the mutterings ceased as he earned their respect. The chancel was replastered and the timbers of the roof over the altar repaired. A stained glass window was installed to rival the ones at Trewarne and a beautiful statue of the Mother of God placed in the Lady Chapel. A lychgate was added to give shelter to any coffin and funeral procession before entry into church.

The old priest had for years taught the children spasmodically in the parish church but now Mister Douglas taught lessons on a regular basis and a schoolroom was established in the nave on weekdays. The parishioners were slow to send the children at first and they could not be compelled to do so but gradually the numbers attending increased on the understanding that they would be kept at home when needed to help with the work. For some months Mister Douglas failed in his efforts to encourage the tinners to send their children but Sir Geoffrey added his support and gradually a few of the children walked three miles each way to attend occasionally.

Babies were born and about half survived, a few parishioners died, the children under three years old, including Amy and Kristy, were confirmed. Two of the farm labourers married girls from the village, both girls wearing dresses kept for the purpose by the parish, the wedding vows taken in the porch before the rest of the service followed inside the church. One of the labourers was discovered to possess a talent for painting on the white plaster and more large murals covered the remaining bare walls. Those who still worshipped God in the parish church did not intend to allow their church to be outshone by the new one at Trewarne.

The lanes leading to the village and to the manor were gradually improved, ponds cleared and the churchyard kept tidy. New churchwardens, appointed annually, dealt with minor misdemeanours and more serious lawbreakers were taken to the manor before Sir Geoffrey or dealt with at petty sessions. The Church had her own courts to deal with complaints concerning matrimony or the clergy.

* * *

Throughout the country devout men and women served God in monasteries, nunneries and parish churches, living good and holy lives in the service of others but the clergy, one of the few available careers at that time, was also composed of many who had no genuine call to the ministry but saw it as providing a comfortable living. There were many complaints, sometimes true, often exaggerated, of drunken and immoral clergy, improper retention of tithes and oblations, absentee clergymen and the holding of more than one post which was forbidden.

Reform was essential to put right many abuses but Cardinal Wolsey, throughout his distinguished career, had paid too much attention to affairs of state and too little to the reform urgently needed of some of the clergy. The Cardinal himself had been the cause of much justified criticism during his lifetime because of his lavish lifestyle. Now the many good holy men and women of the Church were to suffer because of the worldliness of others. Parliament, encouraged by an increasingly frustrated king, was planning to make its own reforms. The whole clergy were indicted for praemunire, accused of putting the authority of the Pope before that of the king.

* * *

Sir Geoffrey had not conversed with Sir William Godolphin so frequently since their term of office as justices of the peace had expired, but now the two men and several other neighbouring gentry and their families were at Trewarne. Lady Margaret had long been planning a visit by her friends, and the weeks before Christmas had been spent with Hannah and Thomas from the kitchen arranging menus, ordering preparation of the guests' rooms and adding intricate stitching to the gowns and jerkins made by Kate for the children. Rose was delighted with a new velvet gown which matched her name whilst Amy looked delightful in a pretty blue dress and matching bonnet, blue silk slippers made by Kate peeping from under the hem of her gown. James was not really interested in the green velvet doublet made for him, knowing that he would be constantly chastised by Kate each time he wore his best clothes for having them covered in dog hairs. Bart had been bought new clothes before leaving Penryn to return home for Christmas.

The children practised new songs with Master Darnwell which they were to perform before the visitors on the first evening. The young tutor himself would accompany them on his lute and Rose planned to stand next to him in her beautiful gown.

The great hall was full of laughter, Lady Margaret in a gown of dark blue velvet edged with gold brocade seated at one end of the long table, her husband at the other. Conversation was cheerful and lighthearted as they ate their meal, lavishly prepared in the kitchen and served by Kate and Samuel. In the hot kitchen Thomas and Hannah worked and cooked quickly while the two scullery maids boiled water and washed the pewter dinner service which Robert Trenwith had brought back from abroad. Kate had placed Kristy on a rush mat up a corner where she played with a wooden doll which Samuel had carved for her, well out of the way of the scurrying feet.

The meal over and the songs charmingly sung, Lady Margaret took the ladies to the sitting room upstairs while the children were sent to play in the schoolroom, watched over by the tutor. Sir Geoffrey and the other men sat on at table, their glasses full and Samuel standing in the background ready to refill them when required. The room was glowing pleasantly in the firelight, the light from the candles and lamps casting shadows around the room. Sir Geoffrey motioned to Samuel to leave them and conversation became more serious.

"I hear there is more trouble up-country," observed Sir William Godolphin. "The people are complaining again that the prior at Bodmin is claiming more than his rightful due and has stopped them gathering firewood and from grazing their animals on the common land."

"That happened before," answered Sir Geoffrey, "but it transpired that the townspeople were cutting down branches higher than they should have done and trespassing further than they ought."

"That isn't the case now. The present prior has a bad name for oppressing the people. The church property which he is responsible for maintaining is being neglected but his own house is extremely well furnished. The burgesses are petitioning King Henry."

"It is a case for the ecclesiastical courts surely," commented Harry Boscawen, a neighbour.

"It is by rights but in this case the townspeople are appealing direct to the king."

"That will please many people in London," observed Sir Geoffrey. "Parliament is already making life difficult for the clergy. Another possible case of extortion and unfairness will be very welcome to the ears of some at court."

"I hear there is a rumour that the clergy are to be fined heavily for putting allegiance to the Pope first," remarked Francis Pengalin.

"So we all should in matters of conscience. The king himself as a Catholic is still subject to Rome in matters concerning his soul."

"Not for much longer if what I hear is correct. The king is privately claiming that the Pope has no supremacy over him."

His listeners were startled by Sir William's words. That King Henry was fast losing patience in his efforts to have his marriage to Catherine declared void was well-known but until now he had as king of a Catholic country accepted the authority of St Peter's successor in Rome.

Francis Pengalin spoke first.

"He may say that privately but he will never say it in public."

"You think not?" Sir William asked. "The clergy is about to be fined a total of £118,000 – £118,000, gentlemen – to remind them that their first duty is to the king and not to the Pope."

"A useful little sum for the king," observed Sir Geoffrey drily. "The country has wasted too much money over the past years and now the treasury must get more from somewhere."

"The Church owns a tremendous amount of land in England."

"Granted, but only because for hundreds of years our fathers and grandfathers made gifts of land to the Church to show their gratitude for God's mercy and love. Now some are saying it should be given back to the king but if your fathers and mine had wanted to give it to the Crown, gentlemen, they would not have left it to the Church in the first place."

There was silence as the other men considered Sir Geoffrey's argument. They had all inherited part of their estates from forebears who had gladly given land on which hospitals and almshouses could be built and churches in which Masses would be said for their souls after departing from this life. None of those present in the great hall had ever begrudged the portion of their inheritance given away in the past as an act of piety for the greater glory of God. They would act in a like manner themselves and had drafted their Wills accordingly.

They were interrupted by the arrival of Samuel to throw more wood on the fire and conversation turned to other matters. Constant rumours from London gave cause for concern but to the Cornishmen sitting in the great hall the condition of their land, the production of tin, the fishing industry and the state of law and order in their own county were of primary importance.

* * *

The weekend at the manor had been a great success and it was with reluctance that the visitors bade farewell to their hosts. The weather remained dry and fine, enabling everyone to reach home in reasonable comfort. The manor was once more alive with activity as the servants cleaned and cooked again ready for the visit of Phillipa and her children for Christmas. Robert was still away at sea so sadly would not be with his wife and family to share the festivities but hopefully he would be home in two months when, providing the winter remained mild, Sir Geoffrey and his family would visit Penvedn.

It was the first Christmas that the little church in the courtyard would be ready for use. The young priest who assisted Mister Douglas at the parish church was paid by Sir Geoffrey to attend to their needs every feast day and Sunday. For their first Christmas in the church of St Mary the Virgin Mister Douglas would ride over to offer the first Mass at midnight.

The children had never known such excitement. Christmas was always wonderful but the added thrill of being allowed to stay up until the middle of the night when they would go across the courtyard into the little church ablaze with candles added to the anticipation. The hearts of both Sir Geoffrey and Lady Margaret were filled with love and gratitude as they stood with their little family in their own church and watched Mister Douglas place the carved figure of the Child in the centre of the crib.

* * *

It was Rose who caused panic amongst the children in the middle of the night soon after Christmas. Her aunt and cousins were staying at the manor until Richard and Bart had to return to school. The additional visitors meant that the children were once again squashed up in bed and Rose, sleeping on the edge of a bed also occupied by Amy and two of her small cousins, found herself suddenly on the cold floor. She had been fast asleep but the pale light from the moon filtering in through the window attracted her across the creaking boards to peep outside into the courtyard. In her half-asleep state the unexpected sight of two figures clad in long dark hooded cloaks silently disappearing round the corner of the church resulted in a piercing shriek which terrified all within earshot.

Amy, Elizabeth and Jane sat bolt upright screaming in bed, not knowing what it was that had resulted in Rose's sudden flight from the window to dive under the covers, crying loudly. Richard and Bart, sleeping with James and two more cousins in the next room, fumbled with a candle and ran into the girls in their nightshirts but the crying would not stop. Exasperated by his sister, resentful at being woken so abruptly from sleep, Bart dragged off the covers to reveal Rose, shaking and sobbing at the bottom of the bed.

"What's the matter, Rose?" Richard asked her, trying to stop Bart from shaking her.

"Ghosts!" sobbed Rose. "I saw two ghosts."

The younger children screamed and scrambled under the covers. James, who had been woken too by the noise, struggled hard to restrain himself from diving under the bedclothes with them but if Richard and Bart could stand bravely in the flickering candlelight he would stand also. Trembling he might be, but he had no intention of letting girls see that he too was afraid.

Richard lit another candle and took it over to the window to look down into the moonlit courtyard. All was still and peaceful out there and he was convinced that Rose had been dreaming. The noise had disturbed Master Darnwell and he came into the room, carrying another candle, so that now the room was fairly well lit and less frightening. Between them they tried hard to calm Rose and the younger children and at last they lay quietly back in the bed, sobbing occasionally. The boys returned to their own bed whilst Master Darnwell kept a solemn promise to Rose and dozed fitfully on a bench by the door until daylight.

* * *

Lady Margaret and Phillipa were startled by the pale faces of the children at breakfast next morning and feared that some sickness had overtaken them. It was Richard who eventually explained. Rose, firmly convinced of what she had seen, would not go to bed without tears for several nights until Jinty offered to sleep in the room with the children. Kate, who suspected her father-in-law of some illicit activity again, renewed her threats if Samuel were involved. Digory, injured and entirely innocent for once, railed back at her.

"I ain't bin out o' bed," he fumed indignantly. "If there be ghosts in the yard they must 'ave bin real ghosts, nothin' to do wi' me."

He stormed outraged to the stable, leaving poor Kate feeling shaken. She very rarely believed Digory's denials of misconduct but this time he seemed to be telling the truth. Kate would have preferred a smuggling father-in-law to ghosts.

* * *

The excitement died down and even Rose began to think that she must have been dreaming. Phillipa and the children returned home, Bart travelling with them on his way back to school at Penryn with Richard. Master Darnwell began the children's lessons again and prevented James from teasing his sister in his earshot. Gratitude now added to adoration, Rose worked harder than ever to please her tutor.

Sir Geoffrey encouraged his labourers to improve the land, the addition of seaweed and sand resulting in better crops and fatter animals. Work was started on reclaiming further wasteland on the moors, the stones and rocks removed being used to build walls to enclose the animals and mark the boundaries of the estate. Sheep farming was tried because of the flourishing wool trade but the cattle were the main animals, providing a regular supply of milk for the labourers and their children. Digory, returning quietly one dark night from a profitable visit to the cove, tripped in the darkness over a bucket filled with milk which had been left in the kitchen by Thomas ready for morning. His indignant denials next day as sulky kitchen maids mopped up the mess were discredited by Jinty who had heard her husband's language. Only the thought of the cargo in the cave kept Digory's temper reasonably sweet.

Robert Trenwith returned from sea again and Sir Geoffrey and Lady Margaret, accompanied by Rose, James and Amy, travelled to Penvedn. It was the longest ride yet undertaken with the young children. Amy rode in front of Sir Geoffrey whilst James rode with Samuel. Lady Margaret and Rose had horses of their own.

Digory waited impatiently that night for Master Darnwell and the rest of the servants to retire to bed before quietly easing himself up from the mattress shared by Jinty who was snoring heavily. He picked up his boots, tiptoed out of the kitchen into the courtyard and across the dark fields. The silent figures returning with him hours later carried various loads on their backs which they stored silently in the stables. No one stirred in the manor as just before dawn Digory quietly slipped back onto his bed. There were turnips and other vegetables to be taken to market in the cart when daylight came. There were other goods carefully concealed underneath the produce.

* * *

Master Darnwell, left by himself but for a few of the servants, decided that a long walk to the cliffs would be beneficial to his health. Taking bread, meat and ale provided by Jinty he enjoyed the brisk walk in the pale February sunlight. He found signs of a track across the fields, past the trees which Sir Geoffrey was planning to use for the new benches. It petered out at intervals over the stony moors but he searched and picked it up again, jumping the streams and climbing over the rocks.

He was puzzled when the track, faint though it was, came to a halt on the cliff top above the thundering ocean. Idly he struck his stick against the bracken as he gazed with pleasure at the pounding surf below and was surprised when a solid looking bush lifted easily into the air, caught on the end of his stick. The narrow path down to the cove ended on a sandy beach covered in footprints.

* * *

The young tutor wrestled uncomfortably with his conscience during the two days before Sir Geoffrey returned with his family from Penvedn. The realisation of what he had discovered had not dawned on him at first. It was only when he descended the path and found the cave that he knew without any doubt. Some time later he replaced the bush and walked back along the cliffs.

That the tracks led right back to Sir Geoffrey's own stables only made him more uneasy. For a second the thought that Sir Geoffrey himself was involved flashed through his mind, only to be dismissed immediately. Apart from being an honourable gentleman and former justice of the peace Sir Geoffrey had no need of extra revenue. Someone else from the manor was obviously involved and he rightly suspected Digory.

His conscience urged him to inform Sir Geoffrey. He also knew from the number of footprints in the sand that other workers must be involved and he was reluctant to be the means of perhaps sending them to prison. Worried and confused, he eventually fetched his horse from the deserted stables. He would confide in Mister Douglas.

He had not previously been inside the house attached to the parish church. He had heard of the lack of comfort endured by Mister Vincent before the old man died and wondered curiously what he would find. The door was opened by Mister Douglas himself and the young tutor stepped into a room still dominated by the large crucifix but now simply furnished, a fire burning in the hearth. Mister Douglas listened to the young man and promised to think about the matter, warning him not to mention it yet to Sir Geoffrey.

Digory returned from market well pleased with the results of his journey. The profits were shared out, the larger portion kept for himself.

* * *

Sir Geoffrey and his family, safely home from the visit to Penvedn, were startled the following Sunday after Mass when a talk on St Peter the fisherman suddenly changed into a seemingly irrelevant but strongly worded sermon on the illegal gain of wealth from unlawful activities at sea. It was preached by Mister Douglas in both the parish church and the church of St Mary the Virgin. Sir Geoffrey, together with the rest of the congregation, was surprised to learn that smuggling could be classed as a mortal sin, punishable in certain circumstances by excommunication from the Catholic church. He had never thought of smuggling like that but he supposed Mister Douglas must be right. He was even more puzzled by a slight wink as the priest bade Master Darnwell good-day.

Digory's black expression and ill-humour was only understood by those who knew of the smuggling. The previous day he had been noisily cheerful, even Jinty's occasional caustic remarks failing to dampen his spirits. For someone who had just come out of church he was in a very bad mood.

It lasted until the end of Lent when Mister Douglas reminded the faithful of their duty to confess their sins at least once a year, and that should be during Eastertide, and the need of restitution as well as penance.

"Why does Mister Douglas keep looking at Digory?" whispered James to Rose who was sitting next to him in the little church but Rose had not really been listening, conscious only of the young tutor sitting closely behind her, and she did not bother to answer.

* * *

The hospital of St John the Baptist at Helston was surprised and delighted to receive a large, unexpected donation towards its upkeep a few days later brought by Mister Douglas from an anonymous source.

CHAPTER EIGHT

VAGRANCY HAD BECOME an increasing problem throughout the country as the unemployed wandered from town to town hoping to find work. In many of the larger cities the genuine cases – men, women and children – were joined by troublemakers, unwilling to work, ready to attack and rob as an alternative to honest toil. The generosity of monasteries was the only means of support for many and queues of wretched, hungry people waited daily at the doors. Sir Geoffrey was accustomed to seeing the crowd waiting outside the Dominican Priory on his visits to Truro.

The law of the land ordered that the vagrants should either find employment or return to their own parishes and there support themselves by begging. Failure to do so could be punished by whipping or a spell in the stocks. Now Parliament had brought in an Act under which an attempt was made to differentiate between those capable of work and those unable to do so. Sir Geoffrey, once again a justice of the peace, and others in similar positions of authority, were ordered to issue licences to those who were to be allowed to beg. It was a difficult task, separating those genuinely unable to work from the lazy. Work was not always available even for the willing. Parish resources in many parts were badly stretched by the growing number of needy dependent upon them.

Sir Geoffrey disliked having to decide who should be allowed to beg and who should not but vagrancy was a growing problem existing even in Cornwall and had to be dealt with as fairly as possible. He respected the monks and friars for their work of charity amongst the poor. Recently Mister Douglas had put forward a suggestion for the building of almshouses for the sick and elderly in his own parish now that the church had been put into a good state of repair. Sir Geoffrey willingly provided the land and some of the unemployed who came before him were put to work on the buildings.

They were to be constructed on the far side of the churchyard and some of the older men and women on Sir Geoffrey's estate, now growing too old to work, were to live there on completion, their work on the land then being continued by the new workers from outside the parish. There was some resentment shown at first to the newcomers but there was plenty of work for those already employed by Sir Geoffrey and the opposition gradually died down. There were people of so many different nationalities in west Cornwall that providing the newcomers spoke Cornish they were usually slowly accepted.

* * *

The building of the almshouses progressed well until Mister Douglas, glancing across at the building on his way into church one morning, was amazed to see the walls which had been nearly three feet high reduced to piles of rubble.

Nothing had disturbed him or his assistant during the night. There had been no storm or tremor of which he was aware. The workers, arriving shortly to carry on with the building, were baffled. None of them were experienced builders but they had been given enough instruction and advice before starting to be sure that they had done their job satisfactorily.

The walls were rebuilt, grew to three feet high, and collapsed again. There were uneasy mutterings about the work of the devil. Sir Geoffrey, called from the manor to inspect the site, wondered with Mister Douglas why on both occasions the walls had collapsed in the dead of the night. One of the servants at the manor remembered Rose's ghosts but no one could recall hearing of a ghost which knocked down walls. Convinced that it must be the work of practical jokers the workers were ordered by Sir Geoffrey to spend the nights watching in pairs, sleeping in the porch of the church.

Work was begun again but this time before it reached its previous heights the ghosts appeared again, crossing the courtyard – once more seen from her window by Rose. It had been six months since her last fright at Christmas and she had long since convinced herself that she must have been dreaming. One hot, airless day in early June the twelve year old child complained of feeling unwell and was put to bed early by Jinty who thought it nothing more than a slight chill. Rose tossed and turned during the night, feeling sick and feverish with a sharp pain which had developed in her side. Amy was asleep in the bed beside her as Rose shakily pushed back the covers and put her feet on the cool wooden boards of the floor, fumbling for the candle. In the darkness she knocked it and it fell unlit to the floor but there was a faint light from the moon. Trying to make her way to her mother she began to cross the room unsteadily, the floor and ceiling moving sickeningly around her in the darkness as though they were trying to push her over. She struggled to fight the nausea which was overcoming her and had almost reached the window when a furtive movement in the dark courtyard below caught her eye. The scream of terror which rose in her throat emerged as a feeble cry and with a crash which woke her sister, Rose fell in a heap upon the floor.

* * *

Samuel was sent galloping on Sir Geoffrey's best horse to fetch the doctor from Helston. For over a week Rose lay ill, half conscious and moaning with pain, rambling deliriously about ghosts to the blurred, worried faces which swam above her. At other times she lapsed into a very deep sleep from which no one could rouse her. Her parents sat constantly by her bedside, their faces white with anxiety and fear, gently holding her hands and stroking the dark curls which lay wet with perspiration against the pillow. They had lost two children already – their first child, a boy, who had lived only two weeks and the other a girl who was born after James and before Amy but had only lived one hour. The anguish of their two previous tragedies were reawakened and served to intensify their present suffering.

Jinty and Kate shared their vigil, all offering constant prayers for the child's recovery. Mister Douglas and his assistant paid regular visits to the worried household whilst the parish church and the chapel in the courtyard were visited regularly by those who could to pray for her. Sir Geoffrey and his family were well-loved by the parishioners who shared now in the suffering of the family at the manor.

The doctor brought by Samuel from Helston called daily and bled Rose, his face grave as he examined her. The potions he suggested were of little use. On his instructions Jinty piled yet more blankets onto the bed, the fire kept burning and the windows closed in the already stuffy, over-heated room.

* * *

"I must confess I am baffled," the doctor admitted reluctantly, gazing down at the small, wasting figure in the bed eight days after he had first been called to the manor. "She has not responded to any of the usual treatment – in fact, I have to say that I fear her condition is worse. If only she were conscious and coherent it would help. All this rambling about ghosts seems only to make her condition worse. A bad dream at Christmas seems to have taken possession of her mind and that is not helping her body."

"Is there nothing more that you can do?" Sir Geoffrey asked and at the desperation in his voice the doctor turned his attention from Rose to look at her parents. It would be hard to recognise the usually confident, well-dressed landowner and his beautiful wife in the distraught untidy couple facing him across the bed. Neither of them had slept apart from short spells when exhaustion had overtaken them. Their clothes were crumpled, Lady Margaret's long flowing fair hair tied back from her drawn face with a piece of ribbon.

"There is so much about the human body that we still do not know," admitted the doctor wearily. "Even in London the king himself is surrounded by charlatans who profess to know miraculous cures for ailments which the best doctors in the country cannot heal but their suggestions seldom help the patient. I can only suggest that I bleed her once again."

"No!"

They were all startled at the vehemence with which the one word came from Lady Margaret's white lips. Her pleading blue eyes were wet with unshed tears as she turned to face her husband.

"The child has suffered enough. If we are to lose her then at least let her die in peace."

There was silence in the room broken only by the quiet sobbing of Kate. Sir Geoffrey moved quickly to put his arms around his wife, his dark dishevelled head against her fair one as he held her closely against his aching heart. The doctor gazed at them and looked again at Rose. All he had done for her so far had failed. Perhaps it was time to suggest the opposite of everything he had tried already.

"Open the window a little and bring me some tepid water," the doctor ordered Jinty abruptly. "I am going to try to cool the fever down."

* * *

It was several weeks before Rose, pale and terribly thin, could be carried carefully in her father's arms down into the great hall and placed gently in a chair close by the window. Lady Margaret and her husband had suffered weeks of anguish. Both of them were gaunt and pale but Rose, though still very weak, was beginning to recover. For a short period each day she could be brought down to watch whilst the other children played quietly beside her. Bart was home from school again having been fetched earlier when Rose was thought to be dying. He spent long hours talking to her to help pass the time as she lay recovering on her sick bed.

Rose's illness had wiped all remembrance of the figures in the courtyard from her mind. She had been ill and delirious for so long that nothing in the past few weeks seemed real to her. She remembered Master Darnwell sitting by the bed, gently playing his lute and singing softly to her and could remember her mother and father constantly in her room each time she awoke, but nothing else stayed in her mind.

Master Darnwell had taken care of Amy in the schoolroom with James during the crisis to keep the little girl out of the way. She was almost three and a half years old and had surprised the tutor by how much she knew already. Rose had obviously taught her fair-haired little sister all the songs and rhymes which she had learnt herself and she could say several prayers.

Amy was delighted to be allowed in the schoolroom with James and one afternoon when Master Darnwell glanced up from his desk he realised with a smile that they had been joined by another. Kristy, standing silently in the doorway, had found her own way up the stone spiral stairs from the great hall. James, for the time being, had two little girls to share his lessons.

85

* * *

The building of the almshouses proceeded without any further incidents following a night on which the two men on watch in the porch heard the sound of horses approaching and muffled voices. The men rushed out, shouting and brandishing pitchforks, and the visitors rapidly turned and galloped away. Sir Geoffrey and Mister Douglas, though commending the bravery of the watchers, wished that they had remembered instructions to try to alert Mister Douglas and others without scaring them away. Now they were no wiser as to the culprits, but at least the rumours of wall demolishing ghosts had been squashed.

Master Darnwell was anxious to speak to Sir Geoffrey and approached him one evening before he retired for the night. The tutor had several beautifully carved wooden toys in his hands which he placed on the table in front of Sir Geoffrey who examined them with great interest.

"They belong to Kristy, sir," Master Darnwell informed him. "They were all carved for her by Samuel."

"Samuel? I had no idea he could carve wood."

Sir Geoffrey ran his fingers over the smooth surface of the wooden animals and dolls laid out on the table before him. The thought of the benches he was waiting to have carved stirred in his mind. There would still be a long delay before the men from Mullion would be ready to start the work for him. Perhaps in his own household there was a carpenter with an undiscovered talent who could complete the task.

Samuel had just finished his evening meal when the summons came from Sir Geoffrey. He hastily pulled on his boots again and ran across the dark courtyard, wondering what could be wrong. He was taken aback when he saw a number of Kristy's toys on the table in front of his master.

"You carved these, Samuel?"

He nodded, swallowing nervously.

"Only jus' lately, sir," he answered. "I only used odd bits o' wood. I ain't never done any 'afore, sir, but I wanted to make somethin' for Kristy."

He fell silent, waiting for the disapproval he felt sure must come. The country was very short of timber and he knew there were strict rules concerning its use.

"What else can you carve?"

Samuel was surprised.

"I don' rightly know, sir – I ain't never tried. I ded'n know I could carve anythin' 'fore I made that doll for Kristy."

"Try some more things," ordered Sir Geoffrey. "Show me everything you make. Try carving figures – see if you can make a crucifix."

He motioned Samuel to pick up the toys and the man gathered them up, still slightly bewildered, and waited for his master to dismiss him.

"You may have made an interesting discovery there, Master Darnwell," said Sir Geoffrey, turning to the young tutor when they were alone again. "How did you come to see the toys?"

The young man cleared his throat. This brought him to the second matter on which he wished to speak to Sir Geoffrey, but this time Kristy herself was the subject, not her toys.

"She is extremely intelligent, sir," Master Darnwell finished his plea. "So is Mistress Amy," he added hastily for fear his employer should misunderstand him, "but your own daughter has learnt from her sister and brothers. To the best of my knowledge Kristy has never been taught before."

Sir Geoffrey sat thoughtfully. He saw the dark haired little girl quite often running across the courtyard behind Kate or Samuel. Occasionally he knew she had been in the great hall playing with his own children but generally Kristy was in the kitchen with Kate or Jinty.

No one would ever know where the child had come from and many times over the last three and a half years since she had been brought to the manor he and Lady Margaret had discussed her, the thought always at the back of their minds that Kristy might have been born to parents who were more than farm labourers or servants. It was a question to which they would probably never have an answer but perhaps Master Darnwell's suggestion might help to satisfy their occasionally uneasy consciences.

"You may teach her with pleasure if you are willing, Master Darnwell. If she proves as bright as you think, she may be a challenge to Amy."

* * *

87

Samuel's carvings which he placed before Sir Geoffrey two weeks later proved that he had a gift which had previously lain undiscovered. The figure on the small crucifix was perfect, the wooden figures of the Mother of God and St John standing one on each side at the foot of the cross skilfully and lovingly carved. Samuel himself had been amazed as he sat whittling at the wood in the evenings. Kate watched her husband's steady hands with a heart full of pride. Master Darnwell had informed them of the decision to educate Kristy in the schoolroom and now Samuel was surprising everyone with his newly found skill.

Sir Geoffrey and Lady Margaret examined and admired the carving, Samuel standing awkwardly twisting his woolly hat. Lady Margaret wanted him to have the crucifix back for his own cottage but he refused.

"I c'n mek another one for Kate and me, my lady," he answered. "If you an' Sir Geoffrey think it's good enough I'd like that 'un to go in the little church."

"It will go in with pleasure, Samuel," Sir Geoffrey answered. "Tomorrow morning you can ride with me and choose the timber for the benches from the wood across the valley. We can spare enough wood for that. I shall tell Digory to take over some of your work around the estate to give you more time for your carving."

Samuel looked startled.

"'E won't like that, sir," he answered but Sir Geoffrey brushed his fears away.

"Nonsense, Digory has been having an easy time just lately since I have done less travelling and taken on more labourers. It will not hurt him to do some more work."

Samuel was apprehensive of his father's reactions but to his surprise after his first indignant oaths Digory took it quite well. He was enjoying the limelight reflected from his only son.

* * *

Sir Geoffrey and Samuel rode across the estate to the small wood next day. The trees were on the side of a hill, planted many years ago as a windbreak to give protection from the gales which regularly blew in from the Atlantic. The wood was well established now and it would do no harm to chop down the small number of trees required to provide the benches.

It was some months since Sir Geoffrey had inspected the trees closely. Most of the branches were bare in the early winter sunlight and leaves still crunched under the feet of the horses. Another of his farmworkers with more knowledge of timber joined them at the wood on Sir Geoffrey's instructions. Together he and Sir Geoffrey discussed which trees to fell. Samuel, who had taken little interest in timber before, preferring to work with the animals, listened and only spoke when he was deliberately drawn into the conversation.

"I think it is time we planted another wood," Sir Geoffrey observed eventually. "We have plenty of new trees growing here. We could plant some further along to give more protection to the fields where the men are ploughing."

He gestured to a large field in the distance where two of the labourers were working with oxen, the shouts of the men as they encouraged the beasts carrying clearly through the air. In past years too much attention had been put into the search for tin in Cornwall, the land being neglected, but the unpredictability of success in the tin trade had made many of the landowners return to farming.

The land had been improved considerably and now the crops were good. Some of Trewarne land was enclosed with hedges or stone walls but part of the estate still consisted of big open fields divided into strips and worked by individual labourers.

Corn ripened quickly in the mild climate and vegetables grew well. The wives and children milked the cows, made butter and cheese, cared for the hens, ducks and geese which provided eggs to be sold at the weekly markets. Their cottages were built of large granite stones, usually with only one or two rooms, no water apart from the nearby stream. The rooms were dark, occasionally plastered, with few windows and a hole in the roof for the smoke to rise. They had little furniture – a few stools, a rough table, a mattress which they had often made themselves and which the family shared. Life was hard but the labourers did not expect it to be otherwise.

* * *

For Kate and Samuel, their lot would now be easier. Samuel was no longer just a servant, he had a craft and Sir Geoffrey, always a fair employer, would increase his wages accordingly.

As a carpenter he could earn more than a farm worker. Samuel, riding slightly behind Sir Geoffrey as the two men discussed the best site for the new wood, had no thought of extra wages. His mind was still in a daze at the changes caused by a few toys for Kristy.

* * *

The trees were felled and split into planks before being left to weather. A new wood was planted which would not reach maturity in Sir Geoffrey's lifetime but the manor with the grace of God would stay in the family for centuries.

* * *

Bart followed Richard to University at Oxford. It would be a long time before he would see his family again now that he was so far away from Cornwall. James entered the grammar school at Penryn. Rose stayed in the schoolroom, joined for part of each day by Amy and Kristy.

* * *

The almshouses were completed. Eight of the older and infirm tenants were moved in, helping with any light work of which they were capable. Mister Douglas went each evening to say prayers in the almshouses. He liked to visit the old people before they retired for the night. Many of his older parishioners lived with their families but these residents were members of his flock who had no one left to care for them.

He bade them goodnight one evening and stepped out into the early darkness. Usually his routine took him across the small field which separated the almshouses from the parish church, which he would then lock for the night before going into his own house for supper with his assistant. A cold breeze was blowing and he paused to look up at the sky. Seconds later he was running swiftly across to his house, shouting to the other young priest as he ran round the back for his horse.

Mister Douglas had seen distant sparks rising up into the dark sky. He spurred his horse urgently down the long lane which led to the manor. His assistant followed closely behind, both men shouting as they passed huts and cottages. The glow in the sky increased rapidly and by the time Mister Douglas galloped into the courtyard others had spotted the flames. Together with Sir Geoffrey, followed by Digory and Samuel on their nags and dozens of other men, women and children running behind, they made their way across the fields, over the stone walls and up the valley to the burning wood.

"Thank God it is only the trees," exclaimed Mister Douglas, jumping down from his horse. Such a great fire was unlikely in stone built dwellings but the fear had been with everyone until they had come within sight of the blazing wood. It was a magnificent sight, the flames shooting high into the air, orange sparks flying in every direction. The villagers crowded noisily around watching, shielding their faces from the scorching heat, shouting and screaming as burning branches crashed to the ground. Suddenly a loud cheer went up as Digory and Samuel with other men were clearly visible in the light from the flames carrying the felled timber to safety.

Sir Geoffrey sat in silent fury on his horse. The woods were isolated from other trees and buildings, there was no danger that the fire would spread but a lot of money was lost with the trees and a lot of timber destroyed for which the country was crying out. There was no way that the fire could have been started accidentally. Someone had deliberately set fire to the wood, just as someone had repeatedly knocked down the walls of the almshouses.

* * *

"'Tis the work of the devil," declared Jinty fearfully to Kate.

The two women, accompanied by Hannah, waited impatiently in the kitchen for the men to return. The two serving girls sat with them at first but they both went to bed as the evening wore on. Kate thought that neither of them looked very well lately and hoped that no other illness was going to attack those who lived at the manor.

The men came in at last, black with smoke, and gave a vivid account of the fire to the waiting women. Sir Geoffrey had stormed angrily into the manor on his return without a word.

"'Tis the devil all right," agreed Digory, "two devils if you ask me – and I know who they be."

He had everyone's attention immediately but he pretended not to notice.

"Who, father?" begged Kate when she could bear the suspense no longer.

"You may well ask. Who was it knocked the walls down, tell me that?"

"We don't know, no more do you," answered Jinty scornfully. "You ain't got no idea, nor 'as Sir Geoffrey."

"I got my ideas all right. Ain't no one as lives 'ere on Trewarne land would cause such mischief. Gotta be someone from outside."

"We all know that, you ol' fool," replied Jinty impatiently, "but you don' know who tis any more'n we do."

"I got my s'picions," answered Digory darkly. "I got my s'picions an' I aim to tell master soon as I sees 'im."

* * *

Digory worked in the stable next morning waiting for Sir Geoffrey to make an appearance but he was forestalled. Mister Douglas galloped into the courtyard and disappeared abruptly inside the manor.

Sir Geoffrey had not long arisen. He had slept badly, fury seething inside him against the unknown troublemaker. Now he stared in disbelief at the white-faced priest in the great hall.

"Stolen!" he exclaimed.

Mister Douglas nodded his head gravely.

"Six large silver altar candlesticks, several smaller candlesticks, two gold chalices, various smaller pieces – all gone!"

Sir Geoffrey paced furiously up and down in front of the fireplace.

"No one saw anything?"

"There was no one about," observed the priest drily. "Everyone had gone to watch the fire – except the old people in the almshouses and they did not see or hear anything. My house is the only one really close to the church."

"But the church is always locked at night, is it not?"

"It is, Sir Geoffrey, but not last night. I was on my way there when I saw the sparks in the sky. I thought no more of locking the church until I opened the door this morning."

Sir Geoffrey sat down, drumming his fingers on the long oak table.

"It is sacrilege, of course," went on the priest. "The candlesticks were valuable but the other items were sacred."

"I cannot believe it would be anyone in the parish," Sir Geoffrey answered after a pause. "The fire must have been deliberately started to attract attention whilst the church was robbed."

"Or the robbery could have been an afterthought. Whoever started the fire could not have known I would forget to lock up in the excitement."

"No, but he could have planned to break in and then found he was luckier than he expected."

Sir Geoffrey stood and walked over to the window.

"Those large silver candlesticks were given by my grandfather. My father gave the smaller ones and the two chalices."

"I am truly sorry, Sir Geoffrey."

"It is not your fault. Someone is responsible though and I intend to find him. Digory!"

Digory jumped at the sudden shout. His master sounded in a bad mood. He ran across the courtyard just as Sir Geoffrey strode out of the front door, followed by Mister Douglas.

"Fetch Samuel," ordered Sir Geoffrey. "Tell your mistress I shall be back later," he added to Kate who had just come out of the kitchen door.

* * *

The four men were joined in the parish church by the assistant priest and watched silently by the old people from the almshouses as they examined both the inside and outside of the church. The thieves, whoever they were, must have escaped along the lane or across the fields but the rain during the night, welcome as it was on the still smouldering trees, had washed away any trace of foot or hoof prints.

With or without evidence Digory was still convinced of the culprits. He had chased off elusive figures on several occasions over the past couple of years. He had never managed to catch them but he was sure that he knew who they were.

"You have seen their faces?" Sir Geoffrey demanded.

"No, sir, I ain't but I know they from passin' on the lanes and I know they be the same ones. Big powerful 'orses they ride, sir, and I ain't seen none others like they 'ereabout. 'Tis my opinion they was the ones that knocked me off my 'orse that time."

Sir Geoffrey and Mister Douglas exchanged looks.

"Why should they be on my land?" asked Sir Geoffrey.

"I dunno, sir. They be troublemakers, I know that. Allus drunk." He stopped as he noticed his master's slightly raised eyebrow and looked indignant. "I like a drop," he defended himself in an aggrieved voice, "but I never go round causin' no trouble to nobody."

"He could be right," the young assistant priest commented. "I know the two he means. Loud-mouthed, arrogant, aggressive if anyone is in their way when they are riding along the lanes. I have heard many complaints from the workers on their father's estate but they dare not say too much for fear of losing their homes."

Sir Geoffrey mounted his horse abruptly and motioned to Digory and Samuel to do the same. Charles Rawlaston's house was ten miles away. They would be there before dinner. One of the old people could take a leisurely walk down to the manor and inform Lady Margaret that he would be back later that afternoon.

* * *

Charles Rawlaston glared across the table as Sir Geoffrey faced him. He had grown fatter since his term as a justice of the peace several years ago. Problems with his sons had already set back his plans to enter Parliament. His closely set eyes in a face now purple with fury shot venomous looks across the table at the three men who had walked uninvited into his room.

"Prove it!" he challenged Sir Geoffrey.

"I will prove it," vowed the other man. "Your sons have been turned off my property several times. Why were they there in the first place?"

"Did your man speak to them?"

"They rode away when he chased them."

"Then you have no proof," Rawlaston stated coldly. "As a justice of the peace you should know better than to make any unsupported accusations."

"Your sons are drunken bullies as most people know."

"Has anyone said so in court?"

Sir Geoffrey was fuming. His questioning of Digory on the ride over had been intense and he was convinced in his own mind. If nothing else the Rawlaston boys were regular trespassers on Trewarne land.

"Where are your sons?"

"How should I know? They are not children. My sons lead their own lives."

"It is a pity you failed in your duty as a father when they were children," answered Sir Geoffrey grimly. "Had you brought them up to respect other people and their property they might behave better."

The other man flushed angrily.

"Have a care, Sir Geoffrey," he warned. "There are laws of slander in this country."

Sir Geoffrey gave one last warning before turning on his heel.

"If your sons are ever caught on my land I shall take the matter to court. And," he added darkly, "if I find proof that they were concerned with the fire or the theft I will have them hanged."

He strode abruptly from the room, inwardly fuming. He knew he had very little chance of proving the boys guilty unless the stolen silver was ever traced.

* * *

Kate watched the two kitchen maids uneasily as they worked. They spent most of their working day helping Thomas and Hannah prepare the food for the household, walking to the weekly market for supplies, replacing the rushes on the stone floors and carrying out any other menial tasks which needed doing. Emmie was always a quiet girl but Agnes not long ago had been given to unexplained bursts of giggling. For some reason lately they had been almost silent as they went about their work. For several weeks Kate worried in case they were sickening for something which would affect them all but one

95

morning the younger girl fled the kitchen abruptly and Kate followed her, feeling concerned. She drew back against the stable wall as she realised that Emmie was being sick.

Kate had not had children of her own but she had heard the other women talk. She made her way back quickly into the kitchen, saying nothing. No one had noticed either Emmie or Kate leave and there was no comment when the girl came back, white faced as she continued her work.

It was only another week before Jinty noticed. Kate knew as she saw her mother-in-law's face when Emmie fainted after arriving wearily back from market that her own fears were correct. The girls had no family. Trewarne had provided work, food and a roof over their heads. Now they stood to lose everything. Jinty berated them for their wickedness, their stupidity – for by now Agnes had also admitted her condition. The pair of them sobbed uncontrollably until the others in the kitchen uneasily tried to calm them and Jinty, relenting slightly, made them warm soothing drinks but neither would name the fathers or even say if the same man was responsible for the condition of both.

They had always slept on mattresses in the same room as several other servants. No one knew how it could have happened unless on the trips on market day and neither girl would say. And then Kate remembered the 'ghosts'. Both girls had been provided with dresses and aprons when they were hired for service at Trewarne. Dark hooded cloaks had been provided the following winter.

Nothing was said for the moment to Sir Geoffrey or Lady Margaret. The girls had begged the other servants not to reveal their condition until it became obvious. Several weeks later they both vanished. Kate saw them go, dark hooded shapes just as Rose had described, silently making their way through the courtyard in the middle of the night. She did not know what had woken her and made her rise from the mattress to look out of the window but she saw them and sighed at their foolishness. She would chastise them strongly herself next morning and threaten to break her silence and inform Lady Margaret.

* * *

It was cold and wet in the woods as Agnes and Emmie waited in the darkness for the familiar sound of horses approaching. Recently they seemed to have waited longer each time for their admirers to join them and Agnes found herself wondering nervously if other more exciting company had now caught the attention of George and Percy. Certainly Emmie had not helped, she thought resentfully and not for the first time. No full-blooded man would enjoy the company of such a tearful, reluctant partner. It would be Emmie's fault if the present opportunity of a more exciting life were lost to them both.

The news which the girls had broken to the two men on their previous meeting had certainly not gone down well. It had been received with oaths followed eventually by moody silence. Emmie had not spoken a word but Agnes had made her demands quite plain. Marriage was not expected but financial support would most definitely be required.

The four had eventually parted in a grim atmosphere of hostility with reluctant arrangements made for the present meeting. Agnes had half feared and Emmie had half hoped that the two men would fail to turn up but presently there was the sound of horses and familiar dark figures dismounted and moved towards the girls.

Agnes turned to her sister, a little smile of triumph about to part her lips, but even in the darkness she could see the revulsion in Emmie's face change suddenly to terror.

"Now what – " began Agnes in exasperation and then a tremendous thud hit the back of her head and mercifully there was oblivion.

* * *

Dawn broke and the servants rose and began their work in the kitchen. Thomas kindled a welcome fire and Jinty brought a bucket of milk in from the cows in the barn. Hannah grumbled that the girls were late and went back into the room to rouse them. There was consternation when she returned to say they were not on their beds.

"They went out again in the night," Kate told them all. "Something woke me and I saw them go."

"Stupid fools," raged Digory. "We shall all lose our places 'ere at this rate. Well, I ain't gonna be the one to tell Sir Geoffrey what 'is scullery maids bin up to."

For once Jinty did not argue with him. They were all becoming very concerned about their own positions. They could not keep the secret much longer.

As it happened the news was broken to Sir Geoffrey in a way none of them expected. A pilgrim travelling along the uneven lane had decided to rest for a while amongst the trees. The bodies of the two sisters lay in a pool of blood a short way from the path.

It was Mister Douglas who brought the news to the manor. The pilgrim had fled along the path until he came to the church and hammered loudly on the door of the house next to it. Mister Douglas, saying his thanksgiving after early morning Mass, hurried from the church on hearing the man's shouts and frantic banging. It took him a moment to make sense of the incoherent words and then, summoning one of the more able-bodied and discreet old men from the almshouse to stay with the shaking man, he galloped swiftly back along the lane. It took him some time to find the right place and the pitiful sight filled him with horror but he said the last rites over the bodies before travelling as quickly as he could to the manor.

Sir Geoffrey was stunned at the news. Summoning Digory the three men returned to the scene. Agnes and Emmie had been stabbed repeatedly and had died clinging to each other. Shocked and horrified, Sir Geoffrey sent Digory back for the cart. He returned accompanied by Samuel and the two tragic young bodies were lifted gently onto the straw.

The servants were summoned from the kitchen and questioned repeatedly. Sir Geoffrey raged at them for not reporting the girls to him. Someone surely must have known they were going out at night. Jinty had been with Lady Margaret and Sir Geoffrey far too long to be afraid to speak her mind.

"When folks work 'ard all day an' go to bed as tired as we, they go to sleep – not lie awake to keep an eye on flighty young girls," she defended them all indignantly.

No one had any information. There were no clues at the gruesome scene. Two constables travelled from Helston to talk to Sir Geoffrey and all his household. All the labourers on the estate were questioned closely. They knew they were all under suspicion.

* * *

A few days following the tragedy John Daniels, one of the tinners, walked down from the moor into the courtyard, his daughter following behind. Sir Geoffrey paused and waited as they crossed over to him.

"Josie 'ere 'as summat to tell, sir," said the tinner, his hand on the girl's shoulder.

Sir Geoffrey waited for the girl to speak. She was dirty, barefooted and clearly nervous of him, standing close to her father.

"I talked to they, sir," she stammered. "At feast day last – I talked to they poor girls."

She started to sob and the two men waited for her to recover.

"They 'ad men friends, sir," she continued at last. "They was laughin' and talkin' about they to me."

"Did they say who they were?"

"No, sir – but they did say as 'ow they 'ad plenty o' money ter spend and wern from this parish."

"Nothing else that you can remember?" urged Sir Geoffrey.

The girl was silent, nervously twisting the corners of her ragged shawl.

"I don' remember no more, sir – 'cept that they said as 'ow they rode big powerful 'orses."

The Rawlaston brothers. They were the only ones within a twenty mile area of the manor who had horses better than Sir Geoffrey owned. They had been seen on Trewarne land by Digory several times over the past year for no apparent reason. The constables who had examined the bodies had stated that two separate weapons had been used. He guessed that the girls, knowing they were both pregnant, had probably tried to obtain money under threats of denouncing the fathers.

* * *

Sir Geoffrey, the two constables, Digory and Samuel rode grimly to the large house built by Charles Rawlaston when he had accumulated large sums of money as a merchant trader. A servant opened the heavy front door and the five men strode into the great hall.

"You are too late, gen'lemen."

Charles Rawlaston sat slumped at the far end of the table, empty bottles beside him, a pewter tankard in his hand. He was drunk, his words slurred and almost incoherent. He pushed the bottles suddenly aside and attempted to stand but he swayed unsteadily on his feet and was forced to grasp the heavy chair for support.

"Too late, I tell you," he repeated, tears streaming down his face. "My sons have gone. I have no knowledge of where they have flown – and I would not tell you if I had."

He slumped back down on to his chair, his great fat body shaking with uncontrolled sobs. The other men looked at him with a strong mixture of pity and distaste.

"We must search the house, sir," said one of the constables.

"Search it – search as much as you like. I doubt if you or I will ever see my boys again."

* * *

The brothers had gone, taking some of their clothes and possessions with them. A chalice from the parish church had rolled under the four-poster bed but there was no trace of the other missing silver. On the floor, hurriedly discarded by the wearer, lay a white silk shirt, bloodstained on one cuff.

They were not seen again. Descriptions and drawings were passed to every part of the country but the boys had vanished. There were plenty of foreign boats trading regularly around the Cornish coast in which fugitives could escape.

* * *

Innocent people were also seeking to escape from England as King Henry became more desperate to divorce his legitimate queen and marry Anne Boleyn. Threats against the clergy who opposed him developed into accusations of treason against the bishops for putting their loyalty to the Pope before loyalty to their King.

Henry's demands that they should submit all authority to him and not to Rome were repeatedly rejected by the bishops but at last they were forced to surrender. The day following the submission of the clergy Thomas More resigned as Chancellor of England because his conscience would not allow him to retain his royal post. It was May 1532.

CHAPTER NINE

THE EVENTS OF the past few months at Trewarne had affected the spirits of all concerned and Phillipa's suggestion that a change of scenery might help was accepted by Lady Margaret eagerly. It had been a bad year, beginning with Rose's severe illness and continuing with the fire, the theft from the parish church and the murder of the two young servant girls.

A smaller group than usual gathered together at Penvedn with Phillipa and her younger children. Robert was away on another sea voyage. James was with them, home on holiday, but Richard and Bart were at Oxford. Sir Geoffrey stayed for two nights but had business in Bodmin. He left Penvedn at daybreak, taking Digory to accompany him.

It was early afternoon when they rode into Bodmin, the largest and busiest town in Cornwall. Ragged, barefooted children ran after them, begging for alms as they rode through the dirty streets. Dull, expressionless faces stared at them from the doorways of decaying old houses. The two men did not stop until they rode up to the priory and entered the gates, seeking hospitality for the night.

There had been continuous trouble between the prior and the people of Bodmin for many years. The townspeople claimed that the right of common pasture had been taken from them, that the prior had a mill pool which flooded the ground, that he dealt in the production of tin and claimed unfair tithes. The prior in return accused the populace of being full of malice, failing to pay their dues, encroaching on his land, disorderly conduct, stealing his wood, poaching his fish – feelings on both sides had run high for many years. Sir Geoffrey, dining that evening with the prior in his private rooms, listened as he poured out his complaints. It was obvious that little love was lost between the prior and his parishioners.

"You have an excellent cellarer," observed Sir Geoffrey, feeling it time to change the subject of their conversation.

"From Padstow," answered the prior. "Brother Thomas is in charge of the kitchen. He has some assistants hired in the town."

"You have many in the community here?"

"Twelve, including myself. You must join us later for Compline. The singing is excellent. Brother Michael is our cantor. He trains us in the chant and rehearses us all very diligently."

"I shall be pleased to attend," answered Sir Geoffrey. "Afterwards I plan to visit friends in the town."

"Ah, then you must warn Brother Benet who is in charge of our guests, otherwise you may find the doors locked against you. We retire early at night and rise very early in the morning whilst most people are still asleep. Are you staying in Bodmin tomorrow, Sir Geoffrey?"

"I am here for a day or two. I have business to which I must attend."

"Join us if you are free," the prior invited. "We have the barber coming to trim our tonsures and let blood if any of the brothers require it."

Sir Geoffrey shuddered.

"No thank you, prior. I have no taste for blood-letting."

"You should, you should," the prior urged, waving his hands enthusiastically. "It clears the blood and many believe it also lets the evil out of our bodies."

"I can think of pleasanter ways." Sir Geoffrey was smiling, his grey eyes showing amusement as he ran his hand through his thick, unruly dark hair. He was almost forty years old and the first few grey hairs had begun to appear over the last stressful year. "I need a barber, I grant you, but I think I will do without his other talent."

"You would feel better for it," persisted the prior. "We undergo it regularly in the infirmary and relax our rules a little for a few days following – more sleep, better food, a little more time to converse and relax before resuming our normal routine. Perhaps," he added thoughtfully, looking at the handsome, well built man across the table and comparing him with his own paunchy, overweight body, "we should also take more exercise."

He rose, wiping his hands, and Sir Geoffrey rose too.

"You have enough sick people in your infirmary without me joining them too," he declined firmly. "I promise to visit the barber whilst I am in town but no blood-letting for me."

* * *

He slept well that night in the small guest room of the priory and attended Mass early next morning before walking into the busy town, accompanied by Digory. It was market day and the dirty streets were crowded. The shops, most of which were houses with the front used as a shop and the shutters let down to form a counter, attracted fewer customers than those selling their wares in the centre of the street and in the market place.

Sir Geoffrey looked around briefly, stepping carefully amongst the filth on the roads. The droppings from the ducks, geese and animals driven in from outlying villages added to the unpleasantness underfoot and the pungent smell which filled the air. He was not sorry when it was time for his business appointment with a local land agent. A wealthy merchant who had owned a small parcel of land adjoining Trewarne had died and Sir Geoffrey hoped to purchase the man's estate.

Matthew Wychcombe welcomed Sir Geoffrey into his small dark office. The two men knew each other well from their days at grammar school and they talked for a long time after concluding the business.

"Stay with us tonight," insisted Matthew. "Mary will be delighted to have company. My nephew is also with us at the moment on his way to Cambridge. He intends to enter the Church – not that I would say he is a particularly suitable candidate," he added drily. "I think his tastes a little too worldly for the religious life."

"It will give me great pleasure, thank you," accepted Sir Geoffrey, "but first I need the services of the barber if he has finished at the priory."

"You have heard of all the trouble of course with the prior?"

"I have heard his side of it," admitted Sir Geoffrey. "No doubt others would tell a different tale."

103

"There are faults on both sides," conceded Matthew. "The Franciscans from the friary are very popular here with their simple way of life and preaching but the Black Friars from the priory are not so well loved."

"For good reason?"

"Some would say so. They give alms and feed the poor each day but the priory possesses a lot of land mainly between here and Padstow and the people are beginning to resent the growing wealth of the Church. They grumble that many of the clergy have an easy life at their expense, but as long as the Church is seen as a comfortable career by many fathers for their sons we shall have trouble. The clergy should consist only of those genuinely dedicated to the service of God."

"As it was originally," agreed Sir Geoffrey.

"Let us hope that in the meantime His genuine followers will not suffer," answered Matthew.

The outlook of his nephew concerning his future had shocked both Matthew and his wife. The religious life was to be but a stepping stone to higher things, a rich benefice or preferably a life at court. The laws of the Church were minor irritations which would be observed when necessary or perhaps convenient. There were too many entering the Church with his young nephew's philosophy. Unless change came from within it could soon be too late.

* * *

Digory had stayed with his master while Sir Geoffrey looked fleetingly at the shops, following slightly behind and keeping a wary eye open for pickpockets, but once Sir Geoffrey had dismissed him he was free for an hour or two. He watched a cockfight for a few moments, joining in the shouts of the onlookers surrounding the birds, but he had business to do of his own.

For several months Digory had followed the same hunch on each occasion he had visited a different town in the service of his master. He had told no one else of his quest. Now he had his opportunity to try his luck in Bodmin. He had been there before, whiling away the time in noisy inns in dirty back streets as he waited for Sir Geoffrey. Occasionally he had met dubious agents to arrange for the disposal of smuggled goods but those days had unfortunately gone. Nevertheless, he still had a few useful contacts in the town and it was not long before he found himself in the dark back room of an almost derelict workshop. Jinty had always told him he looked a villain and now Digory practised what he hoped was his most cunning expression.

The man he was talking to ignored him at first so Digory increased his price.

"Who be wantin' they?" asked the other man guardedly.

"I ain't tellin' – let's jus' say a cust'mer. I 'eard as 'ow ee might 'ave some at the right price."

"'Ow do I know I can trust ee?"

Digory leaned towards the man with a sly leer.

"Let me 'ave they an' I can sell they at a good price. They ain't worth so much to ee if they 'ave to be melted down. It's my last offer – tek it or not."

The man hesitated, looking closely at his visitor. Digory bared his discoloured teeth in what he hoped was a conspiratorial grin. His hand stretched out invitingly and the grimy hand of the other man abruptly took the money. The deal was made. Moments later Digory stepped out into the alleyway, blinking in the sunlight, a heavy sack clutched firmly in his arms.

* * *

Sir Geoffrey was annoyed. He had left Matthew Wychcombe expecting to find Digory waiting in the street outside. There was no sign of the man and Sir Geoffrey strode impatiently back through the town. He would visit the barber and then if Digory had not appeared he would return to the priory. Digory could look for him there.

A message from one of the servants at the priory sent Sir Geoffrey hurrying round to the stables, fearing that something had happened to his horse but he could see the black mare standing quietly as he entered. Digory was sitting in the straw at her side, grinning with delight as he hugged his knees, a large sack clutched closely against him.

"What the devil are you doing, man?" demanded Sir Geoffrey irritably.

Digory had not noticed his master enter the stable, so delighted had he been with his own thoughts. He scrambled to his feet, pulling off his woolly hat as he did so. Sir Geoffrey had never seen his ugly servant beaming with such pleasure and suspected for a moment that he was drunk but Digory had been too busy with other matters to pursue his usual activity. Now his great moment had come and he tipped up the sack. Two large silver candlesticks, two smaller ones, a chalice and paten fell out onto the straw.

For a moment Sir Geoffrey was speechless. He had never for one moment hoped that the silver would be found, believing it to be well out of Cornwall months previously.

"I ain't found the rest of it yet, sir," Digory was saying, "but I reckon as 'ow that's a good start."

Sir Geoffrey dropped to his knees, examining the silver incredulously.

"I dedn' much like 'avin ter put the chalice and they other 'oly things in the sack, sir," Digory went on, "but I reck'n as 'ow I 'and't much choice."

"It's no matter, Digory. Where did you find them, man?"

"I 'ad an 'unch, sir," explained Digory. "I thought 'bout what I would 'a dun with they if I 'ad pinched they – not that I would, sir," he added hastily for fear his master should misunderstand him, "so I jus' kep' askin' every time we went anywhere."

Sir Geoffrey was still shaking his head in disbelief. It was not so much the value of the stolen silver which had upset him at the time but the act of sacrilege and the fact that his own ancestors had given the gifts to the church. It was incredible luck that Digory had found it. The old saying that it took a thief to catch a thief shot fleetingly through his head but he dismissed it immediately as unworthy of him. Digory would certainly have to receive a reward.

* * *

The excitement caused in the parish by the return of some at least of the missing silver lasted for weeks. Digory told his story over and over again, colouring it a little each time, until even Jinty was impressed by her husband's bravery in his single-handed fight to regain the silver from a belligerent shopkeeper and his powerful assistants. That Digory bore no marks of a struggle and the number of powerful aggressors increased daily was a slight cause of wonder but the reward which Sir Geoffrey gave his servant was real enough. Jinty would have been even more surprised had she known the full amount her husband received. A special service of thanksgiving was held in the parish church when Mister Douglas publicly thanked Digory and some weeks later a grateful parish elected him as a churchwarden.

* * *

In the middle of the year William Warham, Archbishop of Canterbury, died. Some months earlier he had denounced the king's tactics in the divorce case and condemned all that Henry had done against the liberty of the Church and the authority of Rome.

After his death Henry chose Thomas Cranmer as his new Archbishop. The Pope, ignoring warnings that Cranmer was unsuitable and unaware that he was a married man, approved the consecration. In March 1533, publicly swearing allegiance to Rome but privately stating that he would consider no oath to the Pope to be binding, Cranmer was consecrated Archbishop of Canterbury.

Meanwhile King Henry, accompanied by Anne Boleyn and 2,000 others, had set sail for Calais for a rendezvous between Henry and Francis I, the king of France. No expense was spared by Henry either for his own wardrobe or for the food and entertainment provided. Great banquets, jousts and revels took place in perfect weather. Expensive gifts of horses, jewels and cash were given to the French and an embarrassed Francis I had to borrow money to return such lavish gifts. Amongst other arrangements made it was agreed that two recently appointed French cardinals should go to Rome, one of their main tasks being to put pressure on the Pope to dissolve Henry's first marriage.

A few months later Henry's marriage to Anne became more urgent. After all his trouble over the past six years Henry had to ensure that the people would consider the new heir, now on its way, legitimate. They were married secretly and bigamously on 25th January.

Henry declared himself to be Supreme Head of the Church in England and Vicar of Christ on Earth as far as his territorial rights extended. He claimed the right to administer the Church, tax it, appoint its dignitaries and officials, control its laws and supervise its courts with no interference from outside the realm. He could and would determine doctrine and ritual.

In May Archbishop Cranmer declared Henry's marriage to Catherine null and void. Anne Boleyn travelled triumphantly by river from Greenwich to the Tower to prepare for her coronation, accompanied by over three hundred other barges and smaller boats, bedecked with flags and ringing with music. She rode to Westminster, carried on a litter under a canopy of gold cloth. Next day, Whit Sunday, she was anointed and crowned by Thomas Cranmer.

The first news that most people outside London heard of the coronation was at Sunday Mass when prayers were said 'for the King and Queen Anne'. In many parts of the country people showed their disapproval by abruptly leaving the church. In London so much indignation was voiced by the people that the Lord Mayor was ordered by Henry to issue a proclamation forbidding any demeaning reference to the new marriage.

In September, the child for whom the king had altered the religious pattern of his country was born. The king's seventeen year old daughter by his first marriage, Princess Mary, as heiress presumptive was required by tradition to be present. The court astrologers and soothsayers had confidently predicted a boy.

* * *

"A girl! After so much trouble!"

Lady Margaret looked at her husband in amazement.

"So I was told. I heard the news in Truro. I also heard that the king was furious when he was told. She is to be called Princess Elizabeth."

"It would be strange if the country were left to a girl after all," mused Lady Margaret, returning to her embroidery. "Is it possible?"

"It is possible but undesirable," answered Sir Geoffrey. "England has never yet been ruled by a queen."

"Well, perhaps there will be a boy next time. Have you seen Samuel's work since you returned?"

"No, I intend to go now. He seems to be making very good progress with the benches."

Sir Geoffrey rose and went out into the barn where Samuel had been working for some months on the weathered timber. The benches were almost finished, each one having beautifully carved ends depicting figures and scenes from the bible stories which Samuel had heard since he was a child. In the top corner of the last one on which he was now working Samuel had carved the year. He stopped, removing his hat when Sir Geoffrey walked into the barn and waited while his master examined his work.

"You have made an excellent job of them, Samuel," Sir Geoffrey declared at last with obvious pleasure. "How soon will they be ready to install?"

"About two weeks more I should think, sir."

"I shall ask Mister Douglas to come over and bless them. We will have a special service and then the rest of the day as a holiday, for the benches will complete the church. After that, Samuel, we will have some more furniture made for the manor."

Samuel flushed proudly. He had seen a carved oak chest when he had accompanied Sir Geoffrey on a visit to Godolphin once and he had other ideas too for pieces of furniture for the manor. His increase in wages had helped him to improve his own cottage and Kristy now had her own small bed and mattress instead of sharing with Samuel and Kate. He would dearly love to take his little family to visit Kate's mother still living in St Ives but he lacked the courage to broach the subject to his master. Sir Geoffrey noticed his hesitation.

"What is it, Samuel? Come now, you need not be afraid to speak."

Samuel twisted his hat and swallowed nervously. Only his pride in Kristy and love for his wife gave him the courage to stammer out his request.

"Of course you can go," Sir Geoffrey answered immediately. "You have worked extremely well. Kate will have to ask Lady Margaret when it will be convenient but take them by all means.

Take the cart – it will be easier and you can bring back some fish. Have a look at the benches in the church while you are there and see how you think yours compare."

Kate was ecstatic. She had only been to her home once in the last five years and then Kristy had been left with Jinty. Now Lady Margaret had given her leave to stay for three days and Sir Geoffrey had agreed. The cart was loaded with fresh straw for Kate and Kristy to sit on. Samuel rode the nag and they set off, jolting along the lane in the late autumn sunlight. Kristy's excitement soon turned to sickness and tears as they lurched along mile after mile but at last they had passed Lelant and were making their way down into St Ives. Kate had lived there as a child and loved the beautiful sweep of the coastline, looking eagerly as Samuel guided the horse gently down into the bay.

The harbour was full of boats, loading and unloading their cargoes, for St Ives was a busy port trading mainly with Brittany, Ireland and Wales. Copper ore, tin, fish and hides were shipped out and salt, wine, linen, canvas and timber came in, together with rugs and white fish from Ireland. Kristy was fascinated by the sea, the boats and the sand.

The sand seemed to be everywhere. Samuel guided the horse past the market hall with the courtrooms above and past the church which was so much larger than their own. He followed Kate's instructions to find the cottage where she had lived but the sand had moved in and many of the houses there were no longer occupied. The inhabitants had fled higher up away from the relentless sand which got into their houses, their food, their clothes, their beds. It was some time before they found Kate's mother and they were able to climb wearily down from the cart.

Samuel left the women clinging to each other and crying with joy as he went to unhitch and feed the tired nag. It was about fifteen years since he had first come with his father to St Ives one feast day and met Kate. Tomorrow he would take Kristy to play on the sand and look more closely at the boats. He had a little money to spend saved from his wages and he would dearly love to buy Kate and Kristy new dresses and perhaps a jerkin for himself.

Kate was distressed to see how much her mother had aged since her last visit but she supposed she must be almost sixty now, like Jinty, and she had worked hard all her life. Kate's father, a fisherman, had been drowned near Zennor and her mother had struggled to support the family on her own until her sons were old enough to work. Kate had two brothers to hug and to whom she proudly showed Kristy. The little girl, a very pretty, lively child now over five years old with long dark tightly curling hair loved the attention, singing and reciting happily the verses she had learnt in the schoolroom with Rose and Amy. Neither of Kate's brothers had married, both still lived at home with their mother. Kristy, with her sparkling dark eyes and long dark lashes, captivated them all.

Samuel asked questions concerning the bargains he wanted to buy. Fish was plentiful everywhere and dresses could be bought ready made at the market next day, made and sold by seamstresses in the town, and if he could not find a jerkin there were three tailors, all from Brittany, who would be only too pleased to make him whatever he required. He would have to look around well before parting with his money.

Kate had other relations she must visit and Samuel went to look closely at the benches in the church while he waited for her. He thought the workmanship was better than his own but it did not detract from his pride in his newly discovered skill and he knew Sir Geoffrey was genuinely pleased with his work. He was anxious for Kate and Kristy to arrive so that he could buy their dresses and at last they were waiting for him, faces flushed with excitement. Kate chose both dresses in blue linen with the addition of a white kerchief for herself to keep her brown hair covered and tidy. Samuel found a green doublet and a rust coloured woollen jerkin. He still had a little money to spare. He would take some oranges as a present for Jinty and Digory.

Their purchases complete, Kristy was taken for a final look at the boats. The sun was setting as they climbed back up the hill, streaking the sky pink and gold in a glorious sunset. Tomorrow they would load the cart with as much fish as they could take for Hannah and the new kitchen maids to salt down for the winter. If they bought some ale, cheese and bread they could pull off the lane into a clearing for a picnic on their journey home.

CHAPTER TEN

IT WAS EARLY evening and Sir Geoffrey and Mister Douglas sat in silence in the great hall at Trewarne. Their earlier conversation had been serious, both men conscious of the events which were taking place so rapidly in London.

Public sympathy continued for Queen Catherine, as Henry's first wife still insisted on calling herself, and because of it Parliament had ordered that everyone in the country over the age of fourteen must take an oath stating his or her belief that any children of Henry and Anne would be the lawful heirs to the throne of England. Anyone who refused to take the oath would be imprisoned for life. Princess Mary had been declared illegitimate, deprived of her title, and was to be known only as Lady Mary.

Most people took the oath when asked, many through fear of the consequences, others through indifference. Bishop John Fisher and Sir Thomas More had refused. They were willing to accept the succession but the oath they were ordered to take covered also an acceptance of the king's rejection of the Pope's authority. Both men had been committed to the Tower of London.

* * *

"Will you take the oath?" Sir Geoffrey asked Mister Douglas quietly.

"As far as the heir to the throne is concerned I see no problem. The king has always had the right to name his successor. I believe his other daughter Mary still claims to be his heir but from what I hear I would not wish the life at court on anyone. She is probably far better away from it."

"If I understand the situation correctly the succession is the only thing to which we have to swear – for the present," replied Sir Geoffrey. "God only knows what will happen next. The justices of the peace are ordered to administer the oath to the heads of households, who are then expected to put it to their own family and servants. I think you will have to take it separately as a member of the clergy."

"And if someone refuses?"

"Prison – fines. I doubt if many will refuse. For most people London and royalty are far removed from their daily lives. They have their own worries and problems to concern them."

Mister Douglas rose to leave.

"It seems an even greater tragedy that England has been torn apart for the sake of another girl. Perhaps there will yet be a boy."

* * *

The country desperately needed money for her defences in case of attack from Spain. Scotland and Ireland were proving troublesome and expensive to control. Thomas Cromwell had already raised a good deal of money by imposing heavy fines on the clergy for real and imaginary offences. It was not enough. The country needed a great deal more. Cathedrals, collegiate churches, parish churches and religious houses throughout the country were compelled to state their exact financial position. Cromwell was determined to provide his master with the money he required.

* * *

Lady Margaret was patiently teaching Amy and Kristy to sew neatly. Amy, like Rose, was clever with a needle but Kristy kept pricking herself and did not like embroidery. She much preferred to be in the schoolroom or helping in the kitchen. When the servants were busy she was expected to keep out of the way but between meals Kate or Hannah would teach her how to make jumbals and other delicious little biscuits.

Rose and Amy liked to go into the kitchen and help too occasionally though Rose, nearly fifteen now and rapidly developing into a very attractive young woman with a strong personality, wide grey eyes which could light up with laughter or flash with annoyance according to her mood and with dark curly hair which reached halfway down her back, still spent a lot of time in the schoolroom, dreading the day when her parents would decide she was too old for a tutor.

James would be home for the summer from grammar school in a few more weeks and Bart would also soon be home from university. It was almost two years since he had gone away and the family could hardly wait for the reunion.

"Kristy, you are not trying to sew neatly," Lady Margaret reproved the little girl. They were in the sitting room upstairs where the children sat several afternoons each week practising their needlecraft. Lady Margaret leaned forward to take Kristy's work but they were all distracted by the sound of a horse cantering into the courtyard below.

"It's a stranger," observed Rose, peering through the latticed window. "No, it is not," she added, seeing the man more clearly. "It is one of Aunt Phillipa's servants. I remember seeing him last Christmas. Perhaps he has brought us another invitation."

Kate tapped as she entered the room a few moments later and bobbed a curtsey to her mistress. She held a letter which she handed to Lady Margaret.

"Is it an invitation, Mother?" asked Amy eagerly.

Lady Margaret read the note but did not answer the child.

"Where is Sir Geoffrey, Kate?" she asked.

"I heard him tell Samuel he was going onto the moors to see the tinners, my lady."

"Take the children out into the garden, Rose," Lady Margaret requested quietly. "I think we have done enough needlework for today."

The children and Kate left her and Lady Margaret opened the letter to read it again, feeling puzzled. It was from Phillipa, asking Lady Margaret and Sir Geoffrey to ride over as soon as possible but without the children. The servant was waiting below for a reply but until Sir Geoffrey returned she could not send a message. The short note was so unlike Phillipa's usual long cheerful letters that Lady Margaret felt a little uneasy. She decided to send Samuel to look for his master.

Phillipa's servant rode off again as soon as he received his reply. He had been given food and ale in the kitchen while he waited. The evenings were long and with luck he would be back at Penvedn while there was still daylight.

* * *

Lady Margaret and Sir Geoffrey followed early next morning, accompanied by Digory. It was strange to ride to Penvedn without the children. The ride along the beautiful lanes would have been a pleasure without the uneasy feeling that something was wrong. Thoughts of Bart and Richard at university at Oxford crossed their minds and of Robert away at sea but neither of them voiced their fears. Perhaps they were imagining the urgency in the note and Phillipa had merely written the letter in a hurry.

It was a long ride to Penvedn and Lady Margaret, who rode far less than her husband, was weary long before she glimpsed the manor on a hillside surrounded by trees. They were met in the courtyard by the servant who had carried the message. Sir Geoffrey lifted his wife down and Digory followed the man to the stables with the horses. To their surprise Robert was home from sea, standing on the steps with Phillipa, and their welcome was as loving as ever, laughing and chattering as they took them into the house.

"Dinner is almost ready so we will eat first and talk later," Robert informed them. "The children are looking forward to seeing you."

"Is anything wrong?" Sir Geoffrey asked, trying to read his brother-in-law's handsome weather-beaten face but the other man seemed cheerful and unconcerned. "We were both a little worried by Phillipa's note."

"Nothing serious," Robert reassured them. "We will tell you all about it later."

Dinner was a happy, cheerful meeting with the children, all eager to exchange news. The beef and chicken were excellent, served with parsnips, swedes and forcemeat, followed by apple and raisin tart. Robert's wine, which he brought into the country himself, was always of superior quality.

After the meal the children were sent out and the adults adjourned to the small private sitting room upstairs, a room with carpets hung on the walls, elegant glass and china ornaments placed on a richly carved oak dresser. The deep comfortable chairs were of a style Lady Margaret had not seen before and she exclaimed with pleasure as she walked round the room with her sister-in-law until she became conscious of the serious subdued tones of the two men standing in front of the fireplace. Her clear blue eyes clouded as she sat down with Phillipa, waiting for her brother-in-law to speak.

"We asked you here without your family because we expect a visitor shortly," Robert began quietly. "Phillipa knows most of the story already and we agreed that the fewer people who know about the visit the better it will be for all of us concerned."

He paused for a moment and his listeners waited silently for him to continue.

"The visitor will be a surprise to you. Someone you have not seen for many years and may not see again for even longer. Your brother Edward, Margaret."

"Edward!" Lady Margaret gasped and stared at Robert first in amazement then delight. "Edward! It must be more than ten years since we saw him last."

Her smile faded as she looked at the serious faces around her.

"Is he ill? Why is he coming here?"

"No, he is not ill," Robert reassured her. "Thank God he is fit and well, but he is in danger."

"Danger – from what?" she asked anxiously.

Robert put his glass down on the table and went over to her side, taking her hand.

"Your brother is a very outspoken priest, Margaret. He has supported Queen Catherine for several years in her struggle to prove her marriage lawful. King Henry has not taken kindly to those who oppose him and since he has married Anne Boleyn no one is allowed to speak out against her. Now it has been made an act of high treason to refuse to acknowledge the king to be the only Supreme Head of the Church in England. Edward will not take the oath and his life is in danger."

"Where is he?" asked Sir Geoffrey.

"He should join us here soon. He is forced to leave the country for the time being. Pray God he will be able to return but for now London is not safe for him, nor any other part of England."

He rose and walked over to the window but no rider was yet in sight.

"How do you know where Edward is?"

"I saw him several months ago when my ship was in London. His parish is away from the docks but I strolled there one evening after the ship was unloaded. I like to see different churches when I go to Holy Mass and on that visit I recognised Edward. His assistant priest spoke to me later when he knew who I was and begged me to get Edward out of London."

"You saw him some time ago?"

"Yes, but I did not send you a message, Margaret. If you had known the danger your brother was in you would have worried. I thought it better to say nothing until my next visit. I hoped events would have quietened down but unfortunately they are worse. When I spoke to Edward some months ago he refused to consider any arrangements to leave his parish but now he has been persuaded by his friends that he must go, however reluctantly. It is not only Edward who will be in danger otherwise, the threat may extend to those who still befriend him."

There was silence in the room, broken by a sudden stifled sob from Lady Margaret. Sir Geoffrey moved towards her but Phillipa was nearer and put her arms around her comfortingly. The sound of hoofbeats sent Robert crossing quickly to the window to look down on the rider dismounting at the front door of the manor.

"He is here," he said quickly and left the silent room. No one spoke until he returned, followed by a tall gentleman, his handsome face thin and clean-shaven, dark eyes lighting up as he saw his sister before him. Lady Margaret hesitated, not recognising for a second the figure before her in fashionable clothes. For as long as she could remember her older brother had worn black clerical garb and ten years ago when she had last seen him his hair had been fair like her own. Now the plumed hat he removed revealed thick grey hair.

"Edward, is it really you!" she exclaimed in amazement, gazing at the smiling richly clad figure before her in his velvet clothes and lace collar. "I have never seen you dressed in this way!"

"And never will again once I am safely out of this country," answered Edward, grimacing at his rich garments. "I hardly think they suit me!"

"Have you eaten, Edward?" asked Phillipa.

"Thank you, yes – I stopped in Truro at an inn. I played my part as a gentleman on business well, I hope."

"Is it as serious in London as Robert tells us?" asked Sir Geoffrey later when, all the greetings over, they sat talking quietly.

"For those who accept the new queen there is no problem. For those whose conscience cannot accept her or the break with Rome then times are bad."

"I cannot understand how it can happen," exclaimed Phillipa, "and in such a short time. We have always been a Catholic country surely?"

"We have been spiritually under the authority of Rome for over a thousand years, Phillipa. Christ gave the keys of the kingdom to St Peter and the Pope has been appointed as Peter's successor since that time to guide all men and women in their search for God. As a human being the Pope can make grave and sinful mistakes like the rest of us but where the teaching of the Church is concerned Christ promised he would always guide him. St Peter's successor is our head spiritually at all times. The king has no authority over Rome."

"But how can all these changes have taken place?" persisted Phillipa. "Why did no one stop them?"

"Because many changes were justified. The Church was in need of reform. She had become too rich, owned too much property. Many of the clergy lived a very comfortable life and were too far away from the simple life of the good holy men and women who converted the country a thousand years ago. Those who wanted to attack the Church for their own purposes did not have to look hard to find faults, then those faults were exaggerated, honest clergy tainted with the same brush."

"What will happen next?" asked Lady Margaret.

"In London? The king has been excommunicated but I do not suppose that will worry him now that he no longer acknowledges Rome. The strange thing is that he is convinced that he is a good Catholic and that everything he has done is right in the sight of God. He believes his first marriage was wrong and now he has put the matter right. God help Queen Anne if she does not give him the son he requires."

His listeners looked at him aghast.

"He cannot divorce her!" exclaimed Phillipa.

"Can he not? Who is to stop him now that he has declared himself to be under no other authority but God?"

"But he waited so long for her!"

"I only know what is being said in London – that the royal marriage is not as happy as everyone expected it to be. The queen argues with King Henry in public. She has only given him a daughter, which he had already."

There was a shocked silence as his listeners tried to take in the implication of his words.

"And your plans, Edward – what now?" asked Sir Geoffrey.

The priest looked at Robert.

"We sail for Spain from Penryn tomorrow," answered Robert. "Edward will be aboard travelling as a gentleman on private business. In Spain we should meet up with another ship, the captain of which I know well and will take Edward to Italy."

"I hope to reach Rome," explained Edward when Robert paused. "I shall stay there for a few months or even years until I am free to return again. I do not go willingly but only because I am urged to do so by those who may suffer if I stay."

He smiled gently at his sister whose eyes were wet with unshed tears.

"You need not look so unhappy, Margaret. A spell in Rome will be a great pleasure to me apart from missing my faithful flock and perhaps there will be souls awaiting my comfort there too."

"And us?" asked Phillipa. "What are we to do – accept the king as head of the Church?"

"There is nothing else you can do, my dear. Many others have tried to stop the king and those who encourage him, but to no avail. John Fisher and Sir Thomas More are imprisoned in the Tower now for their outspoken criticism and others like myself are forced into hiding. I feel myself a coward to leave but my friends constantly remind me that our Blessed Lord himself fled and hid from those who would kill him on several occasions."

He rose and kissed his sister.

"I must take my leave or I shall not be in Penryn before dark."

"Stay the night with us," urged Phillipa but he shook his head.

"Thank you, but I must refuse. I have an old friend who is one of the canons at Glasney. I shall stay the night with him and go aboard ship tomorrow. Goodbye, my dear. God bless you and all your family."

Lady Margaret sprang up and appealed to her husband, the tears now running unchecked down her cheeks.

"This cannot be right," she exclaimed, greatly agitated. "Surely there is something we can do!"

Edward shook his head sadly, smiling at his sister as he took both her hands in his own.

"We cannot always fight to put the world to right, Margaret. Sometimes we have to bide our time. These things could not happen if they were not allowed to do so by the will of God. Somehow, in a way we cannot understand, they are part of His great plan and we must play our parts as He intends us to do. Kneel now while I give you all a blessing."

They knelt before him and he raised his hands above their heads.

"O Lord, holy Father and eternal God, bless our troubled country and those of us here present and our families. Free us of any sins we have committed in this life and which we can never hope to hide from you. Fill the hearts of all your servants with every grace and blessing that they may live in Thy peace and love, filled with the Holy Spirit, for Thou only art God and Thy Kingdom will endure forever. Amen."

He turned on his heel and left them abruptly, struggling to control his emotion. Robert followed and called for Edward's horse.

"Tomorrow then," said Robert and the priest nodded, looking up for a moment at the faces watching sadly from the window above him. He waved briefly, spurred his horse forward and rode out of their sight.

* * *

They did not see him again. Shortly after Edward sailed from Penryn, England became even more dangerous for priests who would not take the oath. Three Carthusian monks from the Charterhouse in London were the first to be dragged on hurdles from the Tower on their way to Tyburn where they were hanged, drawn and quartered. John Fisher was executed in June. Sir Thomas More was executed shortly after, stating from the scaffold that he died in and for the faith of the Holy Catholic Church 'as the King's good servant, but God's first'. His head was exposed on London Bridge until his daughter bribed the executioner to let her take it down.

* * *

Richard and Bart returned home for the summer. They were met at Penryn by Sir Geoffrey and Digory. Sir Geoffrey hardly recognised his son when the two young men disembarked from the boat. Richard was twenty years old, his thick auburn hair making him stand out instantly from the other passengers. He had changed little but Bart had grown from a boy into a fine, tall young man with strong shoulders, his dark wavy hair cut short in the style now favoured at court and his grey eyes alight with pleasure as he greeted his father. For once even Digory failed to complain as he loaded their luggage on to the waiting horses amidst all the noise and clatter, so pleased was he to see his master's young son home again with his cousin from Penvedn.

"I will help you with all that, Digory," said Bart cheerfully but Digory would have none of it.

"I ain't old yet, Master Bart," he protested. "I reck'n as 'ow I still be tougher'n you in spite of your size an' fancy clothes."

"I doubt if any of us will ever be as tough as you, Digory," Bart answered to placate him and the little group mounted the waiting horses, the young cousins asking eagerly for news of their families as they rode first to Richard's home at Penvedn.

* * *

Listening to their animated conversation over dinner Phillipa wished that Robert was home to welcome his auburn-haired son but God willing he would return from sea before Richard left home again and this time the young man would not be far away. He had gained his M.A. at Oxford and had been accepted to teach in the grammar school at Penryn where he had once been a pupil. The Provost at Glasney had talked with Richard several times over the past few years, listening sympathetically as the young man tried to make up his mind whether to enter Holy Orders or not. The suggestion that he should take a vacant post as school teacher whilst living with the religious community had been made by the Provost to give Richard time to come to a decision.

"I do not know whether I wish to enter the Church or remain a teacher," Richard admitted over dinner, trying to answer all his Mother's questions. "I thought if I started as a teacher it would help me to decide. The clergy at Glasney live a communal life, similar to that of monks, but they also have responsibilities to the members of the parish and I think I might like that. I cannot see myself as a completely enclosed monk. What do you think, sir?" he asked, turning to his uncle who sat next to him at table.

"A few years as a teacher would be very wise under the present circumstances," advised Sir Geoffrey. "There are so many changes taking place in the Church at the moment it would be as well to wait before making an irrevocable decision. None of us know at the moment what the king will do next."

* * *

"Is there any news of Edward?" Phillipa asked her brother later when the younger children had cajoled the new arrivals into the garden and the servants were no longer within earshot.

"Only that he reached Spain safely. Perhaps by now he may be safely in Rome but it may be years before we hear anything more. Margaret is still extremely worried and upset but hopefully Bart's return for the summer will take her mind off Edward a little."

He called to his son who was passing the open window, Phillipa's youngest child riding high on his shoulders.

"Are you ready now, Bart? Your mother will be waiting impatiently to see you."

A short while later Phillipa stood with Richard and her other children to wave farewell and Sir Geoffrey and Bart, followed by Digory, set off for Trewarne where an excited welcome awaited them. Lady Margaret could hardly believe that the tall handsome young man jumping down from his horse was her son, and Bart was amazed at the changes in his brother and sisters.

"Why, Rose, you have grown into a beautiful young lady," he exclaimed as he hugged her. "And you, too, Amy. James, I would hardly have known you."

"I shall join you at Oxford soon," James informed him proudly, following Bart into the manor. "I am almost fourteen now and have only one more year at St Gluvias."

"You will have to behave yourself with Richard there, teaching you. Did you know he will be there? After that you will work harder than ever at university. Where is Kristy?"

"In the kitchen," answered Amy. "Kate would not let her come in until we had all met you again."

"Let's find her," said Bart. "I want to see Jinty and everyone else too."

"Be sure not to hinder them," warned Lady Margaret. "Dinner should be ready to serve and they will not want you in the way."

Bart strode into the kitchen, holding Amy's hand. Thomas stood at the large open fireplace stirring a steaming cauldron whilst Hannah and Jinty bustled about and Kate brought in a bucket of milk. Kristy was setting the table ready for their own meal after the family had been served in the great hall.

"Master Bart!" exclaimed Jinty and Bart hugged his old nurse and Kate.

"It's a treat to see ye 'ome again, sir," said Thomas, looking up briefly from his cooking, and Hannah bobbed a curtsey to him.

"Kristy, let me look at you," said Bart. "Why, you have grown even taller than Amy."

Amy giggled but the other little girl tried to hide behind Kate.

"You have forgotten me!" reproved Bart. "Kristy, how could you!"

"She is always shy with strangers," Amy defended her.

"Strangers! Now you really have hurt me," Bart teased his sister. "Come, Kristy, at least we can shake hands."

Kate pushed her forward, brushing the dark curls from the child's flushed face, and Kristy reluctantly allowed Bart to take her small hand.

"You are both prettier than ever," he exclaimed, looking from his fair-haired little sister to Kristy. Amy glowed with delight but Kristy stepped back behind Kate, unable to hide her embarrassment until Bart took pity on her and turned away.

"Thomas, something smells wonderful."

"It might taste wonderful too if you would get out of our way," added Jinty and Bart laughed.

"When Jinty starts shouting at me then I know I am home. Come, Amy, we must go or there will be nothing to eat today."

* * *

The family sat around the table in the great hall and Bart looked at them all, delighted to be with them again. He had missed them during his two years away. His parents had hardly changed but Rose was now an attractive young lady, her cheeks pink with excitement at her brother's homecoming. Bart watched John Darnwell's expression soften each time the young tutor looked at Rose. It was obvious that the quiet man was devoted to her in spite of his attempt to hide his love and Bart wondered whether Rose had outgrown her childhood adoration of him. He saw her face as she listened to Master Darnwell answer a question from Sir Geoffrey and it was clear from the expression in her grey eyes that her feelings towards him had not changed.

Lady Margaret quietly watched her daughter too. She and her husband had been aware for some time of the deep and long lasting attachment of the young couple to each other and they had discussed the situation privately between themselves. When Master Darnwell had first arrived in the household as a shy young man Rose's adoration had amused them. Now Rose was almost sixteen, an age when many girls thought of marriage. Master Darnwell was eleven years older. His quiet, courteous manner, good background and immediate success with the children had quickly earned the respect of Sir Geoffrey and his wife, but Rose had met very few other young men. Lady Margaret looked at her daughter and made up her mind. Bart's homecoming was an opportunity to change that situation. The new wing on the manor had not long been completed. It was time to entertain neighbours and friends, particularly those with eligible young sons.

* * *

The invitations had been sent out, delivered by Samuel and Digory. The Arundells, Sir William Godolphin, Matthew Wychcombe, John Wynslade and several neighbours were invited to attend, all accompanied by their wives and families. The guest rooms were made ready, new gowns and doublets bought or made and for weeks the kitchen was a hive of activity as food was prepared. Chickens, geese, ducks were plucked by Hannah and Jinty ready for Thomas to cook, forcemeats prepared, fish from St Ives baked. Tongue and ham pies with a lovely golden crust stood ready on the kitchen table. Kate made fruit pies and jellies, helped by Kristy, whilst Digory and Samuel fetched what seemed like unending supplies from the markets nearby.

There was plenty of wine and ale brewed ready to drink, musicians hired for the evening and the rushes cleared from the floor of the great hall so that guests who wished to dance could do so. Trewarne had not been the scene of such bustle and excitement since Sir Geoffrey had married Lady Margaret more than twenty years previously.

* * *

The day the guests were expected at last arrived and was spent in last minute preparations, the great hall decorated with greenery, fresh flowers and herbs by Bart and Rose, helped by the younger children. The perfume from the flowers filled the room as the family prepared to welcome their guests.

Matthew Wychcombe from Bodmin with his wife Mary and his nephew, also home from university, were the first arrivals, having broken their journey the previous night to stay with friends in Truro. The Arundells had also stayed overnight near Mitchell. They were followed almost immediately by Phillipa and Robert with their children. All the visitors were greeted, then shown to their rooms by Kate or Jinty. Sir William Godolphin arrived with his family and other neighbours. There was only one more party expected.

It was almost five o'clock when John Wynslade and his wife and children rode into the courtyard accompanied by his niece, Isobel. Bart was standing beside his parents to greet them and thought that everyone in the hall must hear the sudden pounding of his heart as he saw the pretty, fair-haired girl standing in front of him.

"I believe you met my son, Bart, some years ago," Sir Geoffrey was saying to her. "Bart, you must remember Isobel."

She raised her dark blue eyes and smiled at him.

"Yes, we have met," he stammered and then could not think of another word to say. All the polite pleasantries he had exchanged such a short while ago with other guests had flown completely from his head. Isobel went past him with her aunt and followed Kate up the stone staircase and Bart felt he desperately needed fresh air.

"Did you notice Bart's face when Isobel arrived?" Lady Margaret asked her husband later as they rested before changing for supper.

Sir Geoffrey had been absently stroking his wife's long fair hair as she lay beside him and did not answer for a moment until a gentle nudge recalled his attention.

"Whose face? Oh, Bart's. No, why do you ask?"

"We arranged this party for Rose to meet possible suitors," answered Lady Margaret, smiling at her thoughts. "I think we may find we have lost our son instead."

Sir Geoffrey raised himself on one elbow and his handsome face looked down at the delicate features of his beautiful young wife. He bent his head and kissed her gently.

"I can bear losing Bart and I can bear losing Rose providing that they are happy. What I could never bear would be to lose you, my love."

* * *

Supper began once all the guests had taken their places along the large oak table. Sir Geoffrey sat at one end, Lady Margaret at the other. The seating arrangements had been carefully planned beforehand but Bart persuaded Richard to change places with him so that he was seated opposite Isobel. Rose had been deliberately separated from Master Darnwell and placed between two other young men but she smiled at the tutor whenever he looked in her direction. She had Matthew Wychcombe's nephew, Andrew, on one side of her and took an instant dislike to him as she listened to his conversation. The young man on her right hand was pleasant but she was always conscious of Master Darnwell, his dark head bent in conversation with her aunt.

"What do you plan to do now that you have finished at Oxford, Richard?" Andrew Wychcombe asked.

"I am to go to Penryn as a schoolteacher. What about you, Andrew?"

"I shall finish at Cambridge and enter the Church on the administrative side – preferably under the patronage of some great man so that I can make my way to the royal court."

"To court? You surely do not want to go to London!" exclaimed Rose.

"Why not? That is where you must be if you wish to be noticed – to become rich and enjoy a good standard of living."

"If that is your ambition you would do better not to enter the Church," Rose commented tartly.

"The poor have no monopoly of God, Mistress Rose," Andrew answered her. "However, perhaps you are right. I may decide to study law instead. What do you think, Mistress Isobel? Shall I become a priest or a lawyer?"

Isobel blushed. Unlike Rose she found the young man very attractive with his black hair and blue eyes, now fixed on her very attentively. His conversation of the court had been so much more interesting than Bart's stammered answers to her remarks. Rose did not know what was wrong with her brother this evening. Usually he had them all enthralled with his stories of his work and friends at Oxford but tonight he seemed tongue-tied. They had all listened to Andrew's opinionated comments on life at Cambridge with hardly a word spoken by Bart. Rose wondered if he was feeling ill until she noticed how his eyes hardly left Isobel's pretty face.

"I think perhaps you should go in for law, Master Wychcombe," Isobel was saying. "Would that interest you?"

"More work – more study!" groaned Andrew in mock despair. "But then perhaps fame as a barrister. Yes, perhaps I might try law. I could go to Lincoln's Inn for several years and then make my fortune from other people's disputes. When you are still a poor teacher, Richard, I may be a rich lawyer."

"I should like to go to London," sighed Isobel. "I have no wish to spend the rest of my life here in Cornwall."

"Why not?" The implication of her words had shaken Bart at last. "What has London to offer?"

"Life – adventure – interesting people! All the things we lack down here. Oh, I did not mean to be unkind," Isobel added hastily, conscious of raised eyebrows around her, "but nothing ever happens down here. Tonight is the first time I have been anywhere for nearly a year! What about you, Rose?"

"I suppose I must say the same," Rose admitted, "but I am happy here. I have no wish to go anywhere else apart from visiting relatives and friends."

"That is the difference," answered Isobel. "I want to see other places, meet exciting people and I do not suppose I ever will."

"Come with me to London!" exclaimed Andrew dramatically. "I will become rich and present you at court."

"Why, Master Wychcombe, what a delightful idea."

It was too much for Bart. To have fallen madly in love with Isobel and to see her so captivated by another all in the same evening was more than he could bear. He stood up abruptly and strode from the room, making his way into the cool courtyard. Lady Margaret was startled by her son's ill manners.

"What is the matter with Bart?" she asked Rose who was seated close to her near the top of the table.

"Nothing, Mother – he just needed some air."

* * *

The meal over, the servants cleared the dishes from the long table and moved it to the end of the room against the wall. The musicians entered and seated themselves, waiting for permission to play. Rose took advantage of the confusion in the room to slip outside to look for her brother.

"Bart!" she called quietly. "Bart, where are you?"

There was no answer but a slight movement inside the stable caught her eye and she went inside to find Bart moodily stroking his horse.

"What is the matter with you tonight?" asked Rose. "Are you ill?"

"No, I am not," answered Bart shortly. "Go back inside, Rose."

"No, not yet. It must be Isobel then."

Bart turned his back on her abruptly but did not answer.

"Bart, you have only just met her," pleaded Rose. "She cannot be important to you already."

"I met her years ago," answered Bart. "I thought about her occasionally but since this afternoon when I saw her again I can think of no one else. I have fallen in love with her, Rose."

"Hiding in the stables is hardly the best way to show it," commented Rose in exasperation. "She is in there listening to every word that awful Andrew Wychcombe is saying. If you like her you must talk to her!"

"I cannot think of anything to say!" answered Bart helplessly. "Every thing that comes into my head seems so stupid when I look at her."

"You can usually talk for hours to anyone. Come on, Bart. If you like her it will do no good hiding out here and leaving her to Andrew. I would never have thought of you as a coward."

"I am not a coward," Bart was stung to reply.

"Then come back inside with me and talk to her. I will try to distract Andrew by talking to him myself but not for long though – I would much rather talk to Master Darnwell."

In spite of himself Bart smiled.

"I had noticed. This party is supposed to be for you to meet other young men, you know that, do you not, Rose?"

"Is it?" Rose was surprised. "I hope not for it would be wasted if that were the only reason. I intend to marry John Darnwell if father will give his permission – if not, I shall stay unwed. No one else I have ever met has interested me and I do not think I will change my mind now. Come on, Bart. We shall be missed if we do not go back inside."

Bart reluctantly followed his sister back into the great hall where she kept her promise and engaged Andrew Wychcombe in conversation. Bart drew a deep breath and began to talk to Isobel. Each time she smiled at him, looking at him with her dark blue eyes, he felt as though he were drowning. At first she kept glancing away from him to where Andrew was dancing with Rose but gradually she turned her attention more to Bart and he relaxed as he found it easier to talk to her. Master Darnwell was now the one to look unhappy as he had to watch Rose giving all her attention to Andrew.

On Saturday morning the older guests slept late, most of them not appearing until it was time for dinner at noon. The younger ones had drifted down at intervals to be given breakfast by Kate and Jinty.

Bart rose early, fearful of missing a moment of Isobel's company, waiting impatiently in the great hall until at last she appeared. He was relieved to see Master Darnwell smiling again at Rose. His sister's attempts to distract Andrew's attention from Isobel the previous evening had been too successful, alarming Rose and leaving the tutor seething with jealous fury. A hurried explanation by Rose between dances had relieved the tension slightly but when the evening ended the tutor still did not look a very happy man.

The other young people had enjoyed a wonderful evening and were now drifting out into the morning sunshine in the garden.

"How far can you shoot an arrow?" Andrew asked Bart.

"About seventy yards. What about you?"

"More than that. How about a contest?"

"If you wish," agreed Bart. "Longbow or crossbow?"

"Longbow, of course. Only lords or very wealthy landowners are allowed crossbows."

"Not down here in the south-west," Bart replied. "Anyone who lives within seven miles of the sea is allowed to have one for defence against the king's enemies. That is something you should know, Andrew, if you are going to be a lawyer."

Samuel brought the arrows and the bows, some of elm, some of yew. The older men had joined them with Sir Geoffrey and were examining them with interest.

"We will all compete," decided Sir Geoffrey. "The butts are set up in the top field. Fetch the crossbows too, Samuel."

* * *

Archery was practised regularly at Trewarne, as it was throughout the country. Parliament had declared other games such as tennis, bowls, skittles and football illegal for the common people because they distracted them from the far more important skill of the archer which would be needed in time of war. Boys over the age of seven must learn to shoot an arrow. Annual musters were held to keep a record of men, weapons, armour and horses available in each parish. The landowners and all their workers between the ages of sixteen and sixty who were capable of fighting were expected to assemble at certain points when called upon in times of crisis.

Competition was keen amongst Sir Geoffrey and his guests. Bart and Andrew shot their arrows further and more accurately than any of the other gentlemen assembled. It had become a personal contest between the two young men. Both were well aware of and resented the interest of the other in Isobel who was watching from the lower end of the field with Rose and other ladies. Andrew inwardly seethed when Bart was eventually declared the winner.

The ringing of a bell in the distance reminded them that it must be dinner time. Andrew succeeded in reaching Isobel first to walk the short distance back to the manor house and this time it was Bart who was annoyed. After dinner a ride was suggested, a few of the young ladies accompanying the men, but Bart was disappointed to find Isobel was not amongst them.

Supper was earlier than usual for entertainment had been arranged, a group of actors hired to perform a Miracle play in the great hall and their spirited performance of the story of Noah and the flood delighted the audience. The servants were allowed in to watch, Kristy squeezing to the front to sit by Amy.

Bart stood at the side of the hall where he could see Isobel throughout the play. He found himself unable to follow the drama being performed with such vigour. His gaze constantly rested on Isobel, her pretty face now laughing, now serious. The blue velvet of her gown deepened the blue of her sparkling eyes, and long fair lashes fluttered on cheeks pink with excitement. Bart was aware of Andrew watching her too and the eyes of the other young man held a challenge as he returned Bart's hostile gaze.

"Stop glaring at him," Rose teased her brother later that evening. "He will be going back to Bodmin tomorrow."

It was a comforting thought. That would leave Bart with the advantage of being thirty miles nearer to Isobel than his rival for the next eight weeks until he had to return to university.

CHAPTER ELEVEN

KATE WAS FRANTIC with worry. Kristy had been missing since the previous day when she had been playing in a nearby field with some of the farming children. She had failed to return for her supper and as the evening wore on everyone on the estate was out searching for her. Kristy was seven and had never failed to return for her meal before. The children she had been with did not know where she had gone.

When darkness fell and the searchers reluctantly returned to their homes for the night Kate sat sobbing in the kitchen at the manor, Jinty and Samuel, red-eyed themselves, trying vainly to comfort her. Heavy rain started to fall during the evening, adding to their distress. In the sitting room above the great hall Sir Geoffrey and Lady Margaret sat with their family, too worried to retire to bed. Bart and James had joined their father with Master Darnwell and the other men searching the estate until long after darkness had fallen but they had found no trace of the child.

"We will start again at first light," Sir Geoffrey decided. "Bart, you ride to Godolphin and ask Sir William to search his land. She may have strayed over that way. The rest of us will divide into groups. Some of the farm labourers can go and help the tinners search the moors."

"I will go with them," volunteered James. "Storm will be useful up there."

"What about us?" asked Rose. "What can we do?"

"Nothing, my dear, except pray and try to help Kate. Kristy may be back by morning when she can see her way home again. No one can do any more until it is light."

* * *

The fire in the kitchen was kept burning all through the night, the servants dozing fitfully in front of it. Kate stared unseeingly into the flames, her mind in turmoil. She tried to pray but her

132

anguished brain seemed to block out the words. She was icily cold in spite of the fire and Samuel's arms about her. All she could think of was Kristy lost somewhere out there in the darkness. She wanted to scream at the silent men in the kitchen to get out there and search, search for the child, but she knew it was useless. There was no moon and the night was pitch dark.

She was vaguely aware of Jinty coaxing her to drink brandy sent in by Sir Geoffrey. Towards morning she must have dozed for she was suddenly wide awake, conscious that the first grey light was stealing into the kitchen and Samuel and Digory had gone. Thomas, too old and crippled with rheumatics to help with the search, threw more wood on the fire when he saw she was awake. They heard the clatter of hooves as Bart galloped off to Godolphin. The farm labourers were in the courtyard listening to Sir Geoffrey's instructions for a thorough search and James headed towards the moors to join the tinners, Storm barking as he ran alongside.

Kate forced herself to move, to go about her routine tasks. Lady Margaret watched her anxiously but Kate seemed not to hear when anyone spoke to her.

"Kate! Kate, listen to me!" Rose shook Kate's arm and tried to make her focus her gaze upon her. "Who was Kristy playing with yesterday?"

"The farm children," answered Kate mechanically.

"Yes, but which ones?"

There were so many different families on the estate. Kate hesitated.

"I'm not sure. Lizzie and Janie were two of them. I don't remember."

"Where do they live, Kate? Which is their cottage?"

Kate pressed her hands to her aching head, trying to remember.

"Could you take me there?" Rose had tossed in her bed all night unable to sleep and now she looked anxiously at Kate. "There's just a chance they may have remembered something. It will be better than staying here doing nothing but wait."

Kate tried to pull herself together. Rose was right, waiting was unbearable. She went to tell Jinty while Rose ran upstairs to inform her mother and change into an old dress and shoes. She had walked miles through muddy fields once before on the day Kristy had first been taken to Trewarne.

Rose had never before visited the cottages on her father's estate. The workers and their families joined the family from the manor on Sundays and feast days at church or for social events in the parish but she had never been close to their homes. She walked with a silent Kate across fields, climbing over stone stiles and trying vainly to avoid the mud until they reached a little cluster of cottages. The women and young children were amazed to see Rose in her mud-spattered dress but she did not care about her appearance. The men had taken all the horses for their search and she had no option but to walk.

Lizzie and Janie were called out of the cottages, looking very scared when they saw the visitors. Rose questioned them closely and two other children were brought over from a nearby cottage but none of them could say anything which would help. Kate sank onto a large stone, weeping quietly, whilst Rose tried again in desperation with the children. Kristy had left them in the field just before supper time. They had thought she was going back to the manor and had run home themselves, not bothering to turn round again. They had no idea where she could have gone.

"What were you talking about when you were with her?" persisted Rose and for a second she thought Lizzie looked uncomfortable.

"Nothin' partic'ler," answered Janie.

"You must have been talking about something – school – your friends – what was it? Lizzie, you know something."

The child started to cry and Rose saw Janie pinching her sister.

"Stop that, Janie," she ordered. "Lizzie, what is it?"

"Janie made 'er cry," sobbed the other little girl. "She told 'er she ent got no real feyther and that she was found on the beach. Kristy started ter cry and then wouldn't play any more."

"I dedn' mean ter mek 'er cry," Janie defended herself, frightened now as everyone stared at her. "She was braggin' 'er feyther made them benches in church an' I sed he wern't really 'er feyther cos 'er real feyther was drowned."

"Did she not know?" Rose asked quietly and Kate dumbly shook her head.

"Did Kristy say anything?" Rose asked Lizzie.

"No, miss. She jus' stared at us fer a minute then started ter cry an' ran off."

* * *

"We hadn't told her," Kate wept as they made their way back across the fields. "We knew Sir Geoffrey had ordered you other children not to say anything. She didn't mix much with the others so we just thought she would never find out. We thought of her as our own, right from the day she was given to us."

Rose was at a loss how to comfort Kate in her grief. Her mind was going over and over what the girls had said but although they now knew why Kristy had gone off they were no nearer to finding her. She was relieved when they reached the lane again and it was easier to avoid the mud. The sound of a horse galloping behind them made them turn and Rose was very thankful to see Bart.

"Any news?" he asked. Rose told him about the girls.

"She may not have meant to go anywhere at first but just got lost after a time." Rose spoke quietly, aware of Kate stumbling wearily slightly ahead. Bart followed her look.

"I will take her back to the manor. Are you all right, Rose?"

"Yes, thank you."

Bart urged his horse forward and stopped level with Kate. She let him help her up without protest and the horse trotted off, disappearing from Rose's sight.

Bart waited until Jinty had Kate safely back in the kitchen and then galloped off across the fields to join the rest of the searchers stretched out across the estate, calling Kristy's name repeatedly. The church bell was ringing at noon but no one would stop for their dinner that day. Mercifully the rain was keeping off but the clouds looked threatening again and Kristy might not survive another night in the open. He guided his horse across the fields to Sir Geoffrey and told him briefly what Rose had discovered.

"I will try over towards the cliffs, sir," suggested Bart. "She might have tried to make her way to the sea if she thinks that is where she was found."

It was a vain hope but the searchers had covered nearly all of the estate now. The search would have to be extended.

* * *

Bart urged his horse forward, calling the child and listening carefully for any reply. It was some time since he had been to the cliffs on the edge of Trewarne land. His last years at university had left him little time at home. He tried to find the route they had taken as children on the day that Amy was born but he must have missed it for he found himself further along the cliffs, the sea looking grey under the dark sky. Occasionally the sun broke through the black clouds, edging them with silver and sending a shaft of light across the water. His horse picked her way carefully along the top of the cliff but in places the rocks were too steep and jagged for her and eventually Bart left her, the reins looped under a boulder as he had to continue on foot.

He found Kristy asleep under a large rock, her clothes wet and torn, but she sat up and burst into tears of relief as he jumped down beside her. He let her cry, holding her in his arms until at last she calmed down then he looked at her.

"What a disgusting sight!" said Bart. Her face was dirty, streaked with tears and her dark curly hair tangled with the wind. She had lost one shoe, her dress was torn but thank God she was alive. He wanted to ask her so many questions but he thought of Kate and Samuel, grief-stricken at the child's disappearance. Lifting the little girl up from the rock he carried her back to his horse and made his way quickly back to the searchers, Kristy seated in front of him. One of the farm workers was sent galloping to the parish church where Mister Douglas rang the bell loudly and quickly in a pre-arranged signal that the child had been found. Dozens of people ran to the manor, gathering in the courtyard as they waited eagerly for Kristy to be brought home. Bart lifted her down into Kate's waiting arms and they clung together, tears pouring down many faces as Samuel ran down from the moors and hugged his wife and Kristy. Even Digory cried, something which he could not remember doing in his life before.

* * *

It was several days before Kate and Samuel recovered fully from the fright they had received. Kristy tearfully answered their questions, telling how she had run away from the children, at first deliberately going in the other direction away from the manor, only to panic when she found herself lost. She had finally fallen asleep under a hedge, waking next morning and, still going the wrong way, found herself on the cliffs where Bart had discovered her.

It was the second time, Lady Margaret reflected later to her husband, that Bart had brought Kristy to Trewarne.

* * *

Isobel came to stay at the manor once more in the following weeks while her guardians were away. Later Rose and Bart paid a return visit, accompanied by Digory. Richard and James returned to the grammar school at Penryn, James in his last year and Richard now a teacher. The unwelcome Visitors sent to Cornwall by Cromwell to report on the state of the monasteries had begun by ejecting all professed priests and monks under the age of twenty four. It was not the time for Richard to pursue his thoughts of taking holy orders.

Bart was very reluctant to return to Oxford away from Isobel but he had no choice. Sir Geoffrey insisted that he should at least gain his B.A. having proceeded so far in his education.

Thomas, the old cook who had worked in the kitchen at Trewarne for over twenty years, died early in the autumn. He had become unsteady on his feet and tripped one day over a bucket of milk on the kitchen floor, breaking his leg and dying ten days later. Hannah, who had been his wife for nearly fifty years, wept quietly as his body was prepared for burial, Jinty and Digory laying out the body in a little room off the kitchen.

"Poor ol' Thomas," mourned Digory, placing a bucket of holy water between the dead man's feet in which they placed a sprig of yew so that visitors could sprinkle the corpse as they paid their last respects, "I reck'n as 'ow this be the las' time as 'e will kick the bucket."

"You shouldn't make jokes about the dead," Kate reproved him.

"Why not?" demanded Digory. "'Tis summat that is comin' to all on we one day an' that's fer sure. Thomas 'ad a good life and if we give 'im a good send off what more can a man want?"

Samuel went with Digory to fetch the empty red coffin from the parish church next day and Thomas was placed inside wrapped in a rough linen cloth. On the eve of the funeral the procession set off to walk the two miles along the lane to the church, the bell tolling slowly as the coffin was carried on the shoulders of Samuel, Digory and two of the stronger farmworkers.

Hannah walked behind, supported by Kate and Jinty, followed by Sir Geoffrey and Lady Margaret with many of the workers from the estate. Mister Douglas waited for them at the lychgate and led the prayers as the coffin was carried into the church where it remained overnight. The following day, after the funeral Mass, it was carried into the churchyard where the body was taken out and buried. Thomas had been a good servant and he would be missed. Hannah, now frail herself, would be allowed to stay in the kitchen until she asked to go into the almshouses.

Without Thomas there was no one able to prepare the meals as well as he had done. Kate and Jinty were good cooks but had too much other work to do inside the manor. Digory was told to hire a cook on his next visit to the fair at St Ives. He came back with a married couple who proved satisfactory and worked cheerfully with the other servants. They coped well with the extra visitors at Christmas and Lady Margaret was very satisfied with them.

CHAPTER TWELVE

FOR SEVERAL MONTHS rumours had circulated that all was not well between King Henry and Queen Anne. The pilgrims on their way to the Mount and other travellers spoke guardedly for fear of being accused of treason but scraps of information from different sources were pieced together and whispered throughout the countryside. Anne had failed to produce a son, several miscarriages occurring in the years following the birth of Princess Elizabeth. King Henry flirted openly with other ladies at court and for some months had hardly spoken to his new queen.

Whilst Catherine was still alive he did not dare to take any action but in January Catherine died and Anne was all that stood in the way of a third marriage. Anne had made many enemies in her time at court. Another miscarriage on the same day that Catherine of Aragon was buried sealed her fate. The lost child had been a son.

In April divorce proceedings were set in motion, Anne accused of adultery with several men and incest with her brother. Only her young musician, under dreadful torture, admitted the offence. In May the Queen and the other accused gentlemen, all proclaiming their innocence, were beheaded.

The day following Anne's execution King Henry's betrothal to Jane Seymour was announced. Ten days later they were married.

* * *

Thomas Cromwell had already begun the dissolution of the monasteries. He dared not close them all at one stroke, therefore he began with the smaller ones, confiscating the buildings, contents and land and disposing of the monks by sending them to a larger house of their own Order. Those who wished to leave the religious life were offered a pension or a benefice. Any debts incurred by the monasteries were taken over by the government and the personal property of any monk who accepted the change without protest was guaranteed to him.

Unease spread throughout the country as the people reeled under the changes. Families who had exchanged visits for years became wary of each other as loyalties were torn between king and the Church. Those who supported the Church were afraid to make their views public for fear of reprisal.

Rumours abounded and first in Lincolnshire, then Yorkshire and its neighbouring counties and finally the North-West a series of rebellions broke out, partly caused by economic and social grievances but mainly as protests against the religious changes forced upon the country.

The leaders of the rebellions demanded that heresy should be halted, Cromwell and Cranmer replaced and all others who had taken a prominent part in the suppression of the monasteries punished. They condemned the divorce and the breach with Rome, together with the changes made by Henry and Cromwell. They demanded that Princess Mary should be declared legitimate again and that the law of 'treason by words' be repealed. By now the rising was known as the Pilgrimage of Grace.

Henry showed no sympathy for the rebels, now numbering thirty thousand, who were firmly but humbly presenting their grievances and petitions. He called them 'false traitors and rebels, full of wretched and devilish intent who must be punished for the detestable and unnatural sin of rebellion against their king, together with the utter destruction of them, their wives and children.' But Henry had not enough forces on hand to deal with the rebellion immediately. He had to play for time with false promises to allow massive royal forces to be gathered to smash the rebels. Accordingly he promised to consider their grievances and grant them all a free pardon.

Trusting in him, the rebels dispersed, convinced that their bloodless and loyal revolution had won the day and that Parliament would soon set right their grievances. It gave Henry the breathing time he needed to muster his troops. A few months later there were minor disturbances again and Henry seized upon them as an excuse.

* * *

Sir Geoffrey received the call to arms when sitting at the courts at Truro. The gentlemen of the county were ordered to assemble at Bodmin with their able-bodied men, horses and weapons ready to march to the king's aid. Farmers, fishermen, tinners and burgesses were summoned from Cornwall to join the men of the Midlands and the South against the northern rebels.

Samuel, four farm labourers and four tinners were to join the muster with Sir Geoffrey from Trewarne. Digory, now over sixty, begged to be allowed to ride with them but he was too old and would be left in charge of the workers remaining at the manor. Rose was devastated when she heard Master Darnwell was to join the muster and begged him not to go.

"I have no choice, Mistress Rose," the tutor answered gently. "All fit men are bound to answer a call to arms. It would not be right if I stayed whilst others went."

They were in the schoolroom, Amy and Kristy seated at their desks oblivious of Rose and the tutor. Master Darnwell had loved Rose for many years but his position with the family and lack of wealth had prevented him from ever speaking of his love, despite the fact that Rose's feelings for him were obvious to all. As the daughter of Sir Geoffrey Trewarne Rose would be eagerly welcomed by any of the families of the gentry in Cornwall or beyond. She would have a rich dowry given to her on marriage. A simple tutor, no matter how deeply he loved her, had no right to ask her to share his life.

So Master Darnwell had told himself repeatedly over the years, watching Rose blossom from a little girl into a beautiful eighteen year old but his resolve was crumbling rapidly as Rose stood before him, her hand on his sleeve and her stricken grey eyes fixed appealingly upon him. He tried to speak but the words would not come. One of her dark curls had escaped from her headdress and the breeze from the open window lifted it gently, caressing her soft cheek. He had given his heart to Rose many years ago. He had never loved anyone else and now looking into her tearful face he knew that there could never be anyone else for either of them.

"I love you," Rose told him quietly. "I know I should not be the first to say this but I have loved you since I was a child. You think that you are only my tutor and older than I am but neither of those things are of any importance to me. I only know that I will always love you and there can never be any other."

He was lost for words. He wanted to take her in his arms and tell her that he had always loved her too and could not face life without her but Amy and Kristy had suddenly become aware of the little drama being played out before them and were watching with undisguised interest.

"Finish your work," John Darnwell ordered them quickly. For once his words had no effect. They bent their heads but both continued to watch and Amy giggled. He drew Rose away from them closer to the window.

"I love you too, Rose – I have always loved you and I always will," he whispered. "I have to ride with the others, my dearest, it is my duty to do so, but I will speak to your father tomorrow. Perhaps he will give his permission for us to marry upon my return."

Rose smiled up at him as he took her in his arms, her eyes shining with love and delight through unshed tears. It would be terrible to be separated for several months from the quiet, gentle tutor she had loved for so long but at least the prospect of separation had brought their love into the open.

* * *

Sir Geoffrey listened without interruption as Master Darnwell asked him for Rose's hand in marriage. The young man had no family, no prospects apart from the living he could earn as a tutor. Rose had been brought up in the manor, well-provided with everything she needed. She could marry someone with a fortune but John Darnwell had always had her heart. It was a situation he and Lady Margaret had discussed occasionally but never sufficiently to reach a conclusion.

For the next few months the young couple were going to be separated. Until the fighting was over he would delay his decision.

* * *

The men were given a week to make their arrangements before assembling for the march north, forming a company of one hundred under Sir William Godolphin. Sir Hugh Trevarion also headed one hundred men, Sir John Arundell of Trerice had forty. Cornwall provided three hundred and sixty four men for King Henry.

Prayers were said in all the parish churches and homes for their safe return. The women and children, joined by those men too old or unfit to take up arms, lined the route as the men journeyed through towns and villages, sleeping in barns or under canvas, their leaders lodged in monasteries or private houses. The company had its own blacksmith, baker and shoe mender. They had bows, arrows, pikes and bills, gunpowder and a few guns, some armour and tin hats.

They marched through rain, mud, fog, snow, sunshine and bitter cold for it was early winter 1536. They were marching to put down a rebellion by their own fellow-countrymen caused by sweeping changes to their faith and way of life brought about by a king desperate for a son, but whatever their private feelings were, loyalty to King Henry must come first. In Tudor England the king was almost a god. King Henry certainly believed himself second only to the Almighty.

* * *

It was a quiet Christmas at Trewarne. Phillipa and her children joined the family but with her husband, Sir Geoffrey and Master Darnwell away from home and Bart at Oxford, as well as Samuel and the men from the estate away, it was difficult to enter into the Christmas spirit.

Richard and James joined them from Penryn but Richard was very quiet. Cromwell's work of dissolving the priories was spreading fast. The priory at Tywardreath, near Fowey, had been the first in Cornwall to be closed. A few months earlier Parliament had issued the Ten Articles of Faith in which four of the seven sacraments had been declared unnecessary and prayers to the saints and for the dead to be of no value. Parliament had struck again at the teaching of the Catholic church and the faith of her devout followers in England for over a thousand years.

Meanwhile King Henry had assembled his troops from all parts of the country. He was ready to take revenge for the rebellion in the north. Those who had taken part some months before thought it to be over but Henry was only waiting for his opportunity. A few minor disturbances were all that he required as an excuse to exact vengeance. Nearly four hundred people were publicly hanged as a lesson to others and the leaders of the earlier uprising were executed. Three of them were executed as traitors because they told the people 'to stay quietly in their houses and not help the rebels'. It was considered treason 'because they had not told them to go outside and help suppress them.'

It was early summer before Sir Geoffrey and his men were back at Trewarne, weary and sickened by the grim events of the previous months. They were thankful to be safely home after their arduous journey but the cruel vengeance carried out in the name of King Henry was something they would find difficult to forget.

The rebellion had also shaken Thomas Cromwell. The dissolution of the monasteries must be speeded up before planned religious changes resulted in further uprisings.

Rose had spent the five and a half months Master Darnwell had been away praying for his safe return and beseeching Lady Margaret to give her approval to their marriage. She was torn between hope of agreement and fear that her parents might feel she should still wait and consider other suitors. Lady Margaret would not give her daughter an answer, only support Sir Geoffrey's decision that they should wait and see what the separation might reveal.

Rose had no doubts of that at all. She tried to pass the time by taking over the tutor's role in the schoolroom with Amy and Kristy which she enjoyed. Both the children were very bright and eager to learn anything which Rose could teach them.

They were all three in Lady Margaret's sitting room with their needlework when the unexpected sound of horses sent them running to the window then down the stairs into the courtyard as fast as their long skirts would allow. Rose was in John Darnwell's arms hugging and kissing him before she remembered others around them and stood back, blushing furiously, but in the general emotion in the courtyard they were unnoticed. Weary and dishevelled as the rest of his men and greatly relieved to have brought them all safely home Sir Geoffrey jumped from his horse to kiss his radiant wife, holding her closely to him as he lifted Amy with his free arm, her soft golden curls hiding her face as she buried her head shyly in her father's hot, dusty neck.

Samuel hugged Kate and Kristy, and the other men were sent off to their own families. Inside the manor food was hastily prepared but the travellers were too weary for much conversation. They were happy to be home but for now all they wanted was to sleep in their own beds.

The months spent in close company with John Darnwell had convinced Sir Geoffrey that his daughter would be in safe hands. The quiet young man might not be wealthy but he had shown integrity and a great deal of courage throughout their ordeal. His loyalty to the king had not changed his allegiance to the Catholic faith. He had done his duty as had many others but the old beliefs still flourished in his heart as in the hearts of most Cornishmen.

* * *

Rose and John Darnwell were to be married in the parish church in August. The next few months following his return were spent in a whirl of excitement and activity, everyone trying hard to forget the worry of the last six months. Tailors and dressmakers travelled to the manor from St Ives bringing samples of silks, satins and velvets for approval and to take measurements. Rose finally chose pink silk and velvet trimmed with silver beads for her wedding gown. Lady Margaret chose dark green velvet for herself and a paler shade of green for Amy. Seeing Kristy's wistful face as she silently watched Amy being fitted with her dress Lady Margaret ordered the dressmaker to make a new gown for Kristy too. The two little girls spent so much of their time together both in and out of the schoolroom it seemed unfair to leave Kristy out of the celebrations.

Invitations were sent out to all their friends and once again the servants were busy baking bread, pies, pastries and puddings, cooking meats and fish, preparing for over a hundred guests. Some would stay overnight, others at neighbouring houses. The great hall was filled with benches to seat all the guests, the long tables covered with damask cloths. The cart trundled backwards and forwards to the markets, carrying Kate and Samuel to purchase the endless supplies needed by the cook and his wife. Jinty and Hannah, both now growing a little frail, made sweetmeats, custards and jellies and brewed ale with Digory. The day following the wedding was to be a holiday for all the workers of Trewarne to relax and have their own celebrations which would include an ox-roast, dancing and wrestling.

Amy was to move into Master Darnwell's old room after the wedding. Rose kept her bedroom and the guest room next to it was refurnished as a sitting room in order to give the young couple privacy apart from meal times. They would live at the manor at least as long as Amy needed a tutor and Amy was only just nine years old.

The banns were read on three following Sundays in both the parish church and the little church of St Mary the Virgin in the courtyard. The sun shone throughout August and everyone prayed that the good weather would last.

Rose awoke early on her wedding day to find the sun streaming through the latticed window again and a beautiful clear blue sky. The wedding procession would have no fear of getting wet riding the two miles to the church where Sir Geoffrey and Lady Margaret had been married twenty three years ago.

The church was decorated with flowers, filling the air with their perfume. Mister Douglas waited with Master Darnwell in the porch, Lady Margaret, Bart, James and Amy standing with them. There came the sound of hooves and Sir Geoffrey rode into sight around the bend in the lane, Rose riding at his side. She was radiant with happiness as her father lifted her from her horse and escorted her through the lychgate and up the path to the porch where Master Darnwell awaited her.

The young couple made their vows in the church porch, their eyes only for one another. Master Darnwell slipped the ring on Rose's finger as he repeated the words after the priest:

> "With this ring I thee wed and this gold
> and silver I thee give; and with my body
> I thee worship and with all my worldly
> chattels I thee honour."

Rose smiled at him, her eyes sparkling with happiness, and the bridal party followed Mister Douglas into the church for the celebration of the Nuptual Mass.

* * *

Bart had come home from Oxford for his sister's wedding, hoping to find Isobel amongst the guests and he was not disappointed. He had worked hard in his last year at university to be sure of getting his B.A. so that he would not have to leave Cornwall and Isobel again. It was almost a year since he had seen her last but he had thought of her constantly and now that he was with her again he thought she had grown prettier than ever. The news that Andrew Wychcombe was to be amongst the guests had annoyed him at first but fortunately Isobel showed no more than a polite interest in Andrew at the wedding, giving her attention wholly to Bart.

"What will you do now that you have finished at university, Bart?" she asked him as they strolled in the quiet garden at the manor, away from the guests.

"I am not sure," Bart confessed. "Help my father with the estate amongst other things. I would like to be a builder but gentlemen's sons are not expected to work with their hands. Perhaps one day people will want houses designed especially for them instead of just building as others have done before. I should like to do that."

"I expect Trewarne will be yours one day."

"Yes, it will, but not for many years yet. My father is some years off fifty and very fit. I hope I shall not inherit for a long time, perhaps twenty years or more."

"Twenty years! What will you do until then?"

"Not go into the Church, that's for sure," laughed Bart. "I want to be free to marry one day. I could teach but to do that I would need to go back to Oxford for my M.A. and I do not want to go away from you again, Isobel. I would rather stay here in Cornwall where I can see you each day."

"You will have a long ride to do that." Isobel deliberately ignored the obvious meaning in Bart's words and the intense expression in his eyes. She was flattered that this tall, handsome young boy, heir to Trewarne Manor, was gazing at her so ardently. His dark curly hair, grey eyes, strong shoulders and firm body made him as physically attractive to her as she was so obviously desirable to him but she had no intention of committing herself to one man until she had explored other opportunities. She sensed that Bart was about to move closer to her and spoke quickly to forestall him.

"It is time we returned indoors, Bart. I can hear the musicians beginning to play."

"Damn the musicians!" but Isobel had already begun to retrace her steps through the garden. Other guests had come to stroll outside in the cooler evening air and they were no longer alone. Bart groaned with frustration and followed Isobel back into the great hall. Sir William Godolphin spoke to him and he was forced to stay for a moment talking politely. When he was free to move away Isobel had moved nearer to the musicians and was talking to Andrew Wychcombe who was paying her great attention.

Bart tried unsuccessfully throughout the evening to speak to her alone again. He had spent months thinking of all the things he would like to say to her but although Isobel would dance with him and spoke charmingly to him in company she appeared to Bart to be deliberately elusive whenever any opportunity arose of being alone with him.

The wedding celebrations continued into the early hours of the morning and dawn was breaking when Jinty and the other servants began to prepare a light breakfast for those who wished to make an early start on the journey home.

* * *

In October the whole country was filled with rejoicing as Queen Jane, the king's third wife, gave birth to a long-awaited son. King Henry at last had his heir but less than two weeks later Queen Jane was dead. She had not recovered after a difficult birth. Within a few hours the English ambassadors abroad had been instructed to look for a new wife for the king who now, in spite of a broken heart, believed it 'his duty' to marry again. A foreign marriage would leave the country less isolated if

France and the Empire ended their hostility towards each other and turned their attention again to England. Over the next two years a dozen or more ladies were considered, five of them required to have their portraits painted by Holbein for the king's inspection.

* * *

Bart, now very much in love with Isobel, rode regularly to visit her at her uncle's home. He was hardly ever alone with her for more than a few minutes but John Wynslade approved of Bart's visits to his niece and welcomed the prospect of her marriage to the heir of Trewarne. Isobel always seemed rather quiet and said little of her feelings but welcomed Bart pleasantly on each visit. It was a shock to everyone when she vanished with Andrew Wychcombe leaving only a brief note in which she thanked her uncle for all his kindness and begged him to forgive her. She did not mention Bart.

Bart had ridden down from Trewarne, eager to see Isobel again after a week's separation. Distraught, he stared speechlessly at John Wynslade standing on the steps of Bochym Manor as the shaken man held out Isobel's short letter for him to read. No one had known that she had stayed in contact with Andrew. One of the young servant girls had apparently been used to pass messages between them. Bart's hand was shaking as he handed Isobel's letter back to her grey-faced guardian and turned his horse back towards Trewarne.

He could not believe that Isobel had gone. He had hoped more and more on each visit that she was beginning to love him if only a fraction as much as he loved her. For over a year he had thought of her and since Rose's wedding six weeks earlier she had been scarcely out of his mind yet she had left him without a word. It hurt more than he would ever admit to anyone. Bitter tears streamed down his face and sobs shook his body as he struggled to compose himself on the long ride home through mist and rain across the desolate moors.

There was nothing now to keep him at Trewarne. He wanted to go away, to hide from sympathetic glances and the concerned face of his mother. He could hardly bear to be in the same room as Rose and John Darnwell. There was nothing for it but to return to Oxford for two more years and push Isobel into the past.

Sir Geoffrey agreed with Bart's decision. Lady Margaret wept in her room but she accepted that it was for the best and preparations were made once again for Bart's leave-taking. His clothes and books were repacked by Kate. Bart himself kept away from family and friends as much as possible, riding his horse over the moors, avoiding anyone he saw who knew him. He preferred to deal with his aching heart alone.

* * *

He let his horse pick her own way over the moors, watching with little interest the tinners working industriously in the valley below him. The sea sparkled in the distance. It was many years since he had been on the beach and he headed his horse over towards the cliffs. Memories of the cove where they had found Kristy stirred in his mind and he wondered vaguely but with no real interest whether he would find it.

It was some time later that the great rocky outlines of the headland began to look slightly familiar and he thought he must be near. Leaving his horse tethered to a bush he wandered along the cliff top, watching the breakers crashing beneath him. The rock where Rose had sat waiting was the first he recognised and then just below it he found the path they had taken down to the cove. He followed it and stopped in surprise when he saw the single line of footprints in the sand. Kristy was sitting alone on a rock, throwing small stones into the advancing sea. She did not know he was there until he called her name.

"What are you doing here?" asked Bart in amazement. "You have not run away again, have you?"

"I often come here now," the child answered, her dark curls blowing in the breeze. "Grandfer brought me so that I could see where I was found."

"But it is miles away from the manor. I should know, I helped carry you most of the way. How did you get here?"

"Grandfer says it is the same way. It never takes long for I run mostly. I like to sit here and wonder who I really am."

Bart was silent, sitting down beside her on the rock. Kristy resumed throwing stones into the water occasionally, continually turning to check that the incoming tide had not cut off their retreat. It was pleasant sitting there on the lonely beach, listening to the crash of the foam-capped waves and watching the water surging between the rocks. For the first time since he had stood on the steps of Bochym Manor five weeks ago listening to John Wynslade telling him that Isobel had gone Bart felt his heart a little less heavy.

"We shall have to go," Kristy said suddenly as a large wave swept higher up the beach towards them. She jumped off the rock, wriggling her bare toes in the hot sand. She was up on the cliff top several minutes before Bart climbed up to join her.

"Which way are you going back?" he asked her.

"The way I always go – past the woods."

"You can come with me if you like and share my horse," Bart offered. Kristy looked up at him with delight.

"I'll catch you up when I have my shoes on," she said happily.

Bart waited for her and swung her up on to the horse, mounting behind her. It was the first time for weeks he felt ready for any supper.

* * *

He returned to Oxford in late October accompanied by James for his first year at university. Soon after Christmas Rose and John Darnwell were delighted to find that Rose was expecting their first child which would be born in the summer. Master Darnwell was also pleasantly surprised to receive a legacy from a relative he had never known in Norfolk. It enabled the young couple to plan with great excitement a home of their own and Sir Geoffrey willingly provided the land.

CHAPTER THIRTEEN

IT WAS EARLY spring and the courts were full of cases of robbery, assault, non-payment of debts and other quarrels. Felons were hanged and persistent troublemakers whipped. Sir Geoffrey had spent the early part of the week passing sentences at Bodmin and was now riding to Truro with Digory for the next session in the court there. The weather had been bad for weeks with much rain and strong winds, making the already poor roads into muddy mires through which the horses squelched as they tried to lift their feet. The heavy rain increased and Sir Geoffrey reined his horse outside an inn. It was futile to try to travel further in such weather. The innkeeper showed his guest to a room and Digory disappeared around the back to the stable.

"A nasty day, sir," the innkeeper sympathised, kindling the fire in the room. "Shall I take your clothes to dry them, sir?"

"No, thank you, they will dry in here. Bring some wine for now. I will eat later."

The man bowed and left the room, returning with a bottle and glass on a tray. He lit the candles and retired, leaving Sir Geoffrey to sit quietly by the fire, gazing into the flames. Approaching fifty, he was still a handsome, well built man, his dark hair showing only slightly grey. Constant riding and active supervision of his estate together with his other work kept him fit. He loved his wife and family dearly. Life would be so pleasant were it not for growing anxiety at the news which regularly trickled down from London.

He must have dozed for suddenly he was jerked awake by the sound of angry voices below, followed by heavy footsteps clumping up the stairs and past his room, then a door banged and he could hear heavy movements in the room next door, the landlord's voice mingling with others. It was no longer quiet and Sir Geoffrey sighed and decided he might as well go downstairs to eat.

The landlord had scarcely finished serving him hot pie, gravy and large chunks of bread before the other travellers came down to supper and rather reluctantly Sir Geoffrey acknowledged them. He had a distinctly uneasy feeling that somehow they were going to cause trouble in Cornwall.

"You are from these parts, sir?" one of the men asked, nodding curtly to Sir Geoffrey as they sat at the table next to him. "A barbarous county," he continued without waiting for a reply. "No roads, foul weather and murderous cut-throats to waylay the traveller. No wonder Cornwall is said to be a savage place."

"You have been attacked?" Sir Geoffrey was surprised to find himself feeling oddly pleased. He was not usually on the side of the attacker but somehow the men sitting so close and eating their food so noisily irritated him.

"Aye, and robbed too. The villains jumped on us a few miles back. Have a care if you are travelling that way. The wretches stole rings, weapons, money, horses. 'Tis well we were close to an inn or we would still be squelching through the mud."

"How many attacked you?"

The man shrugged. "Three – four. They jumped on us without warning and were gone in seconds. My servants stood little chance of following them. I shall report the attack when I reach Bodmin tomorrow if ever I arrive there. Are there no good roads in this uncivilised county?"

"No good roads," answered Sir Geoffrey stiffly, "but we are not uncivilised. You have been unfortunate in your experience but London roads are little better and equally dangerous for the traveller if not more so. You are down here on business?"

"On the king's business," retorted the man and said no more. Sir Geoffrey finished his meal and rose to retire to his room. He did not like the mean looking men and had no wish to spend the evening in their company.

"I fear you have the worst part of your journey still before you," he commented, not without a little hidden pleasure. "Bodmin moor is notorious for its poor weather and difficult progress. I wish you good night, gentlemen."

* * *

It rained heavily all night but by dawn it was dry again. Sir Geoffrey and Digory left the inn soon after daybreak. It would be a slow and difficult journey along the muddy lane leading to Truro and the court would begin sitting early that morning. There was a murder trial to be held and it would create a great deal of interest in the town. The church bell was ringing to call the people to Mass as the riders made their way along to the courtroom.

Sir William Godolphin, now in office as Sheriff of Cornwall for another year, greeted Sir Geoffrey but there was little time for conversation before the court began. Later when they adjourned for dinner the two men sat discussing the tin industry. The Godolphin riches had all been derived from the rich tin streams on the moors below and the hills above the great house but the streams were becoming exhausted and it was necessary to tap the lode itself and mine for the tin.

"Germany has the experts," Sir William was saying. "They know far more at present than our own Cornish engineers. They are more advanced with survey work and the sinking of shafts."

"Sinking of shafts? Will that be necessary?"

"Unless the tin industry is to die out it will be essential. We have streamed for tin for thousands of years. There's little more to be found on the surface. Are your tinners making a living?"

"A bare one," admitted Sir Geoffrey. "Occasionally they have a good find. I heard one found a nugget of gold last week but that will probably never happen again. I know they are digging more and more into the rock but no one has yet suggested sinking a shaft. It will be an expensive business."

"It will need financial backing," agreed Sir William, "but I believe it will be worth it. The alternative is to throw hundreds of men out of work. The tinners themselves are convinced that there is an enormous amount of tin and other minerals under the ground – copper, lead, silver. Either we invest in the machinery to help us get it out or leave it where it is for future generations to discover. Will you have your land surveyed?"

"I had not given any thought to it. I have good farming land. Too much searching for tin could ruin it."

"There is far more profit in tin than farming," advised Sir William. "I intend to arrange for some German engineers – mining experts – to come over here and give me their opinion. If they consider that sinking shafts will be worth the expense I shall try to raise the money – form a company perhaps. You could ask them to survey Trewarne land at the same time."

"Do you expect to raise the money without difficulty?"

"I have no doubt of it. The tin industry in Cornwall supplies most of the world. It is one of our greatest exports and where there are profits to be made there are plenty who will gamble for their share."

The two men finished their meal before Sir Geoffrey remembered the men at the inn the previous evening and mentioned them to Sir William.

"On the king's business? No doubt that is something to do with the attack on church property," mused Sir William. "I fear we shall hear more of them."

They rose and walked back across the street to the courtroom again. Sir William had given his neighbour from Trewarne Manor much food for thought but the eager noisy spectators in the courtroom at Truro were anxious for the murder trial to resume.

* * *

The Lenten fast was undertaken even more fervently by those of the old faith who were troubled by the closure of monasteries, priories and nunneries throughout the country and the execution of those too openly opposed to King Henry. The lands confiscated by Cromwell on behalf of the king were either given as gifts to those who helped in the dissolution or sold to raise revenue for the crown. Sir William Godolphin showed interest in the purchase of Tywardreath Priory near Fowey but it was given to the brother of the dead Queen Jane.

Over-zealous supporters of the new Protestant religion attacked Catholic churches and smashed statues and other relics. The ashes used by Mister Douglas to mark the foreheads of the faithful at Trewarne on Ash Wednesday were soon to be abolished, along with many other customs and the observance of holy days. The priest appealed to his parishioners to pray for their king and their Catholic faith. It was becoming increasingly difficult to be loyal to both.

No meat was eaten during Lent, a custom which was always popular with the fishermen along the coast, no food or drink allowed before midday. Statues and crosses were veiled, the metal processional cross put aside and replaced by a plain wooden cross painted red to represent the Precious Blood of Christ.

Confessions were heard by the parish priest in the open church, away from listening ears. It was an opportunity to check that the penitent could say the *Pater Noster*, *Ave* and *Credo* in Latin as well as understand the meaning of the words. It was also an occasion to ensure that each person knew the ten commandments, the teaching of the Church and the seven deadly sins.

Lent had always been considered a time for increased almsgiving and the tinning and farming families were as anxious to make sacrifices to offer alms as those at the manor. Even Digory began Lent as he always did by renouncing drink but his good intentions seldom survived the first week.

* * *

Jinty, much older than her husband, was now almost seventy and her movements in the kitchen became slower and more unsteady. Kate watched her mother with concern but Jinty would not listen to her pleas to rest. She had been with Sir Geoffrey and Lady Margaret for twenty-five years. Her one hope now was to live long enough to see their first grandchild born. Rose, radiant and healthy, passed the months of waiting stitching tiny garments with Lady Margaret in her sitting room whilst her husband continued to teach Amy and Kristy. Their new home was already planned and the builders would commence work soon after the baby arrived.

The day before Palm Sunday a shrine was erected by tradition in the grounds of the parish church and bedecked with spring flowers. During Mass next day Mister Douglas, bearing a covered cross and followed by some of the congregation bearing palms, walked from the church to the shrine where he read the gospel. As they walked the children sang *Blessed is He that cometh in the name of the Lord* and alms were distributed to the needy before everyone returned inside the church for the rest of the service.

It was only when the priest left the altar and the congregation began to disperse outside that it was discovered that Hannah, the other old servant who had worked in the kitchen with her husband Thomas, had died peacefully as she sat on the stone bench with her back resting against the wall of the church.

* * *

Easter Monday was a holiday but the festivities were dampened by the wet weather. Food and ale were provided in the barn for those who ventured out but the rain lashed down and most of the women and children stayed at home. The men gathered together, wrestled and practised archery as they discussed the prospects of a good harvest after such a wet spring.

By early May the sun was shining continuously again and the oxen out in the muddy fields. Some of the children were able to attend school in the parish church again now that the excessively wet weather had come to an end, but many were needed at home to help with the work in the valleys which the rain had delayed.

In the third week of May Rose surprised everyone, including herself, by giving birth to twins, a boy and a girl. Barnaby and Clemency entered the world within half an hour of each other, six weeks earlier than expected. Rose could hardly believe her good fortune. The babies were fit and well, crying lustily, both with blue eyes and soft dark hair.

The happiness which followed the arrival of the babies was only marred by the peaceful death of Jinty two weeks later. She had been present at their birth and at their baptism in the parish church. Digory, after more than forty years of companionship, during which they had fought and argued constantly, was silent in his grief. Only Kristy, slipping her small hand into his as he sat slumped on a bench in the corner of the kitchen, could provoke even the slightest response from him. She was away from the schoolroom for weeks as she stayed quietly by the side of the man she loved as her grandfather.

Barnaby and Clemency were the first babies to be registered by Mister Douglas, and Jinty the first death, under the new ruling by Parliament requiring the recording of all births,

157

marriages and deaths in every parish in the country. It was an innovation greeted suspiciously throughout Cornwall as a prelude to increased taxation.

* * *

It took a trip to the cove with Kristy some weeks later to shake Digory out of the lethargy into which he had fallen following Jinty's death. It was a holy day, the Feast of St Peter and St Paul, and the workers had the day free. Encouraged by Kate, who was worried about her father, Kristy cajoled Digory into accompanying her on a trip to the beach after Mass and eventually, carrying pasties and ale, they left the manor to walk over the fields and moors.

It was a beautiful day and Kristy skipped along in front of Digory, jumping backwards and forwards over the streams, scrambling over the boulders, the sun warm on their faces. Digory had not been to the cove for several years since he had shown Kristy where she had been found. Nostalgic memories of his smuggling days stirred in his thoughts. He had enjoyed the excitement and the extra money which came his way but it was a long time ago. He remembered the route well and followed Kristy down the path onto the beach, showing her how to flick stones so that they just skimmed the top of the sparkling water.

"I'm hungry," Kristy announced after a while and they walked back up the beach to sit on a large rock. Kristy pulled a face at the ale but she ate the pasty and apple which Kate had packed for them before returning back to the edge of the water.

It was pleasant to lie in the warmth of the sun and watch the little girl jumping over the incoming waves. She had brought a great deal of happiness into the lives of Digory and Jinty as well as to Kate and Samuel. Her brown eyes were always sparkling in her oval face and she had been a great comfort to Digory during the past few weeks. Digory sat up, shaking his head sadly. For a short time at the cove he had forgotten his loss but now thoughts of Jinty were coming back again. It was time to stand up and explore.

He wandered along the beach, keeping an eye on the tide but it had not long turned. He had not shown Kristy the cave when he had brought her down some years ago but he would take her in there today. With some of his old agility Digory climbed over the rocks and entered the cold, dark cave where he had been so often before.

He could hardly believe his own eyes. Stacked at the back of the cave, well out of sight just as they had been many years before, were casks of brandy and rum. Someone else was now using his cave. He could hardly wait to get back to find out who was responsible. Kristy protested in vain that it was too soon to return but Digory was seething with indignation. To have had to give up his illegal, enjoyable activities had been a big enough blow. To find they were being carried on without him was even worse. For the moment he had even forgotten Jinty.

* * *

The meeting of Digory and the other men who had once been involved in the smuggling was a stormy one as Digory loudly swore at them for carrying on their activities, but gradually he became aware that they were all denying it.

"Ain't none o' we bin near the cove since that time," one of them raged back at him. "Why don' ee lissen, you ol' fool. If there be smugglin' goin' on there agen 'tis somebody else, not we."

"Aye, an' mebbe not from Trewarne neither," interrupted one of the others. "C'd be Godolphin men or any o' they from Zennor or St. Ives."

"If it be, they ain't gonna use Trewarne property," said Digory indignantly. "I don' aim ter be in trouble for wot I ain't dun nor got ben'fit of. We must stop 'em."

"Tha's very true, m'dear, but 'ow?"

"I'll tell 'ee 'ow, boy," answered Digory. "That stuff's bin put there for c'lection so we gonna be there when they do come."

"They mos' likely gonna be younger'n us," said one of the tinners cautiously.

"ou ain't scared?" demanded another.

"I ded'n say that but sum o' we ain't as fit as used to be an' we don' know 'ow many'll be there."

His argument made sense. A few more younger ones would have to accompany them. It might even mean several nights on the cliffs before the trespassers came. Samuel for one could not refuse to protect Sir Geoffrey's land and he was a champion wrestler.

Digory rubbed his hands together cheerfully. It felt good to have a bit of excitement afoot again.

* * *

Kate objected at first but, assured that Digory was not up to his old tricks again, she let Samuel go. There was a waning moon and a dry night which might prove the ideal conditions for which the smugglers were waiting. Digory stayed in Samuel's cottage that evening waiting for darkness to fall but the midsummer evenings were long and it was late before they could venture forth. It was as if they had never ceased their activities as the silent figures joined them, running across the dark fields. Only the fact that some ran slower now reminded them that it had been many years since they last travelled that way.

They planned to hide at the top of the cliff path, staying until almost dawn. The sound of the sea crashing continually below them almost lulled Digory to sleep. He was just beginning to snore gently when Samuel shook him and he was instantly alert. A straggling line of men were quietly coming along the cliff top, silhouetted against the skyline.

Digory had ordered his men to let the smugglers descend to the beach. They had less chance of escaping there. The last one finally disappeared around the bend in the path and Samuel cautiously worked his way forward on his stomach to peer over the edge. The men had gone into the cave and that was the moment to descend after them. Twelve men had gone down to the cove. Ten men from Trewarne climbed quietly down after them.

It was the best fight Digory had enjoyed for many years. Halfway across the beach before the intruders spotted them, they rushed at each other, fists flying, shouts and oaths filling the night air. Digory found himself rolling over and over in the icy water as he struggled with a man much larger than himself but Digory was fit and wiry and managed to overcome his opponent. He left him crawling out of the water and charged back into the fight, jumping on the back of a man who was banging the head of a tinner against a rock.

Several men together were trying to attack Samuel but he was too strong to be overpowered by them. Digory just had time to shout encouragement to his son before he was attacked from behind and he found himself rolling on the sand again in the middle of another fight. He could have gone on like that for hours had he not suddenly found himself without an opponent, most of the men sitting on the beach nursing cut heads and battered faces as they shouted and swore at each other.

"They ain't St Ives men," declared Digory, peering at the bloody faces around him. "They be from Penzance."

Some of the smugglers had regained their strength and looked ready to start the fight again but the Trewarne men swiftly got to their feet and the others thought better of it. There were sore heads and broken bones on both sides and a good many black eyes and swollen faces would take some explaining in daylight.

"You ain't got no call ter do this," one of the injured men snarled at Digory. "We on'y kep goin' where ee left off."

"That's mebbe," agreed Digory, "but you ain't usin' our cove. There be plenty o' places Penzance way wi'out comin' out 'ere. Clear off now, all on ee, and don' ee ever come back."

The Trewarne men waited on the beach, exchanging insults as the others helped their wounded back across the sand and up the treacherous path. Samuel followed to make sure they dispersed and did not set their own ambush. Inside the cave Digory supervised the rescue of the contraband goods. Mister Douglas could surely not criticise them for taking the spoils of war.

Sir Geoffrey looked with amazement next morning at the battered face of Digory and his cut hands.

"Just a bit of a fight with Samuel, sir," declared Digory honestly and left it at that. There was no reason to add that he and Samuel had both been fighting on the same side. Sir Geoffrey might start asking difficult questions.

* * *

It had been a good harvest in spite of the wet spring. The old custom of Crying the Neck as the last sheaf of corn in the fields was cut took place on a beautiful late summer evening. Mister Douglas said the prayers of thanksgiving in the field and afterwards there was supper and dancing in the largest barn.

Amy and Kristy proudly brought the two babies out for a few moments to be admired. Barnie and Clemency, now three months old, had plenty of willing nursemaids.

* * *

In October Sir Geoffrey rode up to Truro again with Digory. It was some months since he had visited Phillipa at Penvedn. He stayed with her and her family for dinner and rode into Truro early in the afternoon and was surprised to find a noisy crowd gathered outside the friary and strangers on horses roughly forcing them back from the doors. Many women were weeping and several stones were hurled, causing one of the horses to rear into the air. The rider struggled to control the animal while his companions lashed out at the crowd pressing around them.

"Thank God you have arrived," spoke Sir William Godolphin behind him. "We need help to control this mob."

"What is happening?" Sir Geoffrey asked in amazement.

"The friary is being closed today by order of Parliament. There are men inside demanding the surrender of the friars. The people are objecting."

He spurred his horse forward and Sir Geoffrey followed closely.

"Surely in God's name we should be objecting too!"

"We have no choice. Our first duty is to the king," answered Sir William abruptly.

He forced his way through the angry crowd, followed reluctantly by Sir Geoffrey. The friars had carried out a great deal of good work in and around Truro for many years, preaching the word of God, feeding the poor, ministering to the sick. They owned nothing themselves and had not been included in earlier acts of suppression because they were popular with the people and had little to add to the wealth of the king. Now what little property they possessed was to be taken and sold on behalf of the crown. Truro friary could not even provide much in the way of lead from its roof for it was listed by The Visitors as 'having only small gutters'.

Inside the friary John Reskarnan and ten other friars were forced to sign the document of surrender. A chest containing title deeds and other documents left in the safe keeping of the friars by the gentlemen of the town was given to the mayor for safe keeping. A chalice and a few pieces of silver plate used in the daily services at the friary were taken to add to the king's wealth. The few pieces of furniture, books, lamps, bells, altar cloths and vestments were sold. The poor friary had debts of £16.13s.4d. which The Visitors paid from the amount raised.

Bodmin friary had been visited for the same purpose two days previously by the same men, one of them John Tregonwell, a Cornishman. Two of the other men Sir Geoffrey recognised as the strangers complaining of robbery at the inn some months ago. They had said then that they were on the king's business.

Most of the crowd eventually dispersed sullenly from the friary gate after The Visitors had left. Sir Geoffrey went inside to find the Brothers kneeling in communal prayer. It grieved him to see the pale faces and listen to their voices as they sang their Office for the last time.

"What will you do now?" he asked John Reskarnan later as the two men sadly left the friary. The friar shrugged his shoulders.

"The future is in the hands of God. We are not allowed to preach any more. We are given the opportunity of becoming ministers under the new religion but I fear that will be so different from the old faith that I would not wish to preach it."

"You think there will be more changes?"

"I am sure of it. King Henry has begun something he will find hard to control. His own intentions may not be for such sweeping changes in the faith but in Europe the new protestantism is gaining ground rapidly."

There were still a few beggars standing uncertainly outside the friary, waiting hopefully for the food which would no longer be given to them. The friar looked at them sadly.

"We have struggled hard to feed their bodies and now we cannot even feed their souls."

He raised his hand in a final blessing and Sir Geoffrey left him, both men sick at heart.

* * *

They were unhappy days in England and for many they were to grow much worse. The following year Bodmin, Launceston and St Germans priories were suppressed in Cornwall, together with St Michael's on The Mount. In three years Thomas Cromwell had crushed monastic life in England, a way of life which had brought education and food to the poor, healing and care to the sick. Sadly it had also provided a comfortable living for many who had no genuine call to the service of God and it was these men who had provided Cromwell with the excuse to effect such radical sweeping changes for the financial benefit of his king.

At first the Crown made little attempt to sell off the monastic lands confiscated throughout England. The land-hungry nobles and gentry were only permitted leases. For the moment the Treasury had enough cash in its coffers raised by the sale of the goods belonging to the monasteries and the lead stripped from the roofs.

Thomas Cromwell, at the height of his power, now made a very great mistake. He negotiated a new wife for Henry – Anne of Cleves. Henry was repulsed at their first meeting by the plainness of his new queen but he was committed to the marriage. He went through with the ceremony because the foreign situation demanded it, but though he reluctantly shared her bed he 'left her as good a maid as he found her'. Shortly afterwards his new wife quite happily agreed to be demoted in rank to 'the king's good sister'. She was well provided for with two houses and a good income by a relieved Henry. A few months later the king was once again officially divorced.

Thomas Cromwell's policies had upset the king by forcing him into a distasteful marriage. He had also made many enemies during his eight years in power and those he had angered were now delighted to accelerate his downfall. He was arrested in June and taken to The Tower. A month later Thomas Cromwell was executed. In spite of years of persecution of the Church he declared on the scaffold that he died in the Catholic faith.

On the same day a corpulent, middle-aged King Henry married Catherine Howard. She was nineteen years old and his fifth wife – the second one he had married that year.

* * *

The summer was the hottest in living memory. The glorious days, welcomed at first, gradually caused concern as springs and ponds dried up, animals died and the earth became scorched.

For Bart and James, home after two years at Oxford, it was a chance of freedom in the open air, riding over the moors, swimming on the beaches. It was the first time the boys had seen Barnie and Clemency, now golden brown, their soft hair turned fair by the sun as they crawled happily over the lawns at the manor. Rose and Lady Margaret sat in the shade of the apple trees whilst Amy and Kristy played with the twins endlessly.

The eldest daughter of Robert and Phillipa was married and the family from Trewarne travelled over for the wedding, leaving the babies in the care of Kate. Robert had good news of Lady Margaret's brother Edward, safely in Rome. He sent his love and blessing to the family. Richard returned from Penryn for the wedding and afterwards rode back to spend the week with his cousins at Trewarne. The collegiate church to which his school was attached had not been affected yet by the suppression of the monasteries but none of the clergy doubted that a sword still hung over their heads.

The boys had been swimming in the clear blue sea and were lying on the hot sand. James had Storm with him, running his fingers through the mongrel's rough white and brown curly coat as he lay by his side. Kristy had taken over the ownership of Storm when James left home for university two years ago but the little dog had given his master an ecstatic welcome and transferred his allegiance back to James immediately upon his return.

"Well, James, and what will you do for a career?" asked Richard lazily.

"I hope to be a Catholic priest," James answered quietly. The other two raised their heads from the sand immediately.

"Don't be a fool, James," Bart retorted. "No one is allowed to train in the old faith any more."

"I can train abroad," James answered. "I shall go to France or Rome and come back when these bad times are over. King Henry cannot live for ever and then with the grace of God England will be Catholic again."

"It may not be," Richard warned his cousin. "From what we see and hear from travellers at Penryn the Protestant faith is gaining in popularity all over Europe as well as in this country. King Henry himself has had to issue statements condemning the rush to change to it. Do your parents know what you are thinking of doing?"

"I have talked to my father about it," answered James. "I think he was going to tell my mother last night."

"She will try to stop you," warned Bart. "It is very unwise to want to be a priest at this time. What did Father say?"

"He tried to dissuade me at first," answered James and in truth Sir Geoffrey had been stunned by his younger son's decision. Mister Douglas had joined him in pointing out to James the difficulties he would have to undergo to pursue his vocation. The young man had listened to them, knowing that it was only concern for his safety which made them try to advise him against the path he had chosen, but in his own mind he had already made his decision.

"What is there to fear when we are in the hands of God who loves us?" James asked his father and the priest, to which neither of the two men could give an answer which would not appear lacking in faith.

Lady Margaret was horrified when Sir Geoffrey told her later that night as they lay in the four-poster bed. She sat up swiftly in agitation, her long fair hair streaming about her as she stared down at her husband's worried face visible in the candlelight.

"Surely we can stop him!" she exclaimed.

"Have we the right to do so?" asked Sir Geoffrey. "James knows the risks. He assured me that it is not a sudden decision but a call which has been with him since he was at grammar school. A few years ago we would have been delighted at his decision."

"But so much has changed! Even Edward found he could not stay in this country and things have become much worse since then. If we encourage James we may be sending him to his death."

"Perhaps for some the death of the body is easier than death of the soul."

He had thought so often of the friars at Truro, tormented by the knowledge that his duty to the king had prevented him from acting on their behalf. His intervention would have been of little use but he could not escape the thought that many of the poor wretched people in the crowd had shown their anger and displeasure more openly than he had done. Priests and monks had been given small pensions but the friars had been left destitute.

Lady Margaret lay awake most of the night, conscious that her husband was also sleepless beside her. She resolved to talk to her son as soon as it was morning but although he listened respectfully to his mother and regretted being the cause of her obvious distress, James felt convinced that he was called by God

166

to carry on His work. Bart and Richard tried to reason with him and it seemed to James that only Rose understood and accepted his decision. He was thankful to escape to the nursery away from the well-meaning arguments of the rest of the family. Barnie played on Rose's knee and Clemency twisted James' fair hair as he held her on his lap.

"How long will you be away?" Rose asked her brother.

"I am not sure – six or seven years perhaps. I shall come back as soon as I am trained if it is safe to do so. These two imps will have changed a good deal by then and you will be living in your new home."

"That should be ready next year. It is close enough to still feel part of the family and yet we shall be entirely on our own. We shall all miss you, James. Six or seven years is a long time."

"I shall come back and find you surrounded by children," James teased her, his blue eyes laughing at his sister's serious face. "How you all worry about me! I shall be safe. Now come, Rose, it is time your husband let the girls out of the schoolroom. Even Richard has longer holidays than Amy and Kristy. Perhaps I should be a school teacher after all."

James left Trewarne a few weeks later, his mother and sisters bidding him a tearful goodbye. Sir Geoffrey and Bart arranged to accompany him to Penvedn where he would join Robert to leave England on his ship.

"Take care of Storm for me," James instructed Kristy, smiling at her and to Kristy's surprise James kissed her. "Don't cry, Amy," he added, turning to his younger sister, "I shall be back in time to marry you to a rich young man."

Lady Margaret clung to her son for a moment, tears streaming down her face in spite of herself. He hugged her, keeping his arm about her until he reached his horse. His father and Bart were waiting for him.

"Pray for me," said James, "just as I will always pray for you."

He rode quickly away, unable to trust himself to take a backward glance.

CHAPTER FOURTEEN

A STRONG WIND blew on All Saints' Day as the people struggled to attend Holy Mass, clutching their clothes tightly around them against the wintry air. Rain followed and the first few days of November were miserably cold with a gale which increased rapidly in strength. Smoke from the fire in the kitchen at the manor blew back into the room causing Kate, who was stirring a cauldron of stew, to cough and choke.

"Tes gettin' worse," observed Digory, struggling to close the heavy door against the wind as he came in from the courtyard. "There'll be no fishin' dun fer a few days if this lot keeps up."

He sat down at table with the other servants. The bread made that morning tasted good with the hot stew and there was little conversation while they all ate.

"Any news from the market today, Samuel?" Kate asked her husband who had not long returned home. Now that the pilgrims had been forbidden to make their way to the former holy shrines the main source of their information was the gossip on market day.

"I did 'ear one bit o' gossip," answered Samuel. "Folks is sayin' that the king is about to get rid of 'is wife agen."

The servants stopped eating and looked at Samuel in astonishment, waiting for him to go on. Samuel glanced quickly around to check that Kristy was not within earshot before imparting the rest of the news.

"Tis sed the young queen 'as bin unfaithful to 'er 'usband," he told his audience then aggravated them all by calmly returning to his food.

"Tell us then," Kate begged him impatiently. "What else did you hear?"

"I'll tell 'ee when I'm finished," Samuel answered and that was all he would say until he had cleared the wooden dish in front of him.

"Now tell us," ordered Kate, "or you won't get nothin' else to eat today."

Samuel gave an exaggerated sigh.

"I 'eard tell as 'ow 'twas discovered she 'ad dun things she should never 'ave dun 'afore she married the king and 'ad carried on doin' 'em after," he said eventually and enjoyed the sensation his pronouncement caused.

"I don' b'lieve it," said Digory. "She wud never dare after she 'ad bin made queen."

Samuel shrugged. "I on'y tell 'ee what folks is sayin', I dedn' say 'twere true."

"No good ever came of a young girl marryin' an old man," Kate commented darkly.

"'E ain't old," began Digory indignantly. "'E ain't fifty yet. I was in this world long 'afore 'im and I ain't old. Don' ee be so free with yer tongue, my girl."

"Well, I hope for the queen's sake the rumours ain't true or I'd not like to be in her shoes," Kate answered.

There were loud voices shouting in the courtyard and they all looked up. Digory left the table and went to investigate. The wind whipped the door out of his hand and sent it crashing back against the wall of the kitchen. Samuel jumped up to help close it.

"Tes a ship in trouble," Digory informed them, listening to the voices in the courtyard. "Better go see what the master ses."

Sir Geoffrey was already out in the courtyard listening to the two men who had come running with the news and stood gasping for breath before him. They were two of the tinners who had seen the ship in distress from the top of the moors and had hurried to spread the word. Samuel and Digory ran over to join them.

"Where is it exactly?" Sir Geoffrey asked.

"Driftin' towards the rocks near Zennor, sir," the older man answered. "We bin watchin' 'er for some time strugglin' towards St Ives but I don' reck'n as 'ow she'll mek it. Tide's turned now an 'tis startin' to sweep 'er in nearer the 'eadland."

"Get all the ropes you can find," Sir Geoffrey ordered Digory. Bart had joined them and he had already started to bring out the horses from the stable. There was no time to lose for the ship would stand little chance in the gale that was blowing her against the treacherous Cornish coast.

The tinners ran off to alert others whilst Sir Geoffrey and Bart, closely followed by Samuel and Digory, galloped across the open moor towards Zennor. The horses struggled against the force of the wind which grew fiercer as they approached the coast, strong gusts continually stopping them in their tracks. Figures could be seen hurrying along the cliff top towards the headland. The driving rain had returned, drenching the anxious watchers through their rough clothes. They were there to help if it proved possible but if not there might be pickings worth having when the ship or her cargo came ashore.

Men from St Ives were already there on the cliff top and figures could be seen running from the moors and from the direction of St Just. Many had watched the ship from early light struggling against the ferocious sea which now threatened to engulf her. She was almost on the rocks and every wave brought her nearer destruction. There were figures clinging desperately to the storm lashed deck, their cries carried on the relentless wind to the ears of the anxious watchers.

Samuel already had a rope tied firmly around his body and Bart quickly wrapped another around his own waist and turned to the man next to him to fix it firmly. Sir Geoffrey looked into his son's eyes with a sense of shock.

"No, Bart, it is not safe," he insisted but Bart had already turned to a group of men on his other side who looked from father to son uncertainly.

"Tie it," Bart ordered but the men still hesitated, looking at Sir Geoffrey. Bart met his father's eyes steadily and Sir Geoffrey paused a brief moment longer before nodding to the men. He had lived with an uneasy conscience since he had failed to help the friars. He had no right to stop Bart now in his determination to help others. He looked at Digory whose face was grey as he helped to tie Samuel's rope.

"Don't worry, we shall be back," promised Bart and made his way to the edge of the cliff. The men had grouped together where they thought survivors might appear in the water after the wreck of the ship which was now inevitable. Bart, Samuel and two other men from St Ives were roped ready to descend the cliffs if rescue seemed possible. They each carried ropes and another around their waist was fastened to the horses on the cliff top. Every one of the watching crowd was ready to seize a rope and hang on to it when the rescuers went over the edge.

The wind howled and enormous waves thundered against the cliffs, soaking those at the top with heavy stinging spray. There was a fearful noise as the ship struck the rocks, pitching screaming men and cattle into the water. Bart and the other three rescuers stepped backwards over the edge, clinging desperately to the ropes as they edged their way down the rocky precipice. The wind blew them dangerously against the rockface, while the men above strained to hold their weight.

Bart heard a terrified shout and was conscious of a figure thrashing about in the water below him. He felt himself engulfed by an icy wave which flattened him against the rock but he came up gasping and spluttering as the water receded for a second. The body in the churning sea had been thrown against him and Bart managed to grasp it. The man struggled frantically and Bart thought he would have to let go but suddenly he went limp and Bart fought to get the rope around him.

"Pull!" shouted Bart, with all the strength he could muster. His voice was lost in the noise of the wind and the sea but the men above had been watching and were ready to heave. Bart breathed a fervent prayer that the rope would hold until they reached the top.

* * *

The rescue continued well into the afternoon. Several other brave men, regardless of their own safety, descended to the wreck which was breaking up rapidly in the raging sea. Bart went down once more but Sir Geoffrey refused to allow him to risk his life a third time for by now he was exhausted. Samuel with his immense strength brought three survivors to the top of the cliff. Digory begged his son not to go down again but Samuel doggedly insisted.

The sea was full of bellowing, terrified cattle swimming for their lives and one more sailor clung desperately to the wreck of the boat. Samuel had the rope fastened around the man's waist when one of the drowning cattle floundered against him and knocked Samuel's head against the rocks. The men on the cliff above heaved with all their strength and brought the two men to the top where Digory eagerly waited to untie his son and the last survivor.

Samuel was dead. His head had cracked open as it struck the jagged rocks. Seven men had been rescued from the wreck of the doomed ship but three rescuers had lost their lives. The other two men were both from St Ives.

* * *

It was several days before Bart recovered from his ordeal and was ready to go downstairs at the manor. He had cuts all over his body where he had been flung against the rocks but he had brought two men to safety. Sir Geoffrey went into his bedroom as his son finished dressing. Bart had to be told about Samuel's death.

Bart listened to his father, sick at heart. Digory had lapsed into the state of lethargy into which Jinty's death had thrown him a few years previously and Kate and Kristy had collapsed with shock. Poor Kate had received a double blow for when news came to Trewarne of the identities of the other two rescuers drowned one had been one of her brothers from St Ives.

* * *

It had been an unhappy year and Christmas 1541 seemed to be the saddest anyone at Trewarne had ever known. Bart had been injured more than he had realised during the rescue and suffered with a painful back. Nothing had been heard of James since he had left them four months ago. Only Rose and her husband, expecting another child and their new home nearly complete, seemed to have any cause to rejoice.

* * *

In London King Henry refused at first to believe the charges of adultery made against Catherine Howard, his young queen, but he was soon convinced. She was beheaded on Tower Green in February, 1542.

Constant trouble with Scotland meant that an English army had to be held in readiness to deal with repeated attacks from across the border. A Scottish force of 20,000 was put to flight by a much smaller English contingent at Solway Moss and three weeks later James V of Scotland died suddenly.

Henry planned to unite Scotland to England by betrothing Edward, his five year old heir, to the infant Mary, Queen of Scots, then a few weeks old, but his plans were thwarted. His next offer to give his daughter Elizabeth (then nine years old) in marriage to the son of the temporary governor of Scotland, providing the two countries united under Henry's kingship and religious doctrine, was not accepted, but some months later a treaty of peace was made between England and Scotland and a treaty of marriage agreed between the children Edward and Mary.

Confident that the war with Scotland was over, massive amounts of money were drained from the Treasury as Henry now enthusiastically ordered guns, ships and men to be gathered ready for war against France. St Mawes Castle was built at Falmouth as part of the new defences of the channel, paid for by money from the monasteries. The construction of Pendennis Castle on the other side of the estuary followed immediately.

Henry's eagerness for war resulted in the clergy and lay people alike being forced to make gifts to the king and loans which they knew would never be repaid. The sale of the monastic lands to eager courtiers and gentry who were only too anxious to take the golden opportunity to increase the value of their estates ensured Henry not only a large influx of money but the support and allegiance of those who benefited from his policies.

* * *

"Will you purchase more land, Geoffrey?" Sir William asked as they rode back together from Truro.

"No, I shall not. My own opinion is that the land does not belong to the Crown to sell. If such action had been taken on a smaller scale by a private citizen to acquire land by force you or I would be trying the offender for theft and violence."

The older man looked at him sharply.

"Dangerous words, Geoffrey. Parliament authorised the seizure of the land and closure of the monasteries as you well know."

"Does that make it right? Most of the land had been given to the Church by our forefathers."

"All the more reason for us to purchase it back from the Crown then, before it falls into the hands of others. There are thousands petitioning already to purchase both the land and the empty properties. Others will not share your scruples."

"If I purchase any of the property I shall be as guilty as those who seized it in the first instance."

Sir William reined in his horse to face the other man.

"You cannot alter what has been done over the past few years, Geoffrey. The Church will never again have the power or the prestige which it formerly enjoyed. I doubt if we have seen the end of the changes yet. Too many of the nobility support the new religion and the poor have little say in the matter. The country will follow the lead of the king and that is how it should be if we are to avoid chaos."

"And you? asked Sir Geoffrey. "Will you follow the king even if it means denial of your own conscience?"

"I shall follow the king because it is my duty to do so," answered Sir William and spurred his horse forward again. Neither man spoke until they reached the lane which led down to Godolphin. Sir William's servant and Digory who had both been ordered to ride slightly ahead out of earshot waited for them.

"Buy the land if you wish your family to prosper," Sir William advised again. "Far better for it to be owned by local landowners who care for it rather than those at court who have no other thought but profit."

He nodded in farewell and Sir Geoffrey followed Digory on to Trewarne. He understood Sir William's arguments but his conscience would not allow him to join the eager rush to purchase which was taking place all over the country.

* * *

Phillipa arrived with her children to join her brother and his family at Trewarne for Easter, bringing with her several new plants for Lady Margaret's garden. Bart had encouraged Digory to help him create and plant a complicated maze where the children happily played. He still suffered badly with his back and had planned the new addition to the garden to help pass the time whilst he was unable to ride, hoping by involving Digory to raise his spirits but it was a difficult task. Kate and Kristy, occupied so much with the lively twins, were slowly recovering from the shock of Samuel's sudden death but Digory was still despondent.

Richard joined them a few days later in April. He had news for Bart but approached the subject warily, unsure of his cousin's reaction.

"Do you remember Isobel, Bart?"

"Yes, I do. I was desperately in love with her years ago. Why do you ask?"

"I saw her recently at Penryn." Richard was undecided whether to continue or not but Bart did not seem concerned at the memory of her. "She was on her way to Spain with her husband. Their ship had to put in for shelter and they stayed with us at Glasney. Very well to do by the look of them."

"Andrew did well for himself after all then," observed Bart.

"No, she married someone else. I gather Andrew abandoned her in London and left her to fend for herself."

"She was a very beautiful girl," recalled Bart. "Did she seem happy?"

"Yes, I would say so. She always wanted to be rich and she certainly appeared to be so. I promised to send a message to her uncle to let him know she is well." Richard paused. "I was a bit worried about telling you that I had met her."

Bart shrugged his shoulders. Isobel had belonged in his life five years ago and had been a very painful experience at the time but he had not thought of her for several years. He had not ridden down to The Lizard either since the day John Wynslade had shown him the note she had left. He had only been back on his horse for a few weeks since his back injury and now the thought struck him that a ride with Richard would be a welcome change.

"We could ride down to see her uncle tomorrow," he suggested, suddenly eager to travel again, and Richard willingly agreed.

* * *

John Wynslade was delighted to see the two young men and they joined his family for dinner. He listened to Richard's message from Isobel without comment. His niece had hurt him deeply by her sudden departure and he preferred not to be overtaken by memories but he was pleased to know that she was safe.

"Are you still teaching at Glasney, Richard?"

"For the moment I am, sir."

"I hear the church buildings there are in a bad state of repair now. It always was a difficult site, built where it is on marshland."

"It has taken a lot of money to maintain over the centuries," agreed Richard. "Now that the Crown has taken over a large part of the income there is hardly enough to pay for all the work needing to be done. Some of the buildings are in danger of collapse and a lot of the timber is rotten."

"It will be a great pity if a beautiful place like that is allowed to deteriorate," observed Bart. "I remember the cloisters and the gardens from the day I started school at Glasney."

"There is a large infirmary too now with its own garden. The church is supposed to be a copy of Exeter Cathedral but I have never been to Exeter so I cannot say."

"If it is left to decline Penryn will decline too," predicted John Wynslade. "The town has built up around the church over the centuries and travellers have always stayed there. Have you seen the new castle built at St Mawes?"

The young men shook their heads.

"Do you think King Henry will declare war on France, sir?" Bart asked.

"I do indeed. Kings have always liked to appear as heroes in the eyes of their people and our King Harry has not had a good fight for some years. Will you two join him?"

"I do not suppose we shall have any option," answered Richard. "If we are told to fight we will have to do so but war always seems to me to cause so much unnecessary suffering and waste of life."

The two young men rose to take their leave and the older man walked to the door with them. Their horses were brought and they mounted, ready for the long ride home.

"Is your father buying any new land?" John Wynslade asked Bart who shook his head.

"No, sir."

"I am pleased to hear it. Neither will I. There are still a few of us left with a conscience which cannot be bought," said their host, and raised his hand in farewell.

* * *

It was late afternoon as they rode back through Helston and the stalls, set in the streets for market day, were just being taken down. The horses picked their way along the dirty untidy street littered with rubbish, weaving their way through the dwindling crowd of noisy people. Sudden shouts caught their attention and a man raced towards them pursued by several others.

"Stop thief!" shouted a furious voice. Bart and Richard tried to pull their horses across the man's path but he was too quick for them and dived between the horses' legs, pursued rapidly by a small, wiry figure. The crowd shouted with frustration at Bart and Richard as the horses stumbled and blocked their way, giving the thief vital seconds to vanish from sight.

"That was Digory chasing him," exclaimed Bart in astonishment as the disappointed crowd dispersed in different directions after their quarry. A young girl ran over to them and the boys were even more surprised to recognise Kristy.

"Someone snatched my purse and Grandfer chased after him," exclaimed Kristy, angry tears on her flushed cheeks. "Where did they go?"

"They cannot be far away," answered Bart. "They must be somewhere in one of these alleyways. Jump up and we will find them."

He was about to swing Kristy up in front of him but he hesitated for a second remembering his injured back. The thought flashed through his mind that Kristy was no longer the little girl who had ridden in front of him some years ago. He jumped down instead and put his hands around her slim waist to steady her as she mounted and smiled at him gratefully.

"You are a very pretty girl now, Kristy," he exclaimed before he could stop himself. Richard gave a little cough and Bart abruptly stepped back.

"You go with Richard – I will try along the passages," he said and vanished into the narrow alleyway down which Digory and the fugitive had disappeared.

"Keep with me," ordered Richard, smiling at Kristy, and the two of them rode up and down the street searching for Digory. Bart found him first, staggering triumphantly along a narrow passageway, blood trickling from a cut on his forehead.

"I caught 'im," Digory grinned, waving Kristy's small leather purse in front of Bart. "I lost 'im agen but 'twas a gud scrap. Reck'n as 'ow I ain't an old 'un yet."

"You certainly can run," Bart answered in honest admiration. "I did not think you could catch him when I saw him shoot beneath my horse."

"Yer've gotta be wiry," Digory informed him, looking at Bart's tall frame and strong shoulders. "'T'aint allus you big 'uns as 'ave got the speed. Us small 'uns 'ave our uses too."

Bart walked with him along the street, thankful to see Digory's face cheerful and beaming again at last. Kristy and Richard saw them and cantered towards them. Kristy jumped down and threw herself into Digory's arms, bursting into tears of relief as she hugged him.

"You ain't got no cause to weep," Digory told her, surprised by her concern but obviously pleased. "I ain't 'urt, my girl. I 'ope as nuthin' 'as bin tek from the cart while we left it."

Luckily the purchases they had made at the market earlier in the day were still safe, guarded hopefully by a small ragged urchin who grinned as he caught the coin tossed by Bart. The two cousins waited until Kristy was seated at the side of Digory.

"Where be ee to, Master Bart?" asked Digory.

"Riding home," he answered and nudged his horse forward with Richard.

They were going to be late for supper that evening at Trewarne.

* * *

The crops grew well and the cart was in regular use throughout the summer making trips to the local markets with surplus vegetables. The tinners had a lucky find and Rose's new son, Luke, arrived and was baptised by Mister Douglas. John

Darnwell began looking for a teaching post. Amy and Kristy, now almost fifteen, would not be in need of his services as a tutor much longer.

Life at the manor seemed to be restored once more to its former pleasant routine and Lady Margaret was thankful to receive several messages from James, prudently making no mention of his training for the priesthood but confirming that he was well and happy.

* * *

The onslaught on the Church seemed to have thankfully ceased. An Act of Parliament which had made it compulsory four years previously for an English Bible to be placed in every parish church was replaced by an Act which only allowed those of the rank above 'gentleman' to read it, but in Cornwall few of the poorer people were affected by either law for they did not read or understand the English language anyway. Cornish was their daily dialect with prayers in Cornish and in Latin taught to them by the priests.

King Henry married Katherine Parr, his sixth and last wife. It was her third marriage, two previous husbands having died. Henry finally settled the crown first on Edward, his only son, then on Mary his first daughter, followed by Elizabeth, his daughter by Anne Boleyn.

Scotland was quiet and Henry was ready to concentrate on war against France. A successful small force was followed the following year by an army of 40,000 men accompanied by Henry himself – 54 years old, excessively fat, unwieldy and sick, he had to be carried throughout the campaign in a litter.

Three hundred Cornishmen under Sir William Godolphin formed part of his army and were the key figures in the siege of Boulogne, using their mining skill to blow up the castle. The town capitulated and Sir William was well rewarded for his valiant efforts but for the rest of his life he bore the scars inflicted on his face during the fighting.

Scotland began to threaten England again. The country awaited invasion from three or four directions. Three armies were assembled – one in Kent, one in Essex and one in the west.

179

Another army stood on the Scottish borders and one at Boulogne. Twelve thousand men were at sea waiting to repel the expected invasion by the French. King Henry ordered processions with hymns and prayers for victory to be held throughout the land.

* * *

None of the men from Trewarne had taken part in the fighting in France but all of Cornwall was involved in the preparations for invasion. Three beacons were prepared on many hills – one to be lit when the enemy was sighted, the second when the enemy was within four miles of the coast and the third if and when men landed. Bulwarks were erected, ditches and trenches dug. Lookouts were posted day and night, for the Cornish coastline with hundreds of little creeks and bays would give easy access to unwelcome visitors. Spies could be landed anywhere, making extreme vigilance essential.

Bart supervised the training of the men and the checking of weapons and armour available at Trewarne. The country expected every able-bodied man to supply himself with a minimum amount of protection for his body and a weapon with which to fight. The men of Cornwall had always fulfilled their obligation in this respect.

A limited amount of guns and powder were available. The Mount was well prepared for defence under Sir Humphrey Arundell. St Ives, which had suffered at the hands of the French many years ago when Porthminster Cove was burnt with the loss of twenty lives, was ready with fort and guns. Along the coast, at strategic places where the enemy might land, rocks and boulders were piled ready to rain down on any attackers. Food stocks were stored in preparation against possible shortages.

* * *

Bart rode into St Ives with Digory to collect a supply of pistols which should have arrived by sea from Bristol. There was a noisy mob gathered around the market stalls under the courthouse where three frightened men cowered on the stairs behind the portreeve and the parish constables, who were struggling to hold the crowd at bay. Bart recognised John Payne, the portreeve, as Kate's brother, one of the men who had helped in the attempted sea rescue when Samuel and Kate's other brother were killed.

John Payne, a large, powerful, usually jovial man was shouting to restore order as the angry crowd jostled noisily in front of him, intent on getting their hands on the three terrified men.

"What is the trouble?" Bart asked a man standing slightly apart from the rest of the crowd.

"Them be foriners, sir," the man answered, nodding to the men cowering on the stairs. "T'ent safe to 'ave pos'ble spies round when we be at war."

"Them ent spies," said Digory scornfully. "They be Bretons an' they've lived 'ere with their fam'lies since 'afore I be born or most of this lot shoutin' 'ere."

"That's mebbe," another man interjected, "but they ent Cornish and we ent aimin' to tek chances. 'Ow do we know they ent sendin' inf'mation to the enemy?"

"Why should they?" asked Bart. "If they have lived here all their lives they are probably as loyal as the rest of us."

He pushed his way to the front of the crowd, the men sullenly making way for him. He was not a St Ives man and in their eyes had no business interfering but he was Sir Geoffrey Trewarne's son and the gentry had to be respected. He was also likely to serve as a future justice of the peace and they might be taken before him at Truro or Bodmin at any time if they failed to keep within the law. John Payne and the two parish constables were happy to have him at their side.

"I'll lock 'em in the courtroom for their own safety," the portreeve decided, nodding towards the three men, and pushed past them to unlock the door. They hurried inside, thankful to be out of reach of the mob, and John Payne stood at the top of the steps to face the crowd again.

"I aim to keep 'em safe in there 'til ee all calm down and come to yer senses agen," he informed them sharply. "I ent allowin' any man to suffer without a fair 'earing while I be portreeve. Six of ee c'n come to a meetin' early in mornin' to talk quietly about this matter and I'll ask parson and churchwardens to be 'ere as well. Clear off now, get back to your 'omes."

The crowd slowly dispersed, arguing among themselves, and John Payne breathed a sigh of relief.

"That were a nasty moment, Master Bart. They poor souls locked up in there were terrified out o' their lives. Some o' that mob chased 'em and threatened to kill 'em."

"Do you think they are spies?" asked Bart.

"Course they ent. They be more loyal than many o' that drunken lot. Nay, most St Ives men will say the same. That were a rowdy crowd wi' some ringleaders wi' too much drink inside 'em. Any more trouble and they c'd well find theyselves in the king's navy." He nodded to the constables. "Keep an eye on they Breton families. We don' want no fools tryin' to tek action agen defenceless women and childern."

The two constables left them. Another group of older men were standing talking under the courthouse.

"They be more sensible," the portreeve informed Bart looking down on them. "We'll sort ourselves out and stay on guard all night in case o' more trouble. I shouldn't doubt if this is goin' on all over the country wi' folks goin' spy and invasion mad. War ent a pleasant thing for ord'nary folks."

"What do you think will happen in the morning?" asked Bart.

"I don' reck'n we shall get much trouble. They Bretons locked in there've allus worked 'ard and lived quietly. The majority o' folk accept 'em and think no ill o' they. The priest will calm things down – tis just a pity 'e was called out to a dyin' man this mornin' or 'e would've bin 'ere. If they leaders o' that mob give more trouble I shall jail 'em for breach o' the peace."

Bart nodded in agreement and decided it was time for him to continue with the purpose of his visit. Digory was standing close by, still holding the reins of the horses, and Bart mounted.

"I ded'n ask ee about my sister, sir, and Kristy," John Payne suddenly remembered.

"They are well," Bart answered. "I will tell them that I have seen you."

He nodded to the man and rode on down towards the harbour. The pistols had at last arrived and were ready for collection. Bart finished his other business in St Ives and rode home late in the afternoon to Trewarne.

John Payne proved correct in his prediction of freedom for the three men. They faced the meeting anxiously the following morning when both sides of the case were argued but no one had any genuine proof or reason to fear the Bretons who had lived among them for so long. They were released and returned thankfully to their homes, giving generous financial help throughout the war, more than they could really afford, to help the community defend the country from the threatened invasion.

The king's fleet gathered at Portsmouth and the Cornish ports were ordered to send all their available ships and mariners too. Robert Trenwith paid a hasty visit to Trewarne with his wife Phillipa before sailing off to join the fleet. He had been disappointed a few years earlier when he had failed to obtain a position on King Henry's flagship the *Mary Rose*, now commanded by a fellow Cornishman. She had two hundred and seven powerful guns, one hundred and twenty oars and could carry one thousand soldiers.

King Henry himself was dining aboard her when the French Armada appeared at Portsmouth. Eighty other English ships were ready including the one captained by Robert Trenwith. The king hurried ashore and the *Mary Rose* sailed into action, chasing the French fleet which was already retreating. Relinquishing the chase, the ship swung round to return to harbour but in the excitement the gunports were left open and the great ship sank with the loss of nearly five hundred lives under the horrified gaze of King Henry and his courtiers. Robert Trenwith helped in the rescue of the thirty survivors from the ship which he had once hoped to command.

CHAPTER FIFTEEN

THE BEAUTIFUL COLLEGIATE church at Glasney was rapidly falling into a very poor state of repair, partly due to the elements and partly to the neglect of the rather worldly provost, Sir John Gentle, but the buildings played a vital part in the defence of Penryn from possible invasion. The walls and towers surrounding the abbey had long been well-fortified with guns for the defence of the town for the tidal river flowed to its door and it was a place of refuge for all in the event of attack. The port and the rapidly expanding harbour at Falmouth adjoining were busy with vessels, hastily loading and unloading or in for repair.

* * *

Robert Trenwith stepped ashore for a few hours while his ship took on further essential supplies for the war. He would not have time to make the journey to Penvedn to see Phillipa but Richard was still teaching at Glasney and Robert could at least see his son. The shock and horror which followed the loss of the *Mary Rose* with his friend Roger Grenville, the captain, and a large number of other Cornishmen aboard had left its mark on Robert. His handsome weather-beaten face was drawn, his hair far greyer than it had been only a short time ago when he had applied to join the ill-fated ship.

Like most of the travellers who disembarked at Penryn he made his way first to the abbey to give fervent thanks for his safe deliverance thus far in the war against France. The bell was ringing clearly over the town, calling the townsfolk to midday service. The church was full and Robert paused for a moment in a vain attempt to pick out Richard before he was hustled forward into one of the last remaining seats. Just as he knelt he saw Richard, his auburn head bent in silent prayer, unaware that his father was kneeling close to him.

Robert had much for which he knew he owed thanks to Almighty God but since that terrible day when he had heard the screams and shouts of so many terrified drowning men and watched their desperate struggles in the water off Portsmouth he had been unable to pray. His own men and those aboard other ships in the area had rowed with every extra ounce of strength they could humanly find to make faster progress to the doomed men but so very few had been saved. Robert sank his head into his hands and tried to let the familiar Latin words of the Mass bring comfort to his tormented mind.

Richard did not notice his father and had gone from the church into the refectory before Robert lifted his head much later and realised that the church was almost empty except for a few still praying silently. The peace and beauty of the place had somehow penetrated his soul and he felt as though a great weight was very slowly lifting from his heart. God had been good to him throughout his life. He had a loving wife, four children – the eldest one somewhere very close at hand – and God in His great mercy had prevented him from joining the ill-fated *Mary Rose*. For the first time in several months he felt his spirits slightly lifted and he found himself once more able to pray.

He rose at last, wondering as he walked slowly down the church if those still silently kneeling were tormented as he had been and if they were he hoped that they too would soon find comfort. He had no idea where Richard had gone. It would be easier to go to the main gates of the church and enquire there where he would find his son.

He found Richard walking slowly up and down the cloisters, absorbed in a book in his hand. Robert stood motionless, waiting until Richard drew level with him and then Richard glanced up, aware of the silent figure standing there. His face lit up with pleasure and delight at the unexpected sight of his father and Robert clasped his son close to him. Richard hugged him and led the way from the silent cloister to the garden where they could talk without disturbing others.

News of the loss of King Henry's flagship had been brought back to Cornwall some weeks ago but nothing had been heard of Robert or his ship since he had sailed to Portsmouth months before. Now Richard was eager to hear all his father's news. Robert still felt unable to speak in detail about the tragedy and Richard understood, tactfully refraining from asking detailed questions as his father glossed over the incident, telling Richard instead of the other activities of King Harry's fleet. The time flew far too quickly and Richard had to return to the classroom before they had exchanged half the news. It was some weeks since Richard himself had been home but at that time the rest of the family had all been well.

"What of you, Richard?" asked his father. "Has Glasney been affected yet by all the changes?"

"Not yet, but we expect developments daily," answered Richard gravely. "Rumour has it that the king is desperate again for money because of this costly war and the collegiate churches with the guilds and chantries will be the next to fall to the Crown."

"If that should happen?"

"Many would like the school here kept open whatever the situation but would I be able to accept the inevitable changes? Part of me still wishes to follow James and train in Rome to become a priest. Perhaps I should have gone earlier."

"It is not a step to be taken unless you are totally convinced that God is calling you," advised his father, "particularly in these dangerous times. Have you considered the new religion?"

"I have discussed it many times with the travellers staying with us at Glasney. I concede it has its good points and the old religion had some bad ones but the old faith is still the only one for me. And you, sir?"

"Sometimes I am not sure," confessed Robert. "I have long spells of doubt and then, God alone knows how, faith comes surging back and I wonder how I could ever have waivered. If only we were not all so afraid to permit each other to find our own way to God. I despair of a country where men break God"s own commandment not to kill because of fear of others of a different faith."

"The Protestants are afraid of us and we are afraid of the Protestants," observed Richard sadly.

"Because of the succession to the throne. The country is so used to following the king's choice of religion each side is afraid of the other gaining control. We tell ourselves we are trying to save the other man's immortal soul but surely God Himself is the only one who can judge whether a man goes to heaven or hell. What right has either side to seek to force its beliefs on those who find another way to God?"

They had reached the school and Richard turned to his father to bid him farewell. Robert Trenwith waited until his son had gone inside the building before retracing his steps back towards the harbour. The visit to Penryn had been a short break and now his ship should be ready to sail once more.

He reached the main street and was forced to stand back against the wall of a house as a group of stony-faced men rode purposefully along the street and turned their horses down towards the church where he had attended Mass a short time ago. Robert knew from the sudden tense silence of the bystanders around him followed by angry muttering that he was not the only one whose heart sank at the clatter of the horses' hooves and the stern, forbidding faces of The Visitors.

* * *

Glasney collegiate church was suppressed that afternoon, the document of surrender signed sadly by an elderly provost who knew he had not always served God and the townspeople of Penryn as well as he might have done had he enjoyed his hawking and hunting a little less. Fourteen other resident priests were forced to sign after him, watched by a bell ringer, a chapel clerk and a white faced young man with auburn hair who gave his name to The Visitors as Richard Trenwith, schoolteacher. Three non-resident priests signed later. For the time being the place would be allowed to stay in use but only as a parish church. A new Provost was appointed, the old one and most of the other priests dismissed with a pension. The young schoolteacher was ordered to carry on with his work in the schoolroom. The Church was no longer his employer. His salary in future would be paid by a representative of the king.

The threat of invasion by France faded, but it was to be another year before peace was officially declared. Little had been gained for England. King Henry boasted that he had fought a successful war but he had only really gained Boulogne and the war had cost the country over two million pounds. The Crown was bankrupt, the people heavily burdened by taxation and forced loans. Prices were rocketing, the coinage debased. The sale of confiscated Church land and buildings had been rushed ahead but the money raised had all been poured into the futile war.

* * *

"You are my heir, Bart. Trewarne and all the land here will one day be your property, God willing. It is time you made up your mind to choose a wife."

Bart listened to his father reluctantly. He had been expecting this conversation for some time but although he would be very happy to marry and have a family of his own not one of the young ladies to whom he had been introduced since Isobel had interested him enough to pursue the friendship with anything deeper in mind.

"You must like some of them, Bart," Lady Margaret urged her usually good natured, handsome son and he shrugged his shoulders.

"I do like them, Mother. They are all very pleasant but I have no particular wish to marry any of them," Bart defended himself.

"You are twenty-seven – most young men are married or at least thinking of it at your age. Your grandfather started Trewarne Manor when he was only a little older than you and now we are responsible for a large number of good tenants and workers. They will need to feel secure when I die."

"But you are not ill, sir," protested Bart. "And even when I do inherit they will be safe under me."

"It would still be better if you found a wife," Sir Geoffrey answered firmly. "There are a number of families showing interest in you."

"Probably only because of Trewarne," sighed Bart, scowling. "If I were poor without any prospects they might not be so eager."

Lady Margaret watched her husband's face as Bart walked gloomily out into the courtyard. Trewarne Manor with its little church and extensive land was very close to Sir Geoffrey's heart. He had dedicated his life to completing the work begun by his own father. Now Sir Geoffrey was fifty-four years old and under his Will Bart would inherit, with ample provision made for Lady Margaret and their other children. James had chosen to become a priest so would have no heirs.

"Leave him a few more months," Lady Margaret suggested. "He will perhaps meet someone suitable in that time. I doubt if he will stay unwed for the rest of his life."

* * *

It was Amy, not Bart, who provided Trewarne with the next wedding celebrations. Seventeen years old, exceedingly pretty with golden curls, she was married in the parish church to Stephen, the younger son of Sir Francis Pengalin, a distant neighbour. Both families were pleased to be united by the marriage and the young couple were blissfully happy together. Trewarne Manor seemed silent and empty when the last guests had gone and Lady Margaret sat sadly in her sitting room with Kate.

Only Bart of her four children now remained at the manor. Amy had left them to live with her husband near Mullion. James had not dared to come home from Rome for the wedding although at least they received news of him occasionally. Rose and John Darnwell with their three children now lived further away. The tutor had found a post teaching a young family further up-country and the distance was too great for him to travel.

The manor which for so long had rung with the sound of voices and laughter was now quiet. Kate, Kristy and Digory were the only ones remaining with them from the old days. Even the kitchen was quiet now fewer servants were needed to care for the small family at Trewarne.

"Kristy will miss Amy badly," Lady Margaret sighed, picking up her sewing.

"She misses them all, my lady," agreed Kate sadly. "She broke her heart when Mistress Rose left with the children."

"Rose offered to take her, I understand."

"She did, and Kristy would have gone but she was unwilling to leave me and Digory."

Lady Margaret smiled as she thought of Kristy and the irascible old man she accepted as her grandfather. Digory had constantly stormed at others, berating them impatiently all his life, but Kristy could twist him around her little finger. He had never shown to anyone, even Jinty in her young days, the love and affection he showered on her and Kristy loved him fiercely in return.

"I suppose it will be Kristy's turn to marry soon," mused Lady Margaret, and was surprised when Kate did not answer. "Do you not think so, Kate?"

"I doubt it, my lady," answered Kate eventually, concentrating on threading her needle.

"Why not? Kate, you must have a reason for saying that. Has she never shown any interest in any of the young men on the estate?"

"Only one, my lady," answered Kate, obviously upset, and rose abruptly. "Excuse me, Lady Margaret. I would rather not discuss it."

Lady Margaret looked after her in astonishment as Kate hurried from the room. She tried to think of any of the young men at Trewarne with whom Kristy could possibly be in love and realised gradually with a sense of shock that there was only one person she had ever seen Kristy's lovely bright eyes follow. It dawned suddenly on Lady Margaret that Kristy, with her mysterious and unknown background, was in love with Bart.

* * *

It was Bart who held Kristy as she sobbed uncontrollably in his arms a few weeks later when Storm died suddenly in a corner of the courtyard. He found Kristy, her face buried in the rough brown and white coat of the little dog who had been rescued from the sea with her, weeping as if her heart would break. Bart took Storm's lifeless body from her and held her closely until her sobbing gradually quietened and she moved from him to gently stroke Storm for the last time.

"He was the only one who knew where I came from," Kristy said sadly in a shaking voice. "If only he could have talked, he could have told me who I am."

* * *

King Henry died on 27th January, 1547. It was three days before the nation was informed that the tyrant who had reigned over them for thirty-seven years and whom they yet accepted and

190

almost worshipped as their king was now dead. The country was stunned and frightened by the news. Three weeks after Henry's death a four mile funeral cortège followed the royal coffin to Windsor Castle for burial.

The following day a glittering procession travelled along icy roads from The Tower escorting a small boy in white velvet decorated with silver, diamonds, rubies and pearls on the first stage of his coronation at Westminster Abbey. Edward VI was crowned King of England. In the place of a majestic fifty-seven year old despot England now had a nine year old boy.

In his Will King Henry had appointed a Council to rule until Edward became of age, no member to be of more importance than another, but within hours of Henry's death the Council had gone against his wishes and agreed to appoint Edward's uncle as Protector of the Realm and Duke of Somerset. A generous though ambitious and haughty man, he was a good soldier but incompetent in politics. Despite having great sympathy with the poor, sadly his policies only succeeded in making their plight far worse. A strong Protestant, he manoeuvred the only devout Catholic off the Council, leaving it composed only of those of the new religion and indifferent members of the old faith on whom he could rely. The young king's tutors were all strong Protestants. The country was about to undergo more radical religious changes and reforms.

* * *

In Cornwall, as in every county, a new commission was set up, this time to make inventories of all the plates, vestments, bells and ornaments belonging to each church. Sir William Godolphin with two other commissioners visited every parish church, systematically writing down its contents. Ostensibly the purpose of the inventories was to prevent any church property being hidden, sold or stolen but to the ordinary people it was another move which would eventually result in confiscation by the Crown.

Mister Douglas stood silently in the parish church as Sir William recorded details of the two statues – one given by Sir Geoffrey and Lady Margaret on their wedding day and the other bought with money raised by his parishioners – the silver candlesticks and chalice retrieved by Digory, the vestments worn when saying Mass. The altar cloths embroidered by the family at Trewarne were noted down, the tabernacle, the bell paid for by the fundraising efforts on Feast Day (no longer allowed to be celebrated). At last Sir William finished. He nodded courteously to the priest and mounted his horse again at the lychgate. His two companions followed as they rode the two miles down the lane which led to Trewarne.

Sir Geoffrey was expecting them. The young assistant priest had sent a hasty warning whilst Mister Douglas and the commissioners were in the parish church. Now he stood waiting for them in the entrance of the little church of St Mary the Virgin which he had built at Trewarne.

Sir William Godolphin did not relish the task in front of him but he had his orders from the Protector of the young king.

"You know why I am here," he stated bluntly, addressing Sir Geoffrey. "I regret in view of our friendship the steps I must now take but you are aware of the new law passed by Parliament."

"I am aware that the king and Parliament are denying us the right to practise our Catholic faith," Sir Geoffrey answered, his grey eyes unflinching and voice as cold as steel.

"The new religion has far more to commend it than the old," began Sir William, but he was interrupted.

"Do you honestly think that, William? Before God, can you honestly say that you believe it, or are you like so many others, growing richer on the land and property seized from the Church?"

Sir William flushed at the implied insult and his eyes flashed angrily but he ignored the taunt.

"I am here to list the valuable items in your church and to order you to close its door permanently. Your chapel here was built to offer Mass for the benefit of the souls of you and your family when you die. Under those terms it is a chantry and Parliament has ordered all chantries closed."

"My church was built for the convenience of my family and household," answered Sir Geoffrey, "to save them from a two mile journey in poor weather."

"And for the benefit of your souls," reaffirmed Sir William flatly. "I was present at the dedication ceremony."

"You were," agreed Sir Geoffrey bitterly, "and in those days you too believed in praying for the dead and many other customs of the Church. Are you so sure of immediately gaining heaven, William, that you do not need anyone to pray for you when you are gone?"

"I believe that I shall be judged on what I have done during my lifetime here on earth and that no prayer said after my death can affect me in any way," answered Sir William after a moment's pause. He was aware that the situation was developing into a religious debate and he had no intention of being further distracted from his duty.

"I would like to enter if you please," he informed Sir Geoffrey stiffly and pushed open the heavy oak door of the little church. Sir Geoffrey followed the men, Lady Margaret now ashen-faced at his side.

The sun shone through the stained glass windows onto the whitewashed walls. The benches carved so lovingly by Samuel and the murals painted by the estate workers gave silent evidence of the faith and devotion which had gone into the building of the church of St Mary the Virgin some twenty years ago. Memories of Mister Vincent, the church lit throughout with candles as he died, of the builders from Lelant, Bart and James falling into the water-logged foundations, the beautiful glass for the windows brought in the cart from Penryn by Digory – all came flooding back as they waited silently for Sir William to complete his list. It did not take long, for the church which they had built so lovingly in the courtyard was only small.

* * *

At Glasney the lands, buildings and entire contents – everything that had been used in the running of the large collegiate church – were sold to the highest bidders. Sir William Godolphin tried to have the buildings retained and used as a grammar school for Penryn and the rest of Cornwall which would rival any in England but he was unsuccessful. Attempts were also made to keep the building permanently as a parish church but the sale went ahead, lead from its roof used in fortifications for the Isles of Scilly.

In London a new proclamation was issued ordering the complete removal of statues and crucifixes from every church.

* * *

Sir Geoffrey was away from home a few weeks later when a group of men on horseback led by a large, fat man with close-set eyes rode purposefully to the lychgate of the parish church and dismounted, leaving one man holding the reins as they strode up the path. Mister Douglas, disturbed by the noise as he knelt quietly making his thanksgiving after Holy Mass, rose to his feet as the men entered. He watched in horror as they pushed past him, systematically smashing the statues, the rood screen, the stained glass windows, slapping whitewash over the murals on the walls. He tried vainly to prevent them but he was pushed roughly out of the way of the jeering men and fell heavily, banging his head against the end of a bench. Charles Rawlaston gave a last satisfied look about him before ordering his men to remount ready for their next assault. He had waited sixteen years for his revenge against Sir Geoffrey Trewarne.

This time it was Bart who faced the grim faced men as they galloped noisily into the courtyard. Kristy leaned against the wall of the barn gasping for breath. She had run over the moors to call back Bart who had just set out to visit the tinners when news of the destruction inside the parish church had been brought to the manor. A small group of labourers gathered behind Bart but only Lady Margaret, Kate and Kristy were at Trewarne that day with a few servants.

Charles Rawlaston surveyed the group gathered in front of him with mounting disappointment. He had planned such a day for so long, waiting through the years for the opportunity to grind the high and mighty Sir Geoffrey Trewarne under his heel and to repay him for the part he had played in the loss of his sons after the nasty business of the two servant girls. Now his frustration boiled over as he realised his enemy was not at home. The people gathered nervously in front of the manor were obviously labourers and servants except for Lady Margaret and the tall, dark haired young man standing defiantly facing him.

"State your business, sir," Bart ordered brusquely and Charles Rawlaston felt his disappointment fade as he realised he was staring at Sir Geoffrey Trewarne's son. He had travelled throughout Cornwall on the Protector's orders for the past few days smashing statues, crucifixes and any other treasures of the Catholic church of which those of the new religion did not approve. It was going to be a pleasure to wreak legal damage at Trewarne.

His men were waiting for him to give the order to enter the little church but Charles Rawlaston had a better idea.

"Smash everything," he ordered Bart grimly. "Smash every blasphemous window, statue and crucifix inside that church."

"I will not," Bart answered steadily. Lady Margaret took a step forward to stand at her son's side but Bart pushed her gently away, his eyes not leaving Charles Rawlaston's face.

"Smash them, I say," roared the man, "or by God I will arrest you and make sure you are hanged for your heresy!"

Bart did not move. The terrified women watching huddled closer and the few labourers looked at each other uncertainly. They were hopelessly outnumbered with no weapons but they would defend Bart and the church in which they had always worshipped if Bart should so decide.

The tension amongst them was at breaking point and all jumped as the door of the church crashed to and there was the sound of a bolt being pushed across. Charles Rawlaston jumped down from his horse and his men followed but they stopped dead in their rush to the church as a crash came from inside and then something was hurled through the first stained glass window, and every other window was broken from the inside to the sound of hysterical sobbing.

By the time the men had forced open the heavy oak door and rushed inside Kristy had broken every statue and window in the church and was slumped sobbing uncontrollably in one of the benches clutching a crucifix which had been made by Samuel and which she had been unable to bring herself to break.

"I could not let them kill Bart," she sobbed in Kate's arms and Bart stared about him aghast at the shattered interior of the little church. Even Charles Rawlaston was stunned for a moment by the unexpected turn of events but then he roared with laughter and the whitewash was slapped all over the murals by his grinning men.

* * *

195

It was several weeks before Bart could bring himself to speak to Kristy. In the shock of that terrible afternoon he could not believe that someone who had shared their lives at Trewarne could wreak such damage to the church which he and his family loved. Even Lady Margaret's insistence that Kristy had acted to save him could not decrease the bitterness he felt towards her. Kristy herself had collapsed after they had reached her and spent a week barely conscious in bed, suffering badly from shock. Sir Geoffrey and Lady Margaret had both visited her in the cottage where she lived with Kate but Bart would not even ask after her.

Kate watched Kristy anxiously, her heart breaking as the lively, dark eyed girl she had brought up as her own daughter and who had grown into a tall, graceful young woman with thick dark, curly hair and a bright smile became steadily thinner, silent and withdrawn. Sir Geoffrey and Lady Margaret tried to talk to Kristy without success. Mister Douglas, recovering from the blow to his head which he had received as he had fallen against the bench end in his own church on that dreadful day, spent many hours with the sick girl, sitting by her bedside or walking the cliff tops with her as she gradually regained her physical strength but Kristy seemed to have withdrawn from them all. She carried out her duties but no one could converse with her. Kristy's mind had still not recovered from her actions in the little church.

Kate sat sewing with Lady Margaret one June afternoon, the sun shining through the diamond panes of the window. Kristy was also with them when there was a knock on the door and Bart entered to speak to his mother. He stopped abruptly when he saw Kate and Kristy and silently Kristy rose and paused only for a brief curtsey to Lady Margaret before going quickly from the room. Bart had deliberately turned his back on her and stared out of the window as she passed him but it was too much for Kate. She stopped behind him on her way to follow Kristy.

"What is it that you blame her for, Master Bart?" she asked quietly, her eyes brimming with unshed tears. "Did Kristy stop you being a hero – is that what really hurts?"

Bart swung round, astonished to hear such insolence, but Kate had not finished yet. She had ceased to care if she lost her position at Trewarne. Kristy was her child as surely as if she had given birth to her and Kate could no longer bear the heartbreak of helplessly watching Kristy's withdrawal from the world around her.

"Kristy broke windows and statues, Master Bart, but she did it to save your life. Which is the bigger sin, I wonder – to break statues or to break someone's heart as coldly and callously as you are doing by your present treatment of her! Perhaps what Kristy did was wrong but I pray that God is more forgiving than you!"

She left the room abruptly and Bart looked furiously at his mother, expecting to see her face outraged at Kate's outburst but to his amazement Lady Margaret's head was bent over her sewing and she spoke not a word. Bart had a sudden uncomfortable feeling that his mother supported Kate in her unexpected attack and he searched his mind indignantly for words in his own defence.

"Kristy had no right to do what she did," he began but Lady Margaret too had begun to lose patience with her obstinate son.

"That man would have arrested you, Bart. He hates your father and that was no idle threat he made. We all know the terrible deaths endured all over the country by those who will not conform. Kristy did not commit sacrilege, she saved your life. Are you really conceited enough to think that your love for God must be greater than hers because you refused to desecrate the church? What would you have done, Bart, had Kristy not acted as she did?"

There was silence in the room as Lady Margaret looked steadily at her son.

"I am not sure," admitted Bart eventually after a long pause. "I have convinced myself that I would never have carried out Charles Rawlaston's orders but perhaps I would have done. Kate could be right and I wanted to appear a hero – in which case Kristy saved my pride too. I do not think I could have lived with the shame of being proved a coward in front of my own mother at Trewarne."

Lady Margaret looked at the troubled face of her elder son but she would not allow herself to be softened by pity for him yet.

"Kristy was braver than any of us, Bart. She loved you – and all of us – enough to do what we were all afraid to do in case we harmed our immortal souls. Can we really think God will blame any of us for actions forced upon us in these terrible times?"

Bart was silent and Lady Margaret returned to her sewing. She pretended not to notice as Bart moved back to the window and after a time she heard him cross the room and descend the spiral stone staircase.

* * *

Bart walked out into the bright sunshine. He had no idea what he intended to do but his footsteps took him towards the stables and he decided to ride his horse up onto the moors where he could think more clearly. A movement in the corner of the kitchen garden arrested his attention and he saw Kristy walking slowly towards him, a bunch of herbs in her hand. She stopped abruptly when she saw Bart but there was nowhere she could go to escape.

Bart looked at her for the first time in several weeks and his conscience hit him as he noticed with a sense of shock her thin body and white face. Kristy's long lashes had always made her beautiful dark eyes seem enormous and suddenly it hurt him to see the black shadows underneath them and Kristy watching him as though afraid. She stood as if poised for flight but in the walled garden Kristy had nowhere she could run.

Bart moved slowly nearer, ashamed now of the bitterness he had felt towards her. He should have been grateful to her and comforted her as his parents and everyone else at Trewarne had tried to do but he had stubbornly rejected her and blamed her for his own feelings of inadequacy in coping with the terrible events. It struck him forcibly as he stopped before her that his own pride and unforgiving attitude had hindered Kristy's recovery and now that he was facing her he could not think what to say.

"I am truly sorry, Kristy," he spoke at last. "Forgive me. I realise now you only acted to save my life."

Kristy slowly raised uncertain eyes to Bart's face. He wanted to say much more but the right words would not come and he no longer struggled to find them. He moved abruptly to take her in his arms, holding her closely to him as he buried his face in her thick soft curly hair before tilting her face to find her lips. The herbs dropped from her hand and shadows lifted from Kristy's tormented soul as she was held tightly in the arms of the man she had always loved.

198

* * *

If Rose's love for her tutor had placed Sir Geoffrey and his wife in a quandary eleven years earlier it had been a small one compared with the problem now facing them as love blossomed between their son and the girl of unknown origin brought up in an in-between world, part of her twenty years spent in the kitchen and part in the schoolroom and company of the family at Trewarne Manor.

Had they been living in normal times the prospect of such a marriage would not even have been considered but their pleasant peaceful lives had gradually crashed about them over the last turbulent years and their values changed. Sir Geoffrey, his hair now almost grey but still handsome and upright, listened to Lady Margaret's suggested solution and thought it wise. Rose and Master Darnwell had been made to endure a test of separation. Kristy would be sent away to help Rose, now expecting her fifth child. There was no doubt that Kristy's love for Bart would stand an endless test of time but they had to be certain of their son.

At first Bart protested strongly but Kristy, well aware of the difficulty of the situation, accepted the decision without protest. She adored the twins, now ten years old, Luke who was six and three year old Rebecca. Helping Rose with the new baby would keep her busy and a year would soon pass. Bart had promised to ride the thirty miles to visit her regularly. Kate was sad to lose the constant company of Kristy but she too recognised the difficulties and Amy was to return to the manor with her small son whilst her husband travelled abroad for a year so there would be compensations.

Poor Digory, deprived of the company of the person he loved most in the world, surprised everybody by taking a new wife. She was ten years younger than Digory, a good cook and well capable of keeping her husband's ill-temper under control.

CHAPTER SIXTEEN

SIR WILLIAM GODOLPHIN and his companions continued their unpopular work of making inventories firmly and courteously but in November 1547 William Body, an unpleasant character, unfortunately arrived on the scene.

Body had caused trouble in Cornwall before. Originally one of Cromwell's agents, an ugly and disreputable man, Body had obtained the archdeaconry of Cornwall almost ten years previously with all its properties and rights. He now decided that he would make a visitation to Penwith. Under the new law each parish was meant to be visited individually for inventory purposes as Sir William Godolphin was doing but William Body had no time or patience for such courtesies. He set up his headquarters in the former church at Glasney and summoned all the incumbents and churchwardens of the area to attend him there.

Suspicious already of the real motive of the Commissioners, Body's arrogant, hostile manner as he addressed them convinced his listeners that the goods of every church throughout the county were about to be confiscated. An angry crowd gathered, rumours quickly spread and Sir William Godolphin, alarmed at growing opposition, sent an urgent report to London of Body's activities.

The Council answered immediately, accusing Body of causing unnecessary trouble and denying that the inventories were for the purpose of confiscation. Body was ordered by the council to be held in custody for a week, and two or three troublemakers sent to prison for a short time until tempers cooled.

For a few weeks all was quiet but then Body began his activities again, leaving a trail of bitter anger as he vigorously carried out the Council's orders to remove all statues and crucifixes from the many churches in the area. A large, angry mob followed him to Helston where he was engaged in despoiling the church. Alarmed at the sight of the noisy crowd approaching, Body shut himself in a nearby house but he had provoked the Cornishmen too far. He was dragged from the house and murdered.

Sir Geoffrey, present in Helston on business as the crowd gathered, faced the sullen mob now numbering hundreds, accompanied only by Digory and a few other constables. He ordered them to hand over the men who had killed Body but they refused. He could do nothing against so many, some of whom also carried arms.

When Sir Geoffrey had prudently withdrawn one of the leaders addressed the crowd, declaring that they would only accept the laws made by the late King Henry himself and none of those made by those acting for his son until he was twenty-four years old. These were the terms of an act made by Henry twelve years previously to safeguard his son should he succeed to the throne as a minor. Henry had rightly feared that the boy would be manipulated and had given Edward the power to repudiate all laws made on his behalf as a child. Even Henry's radical changes were now seen as more acceptable than those being made in the name of his son.

* * *

Next day Sir Geoffrey returned accompanied by Sir William Godolphin and other justices of the peace but they were still unable to force the crowd to hand over Body's murderers. By the following day the number surging through the streets of Helston had increased to over three thousand and the magistrates were powerless to do anything but threaten and appeal to the mob. Only respect for Sir William, Sir Geoffrey and the other justices saved them and their men from being attacked.

The court sessions were due to be held at Helston the following week but the mutinous crowd threatened to be present to ensure that no action was taken against any of their number. Sir William managed to send a written note to London requesting immediate assistance and the messenger was ordered to raise the alarm as he galloped across Cornwall. Other parts of the county did not support the rebels and a force was soon assembled which enabled Sir William to arrest twenty-eight of the ringleaders. The rest dispersed back to their homes.

Those who had struck the fatal blow pleaded guilty and following orders from London were hanged, drawn and quartered, as also was a priest who had taken a prominent part in the affair. Others were hanged as an example to a rebellious population, some pardoned. Much bitterness remained under the outward appearance of calm.

The Act of Uniformity passed in January the following year, followed by the introduction of the Book of Common Prayer which abolished the Mass in favour of a compulsory simple service in English, was to spark a rebellion which would cost thousands of west countrymen their lives.

* * *

"There is trouble in the air," Bart commented uneasily to his father as the family rode home together from Penvedn. The visits to Sir Geoffrey's sister, though still friendly, had become less frequent since Phillipa and Robert had accepted the new religion for themselves and their family. Only Richard, still teaching at the grammar school at Glasney, retained the old faith.

Lady Margaret with Amy and the servants were riding in front of them, well out of hearing.

"You sense it too?" Sir Geoffrey asked.

"I feel it everywhere we go. Amongst our own families there is an air of tension and out in the streets I have the unpleasant feeling that something is going to suddenly erupt. The people stand in little groups and become strangely silent as we pass by, giving us odd looks as though they are uncertain whether they can trust us or not."

"And can they?" asked his father gravely. "I wish in God's name I knew how I should react when the people finally decide they will stand no more interference in their spiritual lives by a Council in London."

"You think they will rebel, sir?"

"I am sure of it. Half the country is in a state of insurrection – the North, Midlands, Norfolk, the South East – even at times London itself. I do not think Cornwall will stay quiet much longer."

"And then?"

"Fifty years ago, Bart, the men of the west marched peacefully to London to protest to the king against heavy taxation – your grandfather amongst them. Many joined them on the way. It is said fifteen thousand reached Blackheath to be confronted by twenty-five thousand of the king's men."

"The march was a failure?"

"Two hundred Cornishmen died. Kings do not take kindly to opposition from the common people. The tragedy could have been far worse but the king was merciful. Now I have a feeling that many are agitating to march again."

They had fallen back behind the other riders as they talked but now those in front were waiting for them.

"You both look so serious!" Amy exclaimed. "Did you not enjoy our stay at Penvedn?"

"Of course we did but now we are discussing more serious business," her father answered.

"Oh, land, tin mining, crops! Gentlemen are always so solemn and talk about such dull things," sighed Amy.

"Your husband, too?" teased Bart.

"Even Stephen can be dull at times but I shall be happy when he returns."

The horses were snorting impatiently and Sir Geoffrey nodded to Digory to ride on again, regarding his manservant's back thoughtfully. Digory's marriage had brought two more members into the household at Trewarne for his new wife, Alice, had brought with her a young nephew whom she had cared for since her younger sister died. The boy, Hugh, who was about fourteen years old, had attached himself to Bart who liked the lad and now Hugh accompanied him whenever he was out riding.

"If anyone knows what is going on Digory will know," remarked Sir Geoffrey to Bart and the conversation was dropped as the lanes became narrower and they were forced to progress in single file.

* * *

Occasionally the thought crossed Sir Geoffrey's mind that Digory must be growing old but the man was as fit and alert as he had ever been and his surprising second marriage seemed to have given him a new lease of life. His thin, wiry frame never appeared to lose its energy and only the extra wrinkles in his ugly face gave any indication of the passage of time. He had served Sir Geoffrey for over thirty-five years and now stood before him in the great hall waiting to be told why he had been summoned to appear before his master and Bart.

"What is going on amongst the people, Digory?" Sir Geoffrey asked, his eyes fixed steadily upon his manservant's face. "Something is being planned and you must know of it."

Digory shuffled awkwardly before he answered. He had felt uneasy for some weeks, he now admitted, wondering whether he should tell Sir Geoffrey of the whispers he had heard but so many wild rumours had flown around the countryside for months that the present mutterings were nothing new. Gossip was the breath of life to those whose drab lives contained no other excitement, as Sir Geoffrey well knew, and all that talk of men being trained at The Mount for rebellion against the Protector was probably only a twist of the truth, for certainly men were being trained there to defend the country against France, Spain or any other country which might suddenly decide to attack. As for the church bells which rumour said were going to be rung backwards as a sign that the rebellion had started they had always been used to warn the country in time of war, as no one could deny.

The people were sullen, resentful of food shortages, rapidly rising prices – and who could blame them, continued Digory, warming to his theme and trying not to use as many colourful adjectives as he would have done had he been holding forth to his audience in the kitchen. They complained of increasing poverty and homelessness brought about by the closure of the monasteries with the loss of all the jobs which had gone with them – work as gatekeepers, cooks, laundresses, servants and many other positions for which ordinary people had been employed. Maybe a good many unworthy clergy had got their comeuppance, for which folks were really glad, but a lot of good ones also suffered and a lot of poor people had been made much worse off in the process.

If they that sat in London making laws on behalf of a small boy had got no more feeling for the common people than to sweep away all the beautiful things which brightened their drab lives on a Sunday and made the weary week worth living – music, singing, stained glass windows, statues, candles, vestments, the likes of which helped poor folk to worship God in all His glory and catch a glimpse of the brighter future in store for them when they departed from this hard world – then they ought not to be in power at all.

Anyone with even a grain of sense should know that the people would accept the law in most things but men should have a right to follow the religion which had been theirs for well over a thousand years. Denying folks the Mass and sacraments meant to most people the loss of their immortal souls and what good was this life of suffering on earth if they could not follow the path they believed would gain them heaven?

Sir Geoffrey listened without interruption, only glancing occasionally at Bart. Digory stopped at last, amazed at his own rhetoric. He had never been asked before to speak so lengthily on any subject in all his years at Trewarne. For one who had never enjoyed listening to sermons he felt he had not done badly at all. In fact, as he told them in the kitchen later that evening, he felt he had done a proper job.

* * *

There was silence for a time after Digory had been dismissed, Sir Geoffrey and Bart both deep in their own thoughts.

"What now, sir?" Bart asked his father eventually.

"What can we do? Digory has told us nothing that we did not know or suspect. I will mention it to Sir William when next I see him but doubtless he knows more than us already."

"I did not mean that exactly," said Bart quietly after a pause.

Sir Geoffrey looked at his son for a moment before he answered.

"I know that is not what you meant," he acknowledged eventually. "You are asking what I will do when this trouble erupts, as it surely will, and my answer to that, Bart, is that I do not know. Part of me tells me that I must be loyal to my king but when I am at prayer another voice deep within me tells me that I should defend my faith."

"Is it disloyal to support the young king but object to those who seek to influence him in defiance of the terms of his father's Will?" asked Bart. "I shall join the people if they decide to march. Perhaps if thousands go to London from all over the country to protest peacefully the Protector and his Council will have to listen to us."

"Protests do not always stay peaceful, no matter how good the intentions of those who organise them. The Pilgrimage of Grace was meant to be peaceful but the broken promises of King Henry turned it into a blood bath, as I well know. Each side incites the other by acts of increasing violence until all reasonable men are swept aside and the devil inevitably takes over. I have no wish to fight my fellow countrymen again."

"But if we do not make a protest?"

"Then God only knows what will happen. I pray that when the time for decision comes He will help us to choose the right way."

Neither spoke again for a long time, the flames of the fire gradually dying down leaving only flickering candles to give light to the room. Sir Geoffrey sat motionless, grateful for the shadows as he struggled with his thoughts and tried to ignore the tightness in his chest which caused him discomfort more frequently now than when it had begun some months previously He was thankful when Bart eventually rose and bade him goodnight, leaving him to sit silently in the candlelight until the pain subsided. Eventually he rose and walked slowly across the room. It was probably nothing serious, simply caused by stress as the situation in the country became more tense and threatened to affect those he so dearly loved. There was no need to mention the recurring pain to his wife or family unless the time came when he could no longer hide the problem from them.

* * *

The country was in ferment and the king's armies, reinforced by mercenaries from Italy, Spain and Germany, were busily engaged in crushing local revolts and fighting against Scotland. The heavy taxes imposed on the country over many years in the struggle to subdue the Scots were bitterly resented by the Cornish who felt Scotland was no concern of theirs as they struggled to make a bare living hundreds of miles away.

The south west corner of England was in a state of uneasy calm and those in London knew little of the county and cared little except for the profit made by those who traded in the tin, mined at great risk to the lives and limbs of impoverished Cornishmen. Cut off as they were from the rest of the country by the Tamar and having close ties with Brittany, the Cornish looked upon themselves almost as a separate race with their own language and rights. Interference by those in authority in London had only made their problems worse and was increasingly resented.

The first outward sign of serious trouble began at Bodmin on the morning of 6th June, 1549.

* * *

Bart had been to visit Kristy and to make arrangements for her return to Trewarne Manor, for the year long separation imposed on the young couple was almost over. Rose was reluctant to lose Kristy who had been a great help to her since the arrival of Tristram, another son, six months previously but she was happy to know that Kristy and Bart would soon be together again.

It was as Bart rode back along the muddy lanes accompanied only by the boy Hugh that he found himself unexpectedly facing a group of ill-clad men surging up the high-banked narrow lane towards him. At sight of him they stopped, completely blocking the way ahead.

"Good day to ee, sir," the man who appeared to be the leader of the group addressed him.

"Good day," answered Bart and waited.

"Ye don't appear to be travellin' our way, sir," the man spoke again ominously. "Will ee tell us the reason why not?"

"Where I travel is no concern of yours," answered Bart stiffly. His eyes swept over the group, conscious of the strong undercurrent of tension surrounding them all. He had an uncomfortable feeling that just one false move could cause the grim-faced men pressing against his horse to attack him and the unarmed boy trying to control his nervous animal behind him. "Pray allow me to pass."

"It is our concern, sir," replied the man grimly. "The common people are risin' at last agenst oppression and either ye travel our way and are for we or ye travel t'other way and must be agenst we."

"Has the rising begun?"

"Aye, sir – this day at Bodmin."

"If I am to join you then I am little use to you as I am," stated Bart, his steady gaze travelling over the sullen ill-assorted group watching him. "I would be of far more use to you if I had more men and horses. Where are you mustering?"

"In Bodmin, sir."

"I may join you there," Bart promised after a brief pause.

The men still blocked his way, unsure whether they could trust him or whether he would alert the authorities and attack them from the rear. They could take him and the boy prisoner to safeguard themselves but that might cause them greater trouble later. Reluctantly they parted and pressed against the bank to allow them to pass. Bart pulled his horse to one side and motioned to Hugh to ride ahead of him. It had crossed his mind that some of the ringleaders might try to seize Hugh as a hostage until Bart returned with the promised men. No one moved as the riders passed between them and Bart could not help smiling at Hugh's audible gasp of relief as they spurred their horses forward around the bend in the lane.

* * *

Mister Douglas was just mounting his horse to carry an urgent message to Trewarne when Bart and Hugh cantered briskly along the lane and they travelled together, exchanging brief snatches of news.

Sir Geoffrey, about to ride up to the tinners on the moor when the riders clattered into the courtyard, dismounted and led the way into the great hall. He looked at the serious faces of his son and Mister Douglas as he poured wine, waiting for them to speak. Bart told briefly of his encounter with the men and their assertion that the rising had begun.

Mister Douglas confirmed his news.

"I had a message from a fellow clergyman in a neighbouring parish a short time ago. There is a large crowd in Bodmin demanding that the men of the west should march to place their petition before the king. A muster has already been called and we are to listen for church bells. If they peal backwards it is a sign that the rising has seriously begun."

"Do you think many will follow?" Bart asked.

"There are many clergy planning to lead the way. I have no doubt that a large number of the people will follow. It is planned as a trouble-free march – pray God it will remain so."

Sir Geoffrey shook his head dubiously.

"It is unlikely. When news travels to London the men will be ordered back to their homes and either they must return or fight their way forward. The king's men will be well armed. Had those men who stopped you any weapons, Bart?"

"Bill hooks, sticks, bows and arrows."

"A genuine call to muster means every man taking whatever weapons and armour he has in order to protect himself. Everyone cannot go. Some will have to stay behind to do the work which the women cannot manage. It will not help if all we men disappear and return after a few months to ruined crops and starving families."

"You intend to go then, father?"

Sir Geoffrey hesitated for one brief moment, realising the implication of his own words. For months he had struggled with his conscience, uncertain as to which side he should place himself upon when the crisis came, and now he found Bart's eyes watching him earnestly and heard his own voice beginning to organise the great revolt.

* * *

Hundreds of Cornishmen flocked to Bodmin, some eagerly, some more reluctantly. Those who survived claimed later in their own defence that they only joined the rebellion under threat of violence if they refused. Many were accompanied by their parish priest. Mister Douglas, Sir Geoffrey and Bart led those who went from Trewarne. Most of the fitter, able-bodied tinners and labourers followed, the older ones left to help the womenfolk and children continue their work. Hugh, who was too young, and Digory, too old, were ordered by Sir Geoffrey to remain behind.

The straggling procession grew at each crossroad as they were joined by groups from other parishes, the men of Gulval and Lelant led by their priests, the men of St Ives led by John Payne, the mayor, brother of Kate. Few of Sir William Godolphin's men joined the rising for he was against the march.

In most parts of England the common people looked to their masters amongst the gentry for leadership and to supply them with horses and weapons in time of need but there were few members of the gentry in Cornwall, for those who sought wealth found it nearer to London than in the remote south west. Those of the gentry who were present in the county but did not support the rising took refuge at St Michael's Mount and the castle at Trematon.

Sir Humphrey Arundell, the captain of the regular garrison at The Mount, became the official leader of the uprising when he was at his home near Bodmin visiting his wife, though he later claimed he was forced to do so by the rebels.

* * *

The hundreds of men on horseback and on foot journeying towards Bodmin early one morning had to make way for a contingent of men travelling in the opposite direction – a group which included men who had trained at The Mount and were familiar with its unique layout. They had been despatched by Sir Humphrey to arrest the gentry sheltering inside the castle for they could not risk attack from the rear. Those inside The Mount tried to defend themselves when the men crossed to the castle at low tide but the attackers carried large trusses of hay in front of themselves to protect them from the arrows and musket balls fired from above and succeeded in reaching the summit, overpowering the gentry. The prisoners were forced to accompany their captors to Bodmin and later imprisoned at Launceston with others of their class who would not join the rising.

Meanwhile the number assembled at Castle Kynoch, half a mile from Bodmin, had grown rapidly and Sir Humphrey Arundell appointed some of the leaders as captains, majors and colonels to establish military discipline and train the thousands of men noisily airing their grievances as they waited for orders. Sir Geoffrey, who had not mentioned to anyone the chest pains and tiredness which had been troubling him for several months, joined those in authority in planning their campaign and drawing up a manifesto which explained their belief in the justice of their cause and their reasons for taking up arms.

A list of their requests despatched by messenger to King Edward asked for the restoration of their traditional Catholic faith and affirmed their loyalty to the young king. The reply received, signed by Edward, reproved them for assembling in a seditious manner but continued that as he considered the people misled 'by evil disposed persons working on their ignorance' he was willing to write a document in reply – one which did not agree to any of their requests and ended 'We have condescended of love to write rather than to war against you as rebels, but unless you repent we will extend our Princely power and draw the sword against you as infidels and Turks'.

"It is only as we expected," commented one of the grave faced men seated around the table to listen to the king's reply read out by Sir Humphrey. "None of us really hoped our requests would be granted so easily."

"No doubt that document was drawn up by the boy's advisers," added Sir Geoffrey. "It certainly does not take his father's wishes into consideration. Nothing should have been changed until Edward himself was old enough to make up his own mind."

Sir Humphrey studied the document in his hand.

"It makes our position very plain, gentlemen. Either we withdraw and accept the king's gracious pardon or we proceed in the sure knowledge that we will have to fight for our cause."

"I would never again trust an offer of pardon." Sir Geoffrey had bitter memories of the rising in the north of the country some years ago when Henry had tricked the people by a similar offer only to wreak terrible vengeance when the opportunity arose.

Mister Douglas sat by Sir Geoffrey's side and now the priest spoke thoughtfully.

"Perhaps another letter to the young king would be worthwhile before we commit ourselves to any other action. Edward is only a boy – we should make our petitions clear to him and ask him to graciously reconsider our requests."

"A waste of time but we will do so if you wish."

Sir Humphrey looked at the faces around him. Several heads nodded and he picked up his quill and prepared to write.

"What do you wish to say?"

* * *

The leaders of the king's subjects assembled around the table that day at Bodmin insisted again on their loyalty to Edward but declared that those acting on the young king's behalf had taken it upon themselves to make decisions concerning religion which should be reserved to God and his vicars. It was to prevent the maladministration on the king's behalf and to urge that there should be no change in the law until Edward became of age as instructed in his father's Will that they were willing to jeopardise their bodies, goods and souls. They admitted reformation within the Church was needed but it should only be carried out on the advice of the bishops. They declared that they would rather sacrifice their lives than relinquish their faith at the bidding of the king's governors.

* * *

Three days after the first outbreak of public unrest at Bodmin, a separate incident occurred at Sampford Courtenay, forty-five miles away in Devonshire. On Whit Sunday morning the parishioners attended church to hear the new compulsory service which replaced the Holy Mass.

The Mass had been a service of prayers and praise of God, sorrow expressed for sins committed, readings from the epistles and gospels, leading to the Consecration when bread and wine were changed by the power of the Holy Spirit into the body and blood of Christ – the Catholic belief in transubstantiation. It was a re-enactment of the Last Supper as commanded by Jesus resulting in the presence of God on the altar in the form of bread and wine which was later distributed among the faithful. At the end of the Mass, following prayers of thanksgiving, any remaining consecrated bread would either be placed by the priest into the tabernacle or into a small closed receptacle, a pyx, for distribution to the sick.

The new instructions banned the celebration of the Mass. The people were forbidden to follow the teaching which was at the heart of their traditional Catholic faith and priests threatened with imprisonment and death if they did not conform. The Mass was branded as 'repugnant superstition'.

The villagers at Sampford Courtenay listened silently as the priest read the new service, now entirely in English. During the day they discussed the new order of prayer and rejected it.

Next morning as William Harper, their elderly priest, prepared for Morning Service a deputation entered the vestry and asked him what form of service he intended to conduct. He replied that he must comply with the law and use the new prayer book as he had done the previous day.

The men forbade him to do so, informing him of the will of the villagers to keep to the old traditions of the Church until the young king came of age and could make his own decisions on the religion of the realm. The rest of the parishioners arrived to confirm their determination and the old priest put on the banned vestments and celebrated Mass.

Before long the local justices of the peace heard of the defiance of the law by the priest and common people of Sampford Courtenay and that men from other parishes had begun to gather there. The magistrates rode into the village, together with armed servants and retainers. The two main leaders of the villagers, William Underhill, a tailor and William Segar, a labourer, refused to discuss the matter unless the justices left their men at a distance. After long talks, nothing was achieved and the magistrates rode away.

A few days later another man rode into Sampford convinced that he could quell the rebellion single handed. He was taken to the upper storey of the house which they had made their headquarters where he 'earnestly reproved and sharply threatened them'. Tempers flared as he turned to leave and the man was viciously murdered on the stone steps leading to the street below. Later the men of Sampford Courtenay set off to join the contingent of Cornishmen now marching to Crediton.

* * *

It was another week before Parliament realised that there was an armed uprising in the west and then two west country men who knew the area were despatched to quell the outbreak of trouble, Sir Gawen Carew and his nephew, Sir Peter Carew. Strongly Protestant, they carried a letter promising a complete pardon to all those who repented of their part in the insurrection provided they promised to behave themselves in future as loving and dutiful subjects. Those who persisted in rebellion would be dealt with severely.

The two knights travelled to Exeter with the letter where they heard that a great number of the people were now assembled at Crediton, seven miles away. They resolved to ride there with their escorts, a total force of nearly two hundred armed men, and speak to the rebel leaders.

Forewarned of the coming visit, those at Crediton had put the town into a state of defence. On either side of the road from Exeter were two barns, the walls of which had been pierced, while men inside waited ready to defend the entrance to the town in the event of attack. Trenches had been dug, ramparts built and great plough chains hung across the road to block the progress of unwelcome visitors. The advance party of the Carews were surprised to find their way obstructed and turned to warn their comrades.

After a hasty consultation with the other gentlemen accompanying them, Sir Peter dismounted with his men and started to walk towards the defences, expecting to be allowed through to talk to the rebels but they did not trust the Carews with their large contingent of armed men and refused them entry. Furious at this unexpected insolence by the peasants, the gentlemen decided to rush the barricades, only to be driven back by a hail of arrows fired through the pierced walls of the barns which they had not noticed, resulting in many casualties.

The rebels had triumphed for the moment but their shouts of joy were short-lived. One of the men in the opposing force set fire to the thatched roofs of the barns. Panic spread amongst the defenders as they rushed to escape the flames and the rebels and inhabitants fled, leaving Sir Peter Carew and his company to enter a deserted town.

It was almost dark and deciding that pursuit was useless the gentlemen returned to Exeter, convinced that the peasants had been taught a lesson which they would never forget. The common people would not rise again.

They were much mistaken. The reports of the callous burning of the barns with men inside spread rapidly throughout the countryside, exaggerated in each telling, until the people were convinced that the gentry were uniting to burn them out of their homes in order to steal their land. The peasants of Cornwall and Devonshire began desperately to arm themselves, fortify their villages and dig trenches across their roads.

The following day at the village of Clyst St Mary, a few miles from Exeter, an old lady on her way to church with rosary beads in her hands was overtaken by a rider, Walter Raleigh, whose son of the same name was to become famous in Queen Elizabeth's reign. Being a strong Protestant the man haughtily ordered the old woman to put away her beads, act like a good Christian woman, be an obedient subject of the king and accept the new religion or he would see that she suffered the punishment of the law. He rode off and the terrified woman fled to the church where the villagers were assembled, claiming loudly that a strange gentleman had threatened her if she did not abandon her Catholic faith and would burn down the village and plunder their homes.

Added to the terrifying reports of the burning of Crediton and the presence so close to them of the Carews with a large contingent of armed men sent on behalf of the king, the result was chaotic. The people poured out of the church, messengers sent hastily into the surrounding district begging immediate help, trenches dug, ramparts erected. Guns were taken from ships moored at Topsham and placed to cover the bridge which formed part of the road into Exeter. Trees were felled to block the road and the villagers waited for what seemed to be an inevitable attack.

* * *

Next morning Sir Peter Carew and his uncle, Sir Gawen, accompanied by other justices of the peace, gentlemen and their servants, all armed, rode to Clyst St Mary, only to find access to the village blocked and heavily guarded. Sir Peter dismounted and began to walk forward when a gun was trained upon him and he would have been shot had not someone seized the gunner's arm. Sir Peter prudently withdrew and a servant was sent forward with a request for a conference.

Dubious at first, the rebels finally agreed to allow three only of the opposing company in for discussion but it was a wasted day and at nightfall talks were abandoned without progress on either side. Sir Peter and his company withdrew again to Exeter.

The Protector still did not realise the seriousness of the position. Sir Humphrey Arundell's prompt action in taking prisoner all the gentry who did not support the rebels early in the revolt had succeeded in preventing any information from being passed to London. So far as the Protector was aware the disturbances in the west were confined to a few small villages and the muster returns for those areas showed little available there in the way of weapons or armour. Lord Russell, a soldier of great experience, was ordered from London with three hundred men to deal with the commotion.

* * *

The recent threat of invasion had resulted in most of the loyal Cornishmen supplying their own needs in the way of weapons and armour as was expected of them and so, despite the lack of support from many of the gentry, the thousands of men now training at Bodmin were very well equipped, over half of them possessing full armour – a helmet, protection for the throat, a coat of leather or canvas with small metal plates sewn inside, and splints to protect the arm or wrist.

Most of their available weapons were bows and arrows, bills – six feet long and with a head which combined a spear point and an axe blade backed by a spike – short swords, daggers and slings. Those who had carried out the raid on The Mount had brought back light cannon and guns. The men of the western rising, gathered together for nearly three weeks, were now well-trained and restless for action. Food was growing scarce and tempers frayed as the Cornishmen waited for the command to march.

Alert to the danger of attack from the rear, a strong contingent was ordered to Plymouth to call the people to support the peasants and imprison dissenting gentry. Plymouth offered little resistance but the defenders of the castle held out, to the disappointment of the rebels who had hoped to seize a supply of guns.

* * *

Encamped at Bodmin, Sir Geoffrey Trewarne had no wish to embarrass his old friend Matthew Wychcombe by a possibly unwelcome visit so a note was sent informing him of Sir Geoffrey's presence in the area – there was no need for further explanation. The messenger returned with a warm invitation and Sir Geoffrey left the camp early one morning accompanied by two labourers training under Bart's command. Matthew Wychcombe lived with his wife Mary not far from Bodmin in a large, pleasant house. He welcomed Sir Geoffrey with great pleasure and his wife stayed for a short while before leaving the two men alone.

"I would join you in your crusade if only I had my health," Matthew sighed. "My old leg wound gives me a great deal of trouble. I hear you have a very large number encamped at Castle Kynoch."

"At times I wonder how we control so many," admitted Sir Geoffrey. "Fortunately they are all filled with enthusiasm for the cause and the days pass fairly quickly with so much training."

"You must find food supplies a problem."

"They are indeed. We are a great drain on the resources of the town – though as always there are some who will grow rich out of the inconvenience. Such a large number of men means a great deal of expense for supplies and other essentials – which brings me to the main purpose of my visit."

Matthew Wychcombe laughed.

"You are going to ask me for a donation to your funds? I will give that gladly though I have given much already. However, in such a cause I can find a little more."

"No, it is not a donation I ask," answered Sir Geoffrey. "I want you to sell something for me. I could get one of my men to take the items into town and sell to any willing buyer but he would not know who is honest and who is not. With our present urgent need of money for our crusade I must be sure I am getting the best price I can obtain."

He picked up a bundle which he had carried into the house with him and Matthew looked in amazement as the silver candlesticks retrieved by Digory many years ago rolled out onto the table.

"They were given by my father and my grandfather to the parish church at Trewarne," Sir Geoffrey informed him. "We are not allowed to use them any more. I brought them in case we ran short of money on this campaign as we are so doing. Several of the clergy accompanying us have done the same, but we shall only sell as much as we are forced to do."

"But surely they are on the inventory taken by the commissioners," protested Matthew. "If they are found to be missing you will be charged with stealing them."

"If we win this campaign for our religious freedom I will replace them. If we lose, it makes no difference anyway, those of us considered leaders will all be hanged. As we feared, we are running desperately short of money. God will not blame us if the need for food at the moment is greater than our need for candlesticks. The armies of the king have been run for many years now on the proceeds from the Church."

"Both Henry and Edward would probably consider their needs greater than yours," chuckled Matthew. "I will not sell them for the moment, Geoffrey, but I will advance you a fair sum against them and you can claim them back when you are ready."

Sir Geoffrey smiled slightly.

"And if I do not come back, Matthew, you will have lost your money."

"Ah, but at least I will have the candlesticks."

He rose and examined them carefully before going to a locked deed box which he opened and turned to hand the contents to Sir Geoffrey.

"I think this should feed the multitude for a while," he began, then his expression changed suddenly as he saw the other man's face. "God's wounds, what is the matter!" he exclaimed.

Sir Geoffrey's contorted face was grey, his hand clutching his chest as he slumped in his chair, gasping for breath. Matthew rushed to ring the bell and pour his friend a drink with shaking hands. A servant appeared and was sent running for Mary and a doctor from the town. The two men who had accompanied Sir Geoffrey sped back to the camp for Bart and Mister Douglas.

* * *

The priest was the first to arrive, having urged his horse into a speedy gallop immediately the news reached him without waiting for Bart to be found. A servant quickly opened the door at his urgent knocking and Mister Douglas hurried inside.

"Thank God you have arrived," exclaimed Matthew Wychcombe. "Is Bart with you?"

"He should be here soon – everyone is searching for him. Is his father very sick?"

"I feared you would not arrive in time. The doctor is with him and my wife, but I was sent from the room to await you. This is a great shock." Matthew was visibly shaking as he spoke. "I did not not even know he was ill."

"None of us did. He has not mentioned any problem."

They reached the door of the room where Sir Geoffrey was being attended and Matthew's wife opened the door to the tentative knocking. The hearts of both men sank as they saw her tearful face but the doctor beckoned to the priest to enter.

"I fear you are almost too late," he said quietly.

Mister Douglas strode swiftly to the bed and took his friend's limp hand. Sir Geoffrey's eyes flickered and the priest motioned to the others present to leave the room.

* * *

It was some time later when Bart was found amongst the thousands of men training outside the town. He jumped on his horse fearfully, spurring him into an urgent gallop, and cursed the misfortune which had made him decide to ride to the very outskirts of the camp that afternoon. The door of the house in Bodmin was opened before he had even dismounted. He stood white faced as the doctor and Matthew Wychcombe spoke quietly to him, restraining him from entering the room where his sick father lay until Mister Douglas opened the door and stood aside for Bart to enter. He ran swiftly across the room to drop on his knees beside the bed but Sir Geoffrey Trewarne was dead.

* * *

"I cannot spare you, Bart. We march to Exeter today and every man is needed. I am sorry, I appreciate your distress, but if I allow you to take your father's body home it will be at least a week before you return."

"I want to be with my mother when she is told the news," answered Bart numbly.

"And if I let you go, we lose one of the few members of the gentry with us on our crusade. I need you if only for that reason, Bart. The men are bitter and disappointed that so few gentlemen have joined us. The loss of your father has been a great blow to all of us."

Sir Humphrey Arundell was sympathetic towards Bart but he had nearly six thousand restless men under his command and his own silent fears that thousands of other wives and mothers would be mourning before the campaign ahead of them was over. He was thirty-six years old, an experienced soldier and had fought for the late King Henry against France. His own parents had died twelve years ago.

Bart had received a severe shock but Sir Humphrey knew from his own painful experience that he would recover.

"I will arrange for your father's body to be taken to Trewarne," he began but Bart interrupted him wearily.

"Thank you, there is no need. My father's friend has offered to do so already."

Indeed Matthew Wychcombe, suspecting that Bart would not be given permission to leave the camp, had offered to make all necessary arrangements and to travel himself with the body to break the sad news to Lady Margaret.

Mister Douglas defied the new rulings and offered a Requiem Mass for Sir Geoffrey at an open-air altar in the camp.

Bart only had time to watch his father's body lifted on to the cart for the sad journey back to Trewarne before Sir Humphrey Arundell gave the command to march.

CHAPTER SEVENTEEN

THOUSANDS OF MEN assembled behind their standard, a banner which fluttered in the late June breeze and which depicted the hands, feet and heart of the wounded Christ. They were led by a priest carrying the consecrated Host beneath a canopy, accompanied by acolytes with crosses, candles and holy water. Behind them rode Sir Humphrey Arundell, other leaders and clergymen.

Their aim was to march to London to lay their grievances before the young king, determined that those whom they believed were unlawfully manipulating him should be removed from their positions of power. No satisfactory answer had been received to their humble requests and the common people would no longer suffer oppression. They had grumbled for years at the changes to their customs and long cherished beliefs but as they left their spirits were jubilant.

Many more joined them on their slow steady progress along the narrow lanes watched by scattered groups of cheering women and children and those too old to take part. It took them nearly a week to reach Exeter, their first destination – a cathedral city, predominantly Catholic, inhabited by wealthy merchants. The weary men marching towards the thick, high walls had no doubt that they would be received joyfully, given generous provisions, their numbers swelled by hundreds willing to join them in their crusade.

They were to be bitterly disappointed. More than a week earlier, as first rumours of trouble had been brought to the city, the mayor and council had debated the situation. Although they had strong sympathy with the uprising they had decided that their first duty was to their king. Exeter had already begun to prepare itself against the rebels.

* * *

Still confidently expecting to be welcomed, Sir Humphrey sent messengers ahead requesting the mayor to open the city gates. There was consternation when the riders returned with a refusal. The leaders ordered a second message to be delivered, demanding that the inhabitants of Exeter should adhere to the old traditional faith and to support those now earnestly trying to uphold it.

There was a tense atmosphere in Sir Humphrey's tent as they awaited a reply.

"Are they with us?" one of the leaders eventually asked following the messengers' return.

Sir Humphrey's face was grim as he stared at the paper in his hand. None of the men watching him spoke a word until finally he looked at them, fury and frustration showing in his bitter eyes.

"No, they are not. They accuse us of being wicked men whom they regard as their enemies and rebels against God, king and country – for which reason they will have nothing to do with us."

"God's blood!" exclaimed a voice and for a moment there was silence in the tent before a clamour of bitter recrimination broke out amongst the incredulous men. Slowly Sir Humphrey rose and prepared to address the thousands of hopeful men waiting for news outside.

* * *

It was a serious set-back to the campaign which had begun so confidently. Not only were the men of Exeter unwilling to support them, the leaders of the rising were reluctant to proceed on their journey and leave an apparently well-armed, hostile city at their rear.

The number of Cornishmen, although large, was insufficient to leave enough behind to protect those who marched forward. They had no alternative but to begin a siege of the city, hoping that sympathisers inside would help to ensure its short duration, but rumours buzzed within the walls predicting rape, theft and violence if the rebels gained entry. The city gates remained securely closed. All able-bodied inhabitants were mustered and enrolled as soldiers, guns were hurriedly placed along the walls and to cover each of the five gates. A watch was posted day and night as Exeter prepared to withstand the siege.

Frustrated at the unexpected turn of events which was delaying the march to London Sir Humphrey began to deal with the situation as quickly as possible. Roads leading into Exeter were blocked with trees, trenches dug, bridges destroyed. Pipes and channels for the water supply to the city were broken up, the lead used to make shot, but the inhabitants were not worried by the threat of a water shortage for they had plenty of fresh springs. Food shortages, however, were a worry and the rebels effectively blockaded their supplies.

Those besieging the city had their own problems. They had no guns large enough to breach the walls but they had one great advantage – many of their men were Cornish tinners, experts in mining. They began to dig beneath the city walls, intending to fill the tunnel with gunpowder which they would then detonate under cover of darkness.

Unfortunately for the success of their plan another experienced miner from Teignmouth happened to be inside the city and, recognising the sound of the tunnelling, informed the authorities who would not at first believe him. Taking a pan of water the man placed it at different points on the ground until it was over a spot where the water would not settle. The mayor was informed and tunnelling began at the same place from inside the walls.

The people living in the area filled tubs and buckets, diverted nearby streams and at a given signal, just as those outside were about to light the fuse, a deluge of water poured down onto the precious gunpowder. A violent thunderstorm added to the torrent and the disappointed attackers, having no more powder left, had to abandon their plan to blow open the city walls. The besiegers tried by various means to wear down the resistance of the city including an unsuccessful attempt to burn down one of the great gates and casualties were inflicted by marksmen of both sides. Spies regularly climbed each way over the walls under cover of darkness and messages were passed in and out of the city. Raiding parties from inside made daring sorties to capture animals grazing nearby, for the food supplies were becoming low.

Frequent truces were called to discuss the situation and those inside complained that although they were called upon to send their most prominent citizens, the leaders of the rebels, apart from a few gentlemen, were 'the refuse, scum and rascals of the whole country'.

* * *

The war of words continued, neither side prepared to give way. A further list of requests was sent to the king, again proclaiming the loyalty of the rebels to Edward personally and beseeching the restoration of the traditional faith. The men also added their complaint that now the services were no longer in Latin but in English most Cornishmen could not understand them. The Protector rudely retorted that he was quite sure they did not understand Latin either.

The siege had reached stalemate but now those in London had at last realised the gravity of the rising. While the inhabitants of Exeter began to fear starvation and the rebels outside grew impatient at the delay, reinforcements for the king's army were beginning to arrive.

Lord Russell had been waiting at Honiton with only three hundred men. Almost four weeks after the siege had begun his army was increased by order of the Protector to three thousand two hundred heavily armed men including German, Spanish and Italian mercenaries. The Italians brought with them their deadly new weapon, the arquebus – a heavy portable gun which was supported by forks when being fired. The men of Devon and Cornwall, though less well equipped, at this stage outnumbered them by about two to one.

* * *

The first serious battle of the campaign took place towards the end of July at Fenny Bridges, two miles west of Honiton. A detachment of rebels was ordered by Sir Humphrey to seize the bridges over the river. After weeks of frustrating inactivity, with many reports from informers of the build-up of royal forces, the order for action came as a relief.

A small group of rebels were left to hold the main bridge while others drew up in the meadow below. Sir Peter and Sir Gawen, still smarting from their earlier failures to disperse the Cornish and Devon men, urged Lord Russell to attack, volunteering to lead the assault themselves. First they had to rush the bridge but the brave determined rebels stood their ground against the heavily armed mercenaries pounding on horseback towards them, until finally they were overcome by sheer numbers and they were forced to fall back, leaving the bridge free for the king's men to pursue them into the meadow beyond.

Hundreds of foot soldiers poured across and the rebels steeled themselves as the royal forces regrouped and charged. Bitter hand to hand fighting continued, the shouts and screams of dying and injured men and horses adding to the horror of the bloody scene. Sir Gawen Carew himself was wounded in the arm by an arrow. The tall, sturdy Cornishmen fought fiercely but they were heavily outnumbered and eventually forced to break ranks and flee.

Convinced that the rebels were defeated the mercenaries began stripping the bodies of any valuables they could find and finishing off the injured with their daggers whilst the gentlemen rested. They were suddenly surprised by an unexpected shower of arrows, for two hundred more Cornishmen led by Bart had been on their way to reinforce those in the meadow and had pressed on in spite of the terrible sight of so many of their badly wounded fellow countrymen retreating past them. They were brave men but they too were overwhelmed by greater numbers and eventually fled back to Exeter. Three hundred rebels lay dead in the bloodsoaked meadow and river. One hundred soldiers lay with them.

Lord Russell pursued those who were retreating for three miles, intending to carry on to the relief of Exeter, but he was stopped by his own household fool who galloped after him screaming that the church bells were ringing and the country had risen in rebellion behind him. He was mistaken but Lord Russell did not know that. Always fearful of attack from the rear he recalled his army and they returned to Honiton.

* * *

Bart had received a wound in his arm in the bloody battle at Fenny Bridges but it was nothing compared to many of the injuries. The women who had followed the rebel army did what they could to bandage the wounded whilst the leaders of the uprising gravely discussed their next move. Exeter was holding out much longer than they had expected. The reports the rebels received from sympathisers inside the walls confirmed that the people, though desperate for food, were divided on whether they should or should not surrender and end the siege.

It was not at all as the rebellion had been planned. The peaceful march to London to protest to the boy king had developed into the bloodbath Sir Geoffrey had predicted, but there was no going back. Several offers of pardon by the Protector had been rejected. The common people had learned to distrust the promises made by and on behalf of kings.

* * *

"God's wounds, if only Exeter had gone with us!" exploded Sir Humphrey but the others sat silent. It was only what they had all said a hundred times. John Wynslade sat at the table with them, his young son outside somewhere with the other men. John Payne from St Ives was present, but the other leaders had been unknown to Bart until the last few weeks.

Those present were Sir Thomas Pomeroy, John Bury, Robert Smyth – he had bravely led the charge with Bart at Fenny Bridges that day – Thomas Holmes and a man called Coffin, servants to Sir John Arundell who was out of the county at the time of the uprising. There were several other men elected as leaders of the campaign but they were somewhere outside amongst the company.

A boy came to Sir Humphrey Arundell with a message and Bart stared at the lad with his familiar freckled face, shock of fair hair and cheerful grin. The boy felt Bart's startled eyes upon him and looked up, his face lighting up when he saw his master.

"Hugh!" exclaimed Bart. "By God's Holy Name, what are you doing here?"

"You know the lad?" Sir Humphrey asked.

"I do indeed," began Bart. He was about to add that the boy was too young to be taking part in any campaign but Hugh was looking at him with pleading eyes and Bart hesitated.

"I will speak to you later," he told the boy and a relieved look flashed across Hugh's face. "Wait for me outside."

Bart had no idea when or how Hugh had joined the company but he was suddenly impatient to speak to him and hear news from Trewarne. Thoughts of his mother had been in his mind frequently, wondering anxiously how well she had taken Sir Geoffrey's death and he longed for news of Kristy.

* * *

The discussions between the leaders continued for a long time but at last Bart was able to leave the tent. Hugh was waiting as instructed and he was not alone. Guessing that the meeting inside would last for some time yet he had shot off in search of someone else and there standing grinning beside the boy was Digory.

They sat on the ground oblivious of the other six thousand noisy men encamped outside Exeter, Bart asking eager questions, still amazed at their presence there. They had joined the uprising the previous day, having ridden up through two counties almost devoid of men. They had searched for Bart and had discovered he was with the leaders but had been unable to speak to him until Hugh had been sent to the tent with a message that afternoon.

Lady Margaret was well. She had taken Sir Geoffrey's death sadly but quietly. Matthew Wychcombe had ridden ahead of the little group which escorted her husband's body back to Trewarne and had spoken to Lady Margaret for some time before the cart had trundled up to the front of the manor. Sir Geoffrey had been buried next day in the churchyard adjoining the parish church. The young priest who had always assisted Mister Douglas and looked after the parish in his absence had carried out the funeral service in the old tradition.

Kate and Kristy were well and they were all now staying with Rose and her husband, including Lady Margaret and Amy whose husband would soon be home from abroad. The manor was empty except for the cook and his wife who had replaced Thomas and Hannah many years ago and Alice, Digory's wife. They were looking after the manor until the family, including Bart, returned. In the meantime, Digory and Hugh had decided to follow the uprising.

"What about John Darnwell?" asked Bart. He had often wondered whether Rose's husband was somewhere in this great throng. Digory threw back his head, showing his broken, discoloured teeth as he roared with laughter.

"Measles!" he informed Bart cheerfully. "Poor man was preparin' ter leave when the childern came out in spots and danged if 'e didn' too. Kristy sed 'e was much worse than the little 'uns – ain't properly recovered yet. But there's summat else to tell yer, Master Bart. I saw a few more stragglers ridin' through the camp this mornin'. I b'aint be too close but I swear one man's back was very f'miliar. He was tall with a very dark ginger 'ead."

* * *

Richard warmly greeted Bart later and the two cousins talked for a long time under the dark starlit sky before settling down to sleep on the hard ground inside the tent.

"By Our Blessed Lady," groaned Richard, "how do you sleep on this solid earth!"

"Be thankful it is not raining," answered Bart. "At least your clothes are not wet with nowhere to dry them. It will do you good to live like one of the peasants for a while."

"I look forward to a soft bed again," sighed Sir Humphrey, blowing out the solitary candle. Sir Thomas Pomeroy was asleep already, snoring gently as he lay on his back.

"I would have joined you before," Richard said half-apologetically to Sir Humphrey in the darkness, "but we have only just finished the school term at Glasney. We have no replacement teacher and it would have been awkward for me to leave."

"Then you had better make sure you do not get yourself killed!" Sir Humphrey commented grimly. "I cannot promise anyone a safe return from this crusade. A few weeks ago, before we left Bodmin, I would have done so. Exeter's refusal to join us has been a bitter blow. God alone knows how the city has held out against us for so long."

It was a question being asked by many who were starving inside the gates.

* * *

Before the week was ended Lord Russell had received nearly four thousand more reinforcements for his army. They were footmen, infantrymen and gunners. Their weapons and ammunition had also arrived.

* * *

On Saturday, 3rd August, the king's army, hoping to avert early detection by avoiding the main road, advanced through Ottery St Mary towards the village of Clyst St Mary where the men of the western rising had made their camp. It was a slow journey for the foot soldiers who were hampered by wagons, guns and baggage in the narrow, muddy country lanes, and the twelve hundred mounted men who had gone ahead were eager to attack without waiting for the remainder of the army to catch up with them. The unsuspecting rebels were still guarding the main road. The vanguard of Lord Russell's men had a good chance of advancing further before their presence was detected, possibly even pushing on to Exeter.

Digory, with his wiry frame and speed of movement, had been ordered to join the number of scouts constantly watching the enemy and reporting their movements. The noise of thousands of mounted soldiers with their guttural foreign voices and heavy armour advancing along the twisted lanes could not remain unnoticed for long. Digory hastily climbed a tree to get a better view of the approaching army and check its size and progress. The leading horsemen were only a short distance away as he jumped down from the leafy branches and onto the back of his patiently waiting horse.

The hooves of the animal pounded along the narrow lane. Only a small group of rebels were stationed in the village but they would have to defend the bridge against the powerful army approaching until reinforcements could arrive. The king's men were much nearer to the bridge than the other men of the western rising. Digory urged his mount to breakneck speed as he raced for help from those he now knew were guarding the wrong position.

Alerted at last, Sir Humphrey ordered Digory back with an urgent message to the small force of rebels stationed in the village. It was imperative to hold the bridge to give additional help time to reach them. Hopelessly outnumbered, they were ordered to attack the royal army and prevent it making progress at all costs. Guided by Digory, they prepared to ambush the thousands of approaching soldiers.

For the first few moments Lord Russell's men were taken by surprise and their superior weapons were of little use in the narrow lane against the unexpected attack of bills and arrows. The courageous rebels fought fiercely but the army quickly rallied. Time after time the Cornish and Devon men hurled themselves against the enemy. Digory rolled in the mud between the rearing hooves of the terrified horses, struggling to force aside a heavy steel blade already dripping with blood which a large heavily armed man was steadily forcing down towards him. He could feel the man's breath upon his face and hear the guttural curses hurled down on him. Pinned down by the enemy's heavy bulk, Digory could do nothing but spit into the man's grinning face before the sharp steel pierced his wiry body and after one last contorted jerk of his limbs Digory fell back dying, only two days after joining the western rising.

* * *

It had been a bloody battle with hopeless odds against them and at last those rebels still remaining alive were forced to flee but they had not fought in vain. They had gained sufficient time for the rest of the rebel force, numbering about two thousand, to reach the village which they then promptly fortified ready for the next assault upon them.

It came next morning. Sometime after nine o'clock the king's army commenced the three mile march towards Clyst St Mary, taking up three battle positions. The men of the west were waiting for them behind a thick hedge but after bitter fighting they were forced back into the village itself. The king's men regrouped and prepared to follow up their attack but in the confusion Sir Thomas Pomeroy had been left behind with a drummer and a trumpeter and all three lay hidden amongst the furze. Sir Thomas waited until the army had passed him in the narrow lane and then ordered the drummer beat a loud tattoo and the trumpeter sound the charge.

Believing themselves about to be attacked from the rear the army panicked, collided with each other and made a chaotic retreat, abandoning weapons, armour, wagon train and anything else which would impede their flight. It was only when they reached their original position that they realised they had been victims of a trick and their own worst fears. The rebels were helping themselves to their discarded weapons, including the dreaded arquebuses though these proved useless in their untrained hands.

The elated rebels retreated into the village, each house being occupied and turned into a stronghold, and this time the army advanced more carefully, setting fire to every thatch until the whole village was ablaze. The defenders were forced out into the street where they were met by a hail of musket fire, the wounded lying where they had fallen and burnt alive.

* * *

Bart had fallen early in the struggle, his right leg hit by gun shot. His unconscious body was dragged desperately from a blazing cottage by Hugh, blood pouring from a wound on the boy's own fair head. The young lad had stayed by his master's side and fought fiercely throughout the battle. Bleeding and terrified he flung himself across Bart and feigned death as the king's army passed close by them in pursuit of the survivors.

The men of the western rising prepared to fall back across the river and a strong rearguard took up a position in the middle of the village to cover their withdrawal. In spite of their bravery the army overwhelmed them. One thousand rebels died that day and many more were taken prisoner but the majority of them were still alive and forming on the opposite bank of the river, determined to hold the bridge.

Lord Grey, in command of the king's army at that point, was determined to get his force across to a more suitable position where his men could make more use of their equipment and fight better on the open plain. Successful at last, the remaining rebels were forced to pull back to Exeter. Lord Grey pressed after them but stopped on top of a hill to survey the countryside behind him. Fear of further uprisings behind him was never far from his mind and he thought mistakenly that he could see in the distance a large army of reinforcements for the rebels marching to attack his army's rear. There was no time to check. The other rebels might return to the offensive at any time.

His own men were handicapped by the presence of hundreds of prisoners. Grimly he gave the order that each one should be slain and nine hundred men of Devon and Cornwall had their throats cut by the king's men guarding them.

* * *

Later that night a young boy, his own head throbbing from a painful gash, silently made his way across fields and under cover of the thick hedges back to the camp where the exhausted survivors were resting. A small group of uninjured men were sent back with Hugh to bring back his barely conscious master and any others they might find still alive.

* * *

Under Sir Humphrey Arundell the rebels made one last courageous attack. They were soon surrounded, the onslaught coming from all sides but they refused to yield and a desperate hand to hand struggle followed until few remained. Lord Grey himself grudgingly reported later that despite the greatness of the slaughter and the cruel fight, throughout all the wars in which he had ever fought on behalf of the king he had never seen such bravery as that shown by the men of the west that day.

* * *

Richard was one of those who died in the bitter battle. The boys of the school at Glasney had lost their much loved conscientious schoolteacher.

* * *

Thousands of reinforcements sent by the Protector were still streaming to join Lord Russell's army and with the loss of such a great number of their comrades and most of their weapons the men of the uprising felt themselves defeated. They had staked everything on what they still believed to be their righteous cause, convinced that God would help them in the defence of their faith and freedom to live their lives in His service as their forefathers had done but God had forsaken them. The roads to the west behind them were still open. Quietly, without anyone inside the walls of Exeter even noticing, the survivors abandoned camp and began to disperse back towards their homes.

The five week siege of Exeter was over. Lord Russell stayed in the relieved city for ten days 'rewarding the good and punishing the evil'. The lands of the ringleaders of the uprising were given to Sir Gawen and Sir Peter Carew amongst others as a reward for their services. Prisoners were handed over 'bodies, goods and lands' to be held for ransom by those who had served the king. Many were executed on the hastily erected gallows. The orders of the Protector – to instil such terror into the population that they would never rebel again – were grimly carried out. He also ordered that the remaining rebels should be followed by Lord Russell's troops and firmly crushed, their leaders publicly executed in different towns to spread the terror as widely as possible. They were to be used as an example which would prevent the common people from ever rising again.

* * *

"How many men have we?" Sir Humphrey asked his grim faced officers camped at Sampford Courtenay. Bart, heavily bandaged and white faced, struggled to sit upright in his seat amongst them.

"Perhaps two thousand, apart from the wounded."

There was silence in the tent, each with his own thoughts. Six thousand men had confidently marched out of Cornwall to be joined by three thousand men of Devon. They had all expected to be safely home by now, the successful march to London and back accomplished. Even the older men such as Sir Geoffrey Trewarne had not foreseen such terrible carnage.

"Russell's men?"

"They are still pouring in. Our information is probably about eight thousand."

Outnumbered four to one. Most of their weapons lost or abandoned in that last fiercesome fight.

"If we give up now we leave hundreds of prisoners in Russell's hands."

"He is as likely to murder them as soon as we attack. God's blood, he had no mercy on the others!"

"I say we should withdraw," Sir Thomas Pomeroy said suddenly. "We have no hope of victory now. We should have gone immediately the siege was over instead of setting up camp again here."

"If we give up now we are betraying all those who have died," argued Bart doggedly. He had lost more than many of them on this crusade. His father, Richard, Digory, several of the tinners – perhaps even more of the workers from Trewarne, he did not know. The men had gathered that morning in the open air for Holy Mass and Mister Douglas had not been amongst the priests present.

"Russell will follow us," John Wynslade stated. "He thinks we are beaten or he would not have delayed so long. Either we stand and fight again or we should disperse."

"As I see the situation, gentlemen," Sir Humphrey announced quietly after a pause, "we have three choices. We make a last desperate effort and win, we lose and die, we run and eventually hang."

"Not necessarily," Sir Thomas Pomeroy protested. "The peasants will probably receive a pardon, the rest of us have the possibility of escape across the sea. Russell thinks he has us firmly penned in down here in the south west but we are surrounded by water."

There was silence inside the tent whilst the others considered his remarks. John Wynslade spoke at last.

"I say we should ask the men."

"I agree with that," said John Payne from St Ives.

Sir Humphrey looked at the faces of the other men around the rough table, most of whom bore vivid evidence of battle. Bart was not the only one amongst the leaders obviously fighting pain and the dreaded possibility of collapse before the campaign was finally over. Sir Thomas looked as if he wanted to argue but finally he capitulated.

"I will speak to the men when we assemble for evening prayers," said Sir Humphrey, and most of the leaders rose, glad to go out of the hot stuffy tent into the cool air.

* * *

The men of Devon and Cornwall stood silently as their leader addressed them in a field one mile beyond the village of Sampford Courtenay. Many of their number had drifted away, disheartened after weeks of defeat, and those of the injured who could travel had been sent back to their homes. There were still a few women who stayed in an attempt to treat the casualties but there was little they could do for many of those who suffered.

The men listened to Sir Humphrey and to several others, priests and laymen, who spoke to them. It was to be their own decision. Prayers were said and the listeners given a short time to decide.

In spite of all they had endured they were willing to stand against the king's army again. They were fighting to defend their faith and surely by now God must be upon their side.

* * *

Sir Humphrey had a rough map before him on the table. The other leaders were bent over it with him, watching in the light of the flickering oil lamp as his finger pointed to various key points on the map and he outlined his plan.

"We shall divide into two forces – the men of one force to dig themselves well in here on this hill where we are encamped and can easily be seen, the remaining men to conceal themselves within the village. The ones left in camp will be the decoy – those in the ambush will be the better armed, under my own command. When Russell attacks he will come straight to the camp where his spies will have seen us making extensive preparation. Once his army is halfway up the hill, those of us hidden in the village will fall on him from the rear."

The others nodded agreement, some questions were asked and details finalised before those leading the campaign joined those outside in the falling darkness. At the far end of the field several priests were hearing the confessions of grave faced, weary but

235

determined men, many already wounded but determined to fight on, making their peace with God before the conflict next day.

* * *

Bart sent for Hugh and the boy stood in front of him, pale but waiting to follow his master's orders. Bart nodded to the ground beside him. He had been told earlier of the boy's actions to save his life and had spoken his thanks already.

"Sit down, Hugh. How is your head?"

"Painful!" answered Hugh ruefully, with a faint trace of his usual cheeky grin as he felt the gash amongst his fair hair.

"That will teach you to stay at home another time when you are ordered to do so." Bart's grey eyes twinkled in spite of the pain in his leg and arm where both musket ball and arrow had found their mark in the last few days. "I am going to give you orders now, Hugh, and this time you will give me your word that you will follow them."

Hugh's head jerked up warily, suspicious eyes searching Bart's face. Bart looked steadily at the lad, his expression stern.

"Tomorrow we go into battle one more time. If I am injured, Hugh, and you are not, I order you to leave me. You acted very bravely yesterday and I have told you already of my gratitude but I do not want you to put your life at risk for me again."

Hugh opened his mouth to protest but Bart firmly silenced him.

"If there is the slightest chance that you can escape I want you – order you – to return to Trewarne. It is important that some of those who have been here with us get back to tell the story of this campaign. So many lives have been tragically lost and they cannot now be forgotten. With God's help we shall yet win but if sadly we lose, you are more likely to be pardoned than many of the older men. Make your way home, Hugh, and tell everyone of our bitter struggle and the bravery of the Cornish and Devon men."

Bart struggled to stand and Hugh scrambled to his feet, his eyes full of indignant tears but also concern for his master.

"You surely will not go into battle again yourself, sir?" he asked anxiously, his eyes travelling over Bart's bloodsoaked bandages and stained torn clothes. "You can hardly walk."

Bart forced himself to laugh cheerfully and placed his hand on the boy's shoulder both for encouragement and for the support of his own unsteady body.

"I cannot walk, Hugh, but there is nothing wrong with my horse. I shall lead my men into battle again tomorrow. Who knows – we may yet succeed!"

He gestured to the boy to leave him and then abruptly called him back. Hugh waited, startled at the sadness which flickered momentarily in Bart's eyes.

"If I do not return with you," Bart spoke eventually in a quiet voice, "tell my Mother and Kristy how much I loved them."

He turned and limped heavily into the tent behind him, leaving Hugh weeping silently under the starlit sky.

* * *

It was a fierce battle in which they almost succeeded in their brave attempt but again the last surviving men under Sir Humphrey's command were overwhelmed by superior numbers and fighting power. Bloody ferocious struggles were waged all day until finally the men of the western rising fled, leaving behind six hundred dead, many injured and hundreds taken prisoner.

Sir Humphrey Arundell fled to Launceston where he was arrested, later taken to London and hanged, drawn and quartered.

* * *

John Wynslade and three of the other leaders shared the same fate. John Wynslade's young son was pardoned.

* * *

Sir Thomas Pomeroy escaped with his life by turning informer against other Catholic gentry who might be sympathetic to the rebels.

* * *

The Devonshire men with their leaders were followed to Tiverton and the Cornishmen followed across the moors to

Okehampton and Launceston where many were hanged and quartered on the spot.

* * *

Many were held prisoner in the hope that their relatives would pay a good ransom for them.

* * *

The property of all rebels was declared forfeit, to be handed over to whoever laid first claim to it. Charles Rawlaston, Sir Geoffrey's old enemy, swiftly claimed Trewarne.

* * *

The bells of the churches of Devon and Cornwall were ordered to be removed except for the smallest one on each church which would be allowed to be rung to call the people to divine service. The bells which had heralded the western rising would never be available for similar use again.

CHAPTER EIGHTEEN

BART REMEMBERED NOTHING after he had been struck and wounded again by an arrow shot by a Spanish mercenary as he fought furiously in the last battle at Sampford Courtenay. He had fallen heavily from his horse, almost trampled underfoot by the frightened animals around him as they reared in terror, crashing into each other in the fearful noise and commotion. A miracle had left him alive but unconscious, his body lying half hidden in a ditch at the side of the bloody field, to be found much later by soldiers of the victorious army. They were stopped from inflicting the final blow by one of their accompanying officers. Bart's heavily bloodstained clothes were of far superior quality to those on most of the bodies. There was no point in killing when a ransom might be obtained.

* * *

Some weeks later, weak from loss of blood and hardly able to walk with the pain of wounds which had not been treated, Bart was taken before Sir Peter Carew to be questioned closely on his part in the uprising. Bart's name had not appeared amongst any of the signatures on the documents sent to the king at the start of 'The Commotion', as it was now being called. It was up to the authorities to decide whether he should be classed as a leader and hanged or whether any money, always useful, might be bartered for his life.

* * *

As Bart awaited his fate in the filthy, evil-smelling prison at Exeter, crowded with other wretched prisoners, he had little hope that he would be released. All his own property and goods, together with that belonging to his late father, were forfeit to the Crown. Lady Margaret would have little hope of raising a ransom. Rose and her husband lived with their five children on a tutor's income, Amy's husband was not a rich man. Kristy, the one he loved most in all the world and had hoped to soon make his wife, had nothing.

* * *

He lay in the cramped, rat-infested dark dungeon awaiting daily the summons to execution. He could not regret taking part in the crusade in which so many thousands of men from Cornwall and Devon had died for they had all believed their cause to be a just one. They had put their loyalty to God before loyalty to the councillors of the eleven year old king. God for His own reasons had not granted them success but they had tried their utmost to defend their faith.

* * *

The young boy found lying unconscious in the narrow lane looked older than his fourteen years, an angry red scar across his freckled face and an arm badly injured by a pistol shot bearing silent evidence of a recent horrific ordeal. Hugh's escape from Sampford Courtenay had been followed by weeks of intense pain and hunger during which he had hidden by day and walked by night, sometimes in the company of other silent, defeated men, sometimes alone.

Sympathetic villagers, fearful of retribution if caught aiding the weary returning rebels, had occasionally given them food. It had finally proved too much for Hugh and his legs had given way beneath him as dawn was breaking one morning in mid-September when he knew he was almost within reach of safety. It was four weeks after the final defeat of the western rising.

By good fortune he was found by John Darnwell as the tutor rode out to instruct his pupils at a neighbouring property for the first time since his illness during the measles epidemic which had prevented him from joining the rebellion. Stunned by his recognition of Hugh, he quickly carried him home to Rose where the boy remained unconscious for several days, nursed by distraught members of the family. It was almost a week before Hugh recovered enough to answer their questions.

Little news of the crusade had filtered back to the south west corner of Cornwall. Only in the last few days as stragglers began to drift home, broken in body and spirit, had anything definite been heard and the population realised that the ill-fated rising, begun with such hope, was finally over and retribution quickly following.

* * *

Sir Anthony Kingston was appointed to complete the punishment and pacification of Cornwall. He proceeded to carry out his new duties with determination. He had already played out a little drama in Bodmin which amused him, at the end of which he had hanged the mayor for his part in the uprising. He rode into St Ives to repeat the macabre performance.

John Payne, Kate's brother, had returned from the unsuccessful march and begun to take up his duties as mayor again in the little fishing town. When a messenger rode in, informing the inhabitants that Sir Anthony Kingston would shortly be arriving and would be pleased to dine with the mayor and other prominent citizens, he greeted the news with relief and a little jubilation. No doubt those in authority had heard of the part he had played in the uprising but obviously he had been pardoned.

Convinced that the visit must be a friendly one to restore peaceful relations throughout the county, a lavish dinner was prepared in The George and Dragon in the market place for their important guest. John Payne with other prominent townsmen waited to welcome their visitor and after their greeting Sir Anthony took the mayor to one side.

"I have a task to perform whilst I am in St Ives," Sir Anthony told him confidentially. "You have a traitor amongst you whom I must execute. See that a gallows be erected outside while we eat."

"A traitor?" asked John Payne. "Who would that be, sir?"

"You will know later," Sir Anthony assured him. "Come, let us rejoin the others now at table and enjoy our meal."

Later that evening Sir Anthony asked John Payne if the gallows were ready and asked to be taken to them.

"Think you they be strong enough?" he asked.

"Yes, sir," replied John Payne, "that they are."

"Well then," said Sir Anthony, "get you up to them for they are provided for you."

John Payne looked at him aghast.

"I trust you mean no such thing to me," he answered nervously.

"Sir, there is no remedy," Sir Anthony Kingston replied grimly. "You have been a busy rebel and therefore this is appointed for your reward. Hang him!" he ordered his waiting men, and the stunned onlookers stood helpless and horrified as John Payne, portreeve of St Ives, was hanged in the market place for his part in the western rising.

* * *

Robert Trenwith and Phillipa had feared for weeks that Richard, their only son, was dead for there had been no message sent to those waiting anxiously at Penvedn. The arrival of Rose, accompanied by John Darnwell, confirmed their worst fears. Hugh had seen Richard killed during the bloody battle at Clyst St Mary before the massacre of the prisoners by the king's men.

Rose sat with her aunt for a long time after the news was broken to her before leaving Phillipa with her own daughters and returning to the library where Robert Trenwith sat staring out of the window with unseeing eyes, the warm sunlight of the autumn evening seeming to mock him in his misery. John Darnwell sat silently with him. Both men stirred as Rose entered the room, her face still pale and wet with the tears she had shed with Phillipa.

"We must not mourn," Robert spoke at last in an unsteady voice. "Richard died for something he believed in and is now with God. He would not wish us to weep for him. What news do you have of Bart?"

John Darnwell shook his head.

"We have none, sir. Hugh said he was alive when he saw him last but that is all he knows."

He hesitated for a moment and Rose spoke in the silence.

"We know you no longer share our beliefs, Uncle Robert, but we desperately need your help. You have far more influence than we have now. We beg you to help us find news of him. It is terrible for all of us not knowing if he is alive or dead."

"I know that, my dear," her uncle answered sadly. "We were sick with worry ourselves for news of Richard. God knows there must be thousands of other families waiting hopelessly. You are right, I do prefer the new teaching of our religion but I cannot find it in my heart to blame those who fought so hard for their right to keep the old faith. If I can help to find news of Bart and any others then I will." He paused for a moment. "How is your mother?"

"Fearful – as we all are. Anxious for news but afraid to hear it. Kristy is broken-hearted."

"Ah, yes. I have been away at sea for so long I had forgotten there was some talk that Bart would marry Kristy. Where is she now?"

"She is at Trewarne Manor, sir," John Darnwell answered. "We know it will be seized from the family but nothing has been done yet and she begged to go back there until it is finally taken. We tried to dissuade her but she was so desperate to return that Kate went with her. Hugh has gone to Trewarne too. He wanted to break the news of Digory's death to Alice, his aunt, himself. Apparently she has looked after Hugh since his own mother died."

"God help us all, what tragic times we live in," sighed Robert. "Most of the men of Cornwall will never come back and we all claim we are acting for love of God. We are taught one commandment which tells us to love our neighbour and we break another and kill him instead. And you, Rose? Will you now follow the new religion as those in London order you to do?"

"I have no choice," answered Rose miserably. "I have not the courage to fight against it any longer. So many have tried and died in vain." She paused, her brimming grey eyes moving from Robert to her husband, tears running down her pale cheeks. "I do not want to go to prison or die. I want to watch my children grow, see them marry, have children of their own. Is that so terrible? I would like to be brave and say I will never abandon the old faith, and I will not in my heart, but outwardly I shall obey the law. If that is cowardice I pray that God will always keep a corner in heaven for cowards like me."

Rose broke down, sobbing, and John Darnwell crossed quickly to her and held her tightly in his arms. When she had recovered they prepared to leave.

"I will do all I can to find news of Bart," her uncle promised as he bade them farewell outside Penvedn Manor.

Rose kissed him gratefully.

"I hope our families will not part," she answered. "That would hurt almost as much as losing my father and Richard."

Robert Trenwith could no longer trust himself to speak. He stepped back, lifting his hand in a gesture of farewell. He watched them ride away until the trees hid them from sight then returned slowly to the house to comfort his grieving wife.

* * *

Sir Peter Carew eyed the man in front of him with interest. It was a good many years since they had met for the grey-haired, well built man with an unmistakable air of authority standing impatiently before him now at Exeter had spent most of his life at sea. Robert Trenwith had served the king loyally for many years. He was not a man Sir Peter was eager to cross or even to keep waiting. He nodded to a soldier standing near the door who left the room, returning shortly afterwards with a prisoner.

Robert looked with horror at the filthy dishevelled figure pushed roughly into the room, his bloodstained clothes crawling with lice, his thick dark curly hair and beard matted, almost covering the white face. Only the sunken grey eyes which sparked with a sudden faint hope as they rested on Robert gave any indication that this weakly swaying body was that of Sir Geoffrey Trewarne's son.

"God's blood!" exclaimed his uncle, turning furiously to Sir Peter Carew. "Could you not at least have treated his wounds? How many more are kept like animals in the dungeon here until they die?"

Sir Peter shrugged.

"We have hundreds of wounded of our own to treat. We have neither time nor doctors to spare for enemies of the king."

"Obviously no food either," said Robert grimly, looking at the gaunt figure of Bart.

"They had no pity for the people of Exeter," Sir Peter answered coldly. "There are thousands of our soldiers still encamped here who must be fed apart from the townspeople. Your nephew made his own decision. He was lucky not to lose his life."

Robert Trenwith's face showed open anger and disgust as he glared back at Sir Peter. He flung the fat leather pouch which he had with him onto the table.

"You have your ransom," he said icily. "Now I presume I may take the prisoner."

Sir Peter did not answer until he had checked the contents of the pouch, then nodded slightly.

"You are responsible for his future loyalty to the king," he reminded his visitor and his face was expressionless as Robert Trenwith helped his stumbling nephew from the room.

* * *

Bart's legs buckled beneath his feeble body as his uncle supported him out into the cold October air. The area around the prison was quiet, the soldiers standing on guard ignoring the well-dressed man half carrying one of the hated rebels who looked as if he had received the punishment he so richly deserved. Robert's servants who had accompanied him from Penvedn saw their master and ran to help him with his burden.

"We must get out of the city – he will get little sympathy here," Robert ordered and they struggled to lift Bart's emaciated body on to the horse they had brought in the hope of finding him. His nephew was in far worse condition than Robert had expected but thanks to Almighty God he was alive. He would have been thankful to find his own son in that dreadful dungeon but Sir Peter Carew had confirmed that Richard was dead.

* * *

There were curious looks but no comment as the group rode through the streets and out of the city gate. Those who still secretly sympathised with the rebels felt hopeful that perhaps this one would survive, whilst those who were bitter against them knew that the gentleman riding amongst them must be considered by those in authority to be loyal to the king.

They rode for almost five miles before Robert ordered the men to stop and carry Bart to a nearby stream where his lice-infested clothes were stripped from him and his filthy body washed in the clear water. Robert looked with great concern at the infected wounds made by the arrows and musket shot. It was only by the grace of God the young man still survived. He had not spoken a word since he had been dragged before Sir Peter Carew some hours ago and he seemed hardly conscious as the men tried to dress him in the clothes Robert had brought with him without causing Bart more pain.

"He is far too weak to travel – we must find an inn," decided Robert. He wished now he had not always travelled by sea for he had little knowledge of the area, most of which had not yet recovered from the recent battles which had raged there. A few curious peasants looked at them as they walked along the nearby lane returning from Exeter where they had sold their provisions and Robert's head jerked up suddenly as he heard the trundle of an approaching cart. His servants stopped the frightened driver as he drew near, his fears subsiding as he realised that he was not being robbed, and Bart was lifted carefully on to the straw in the back of the cart before it moved slowly on followed by Robert and the other two men. The driver took them to a small inn two miles distant where he was paid well for his services before departing.

* * *

Robert was anxious to move on for his ship was due to sail again shortly from Penryn. Bart was very weak but food and four days of rest, together with treatment for his wounds, had made a difference to him already. The knowledge that he was free and being taken back to Cornwall, to Kristy and his family was a greater spur to his recovery but Robert knew it could be some weeks before his nephew would be fit to make the eighty mile journey. Bart would have to be left in the sympathetic care of the innkeeper and his kindly wife, one of Robert's own servants remaining with him.

Bart opened his eyes as his uncle came into the room to say goodbye. Robert sat on the edge of the bed and regarded the young man's gradually improving appearance with relief and satisfaction. The hair and beard were now tidy, the handsome face had lost a little of its gauntness and the dark shadows had faded slightly from beneath the grey eyes. Bart's likeness to his father was returning again, jolting Robert with a vivid reminder of a young Sir Geoffrey in happier days, owner of Trewarne Manor which meant so much to him, devoted to his family and much loved by all who loyally served him on his large estate which would now be taken from his son.

He became conscious that Bart was watching him with a puzzled expression in his eyes as if he recognised that a struggle of which he was not yet aware was taking place inside his uncle's head. He shook himself and brought his mind back to the present.

"I am ready to leave," he informed Bart, "but you will be well looked after. Stay here until you feel fit to travel. I will send a message to your family as soon as I arrive to let them know that you are safe."

Bart nodded gratefully. He had spoken little to anyone since his release for he had been too ill and exhausted but now he could not let his uncle leave without expressing to him his gratitude for all that he had done. Robert listened as Bart thanked him but he had only done what he knew Sir Geoffrey would have done for Richard had their roles been reversed. He was not sure whether Bart realised he would have to forfeit all his inheritance at Trewarne to the Crown but Bart only gave a wry smile.

"I am alive and that is the important thing," he answered his uncle. "I can earn a living somehow – perhaps I will even build houses after all, which is what I always longed to do. I shall earn enough to support my mother, Kate and Kristy. The other servants are strong and will probably find work."

Robert hesitated, his eyes fixed on his nephew's exhausted face but there was still something troubling him which Bart would have to know.

"Charles Rawlaston claimed Trewarne," Robert told him gravely and regretted his words when he saw the stunned look in Bart's pained eyes. "He did not succeed," he added hastily, "but someone else with a stronger claim had to stop him. I claimed it, Bart."

Bart looked at his uncle in astonishment and Robert continued to explain.

"If I had not, Rawlaston would have gained Trewarne. He made the first claim and as a loyal supporter of the king he had the right to do so. Only someone who had served the Crown much longer could stop him and fortunately I have done so. I thought your father – and you – would understand my motives."

"I do and I am grateful, as he would be," answered Bart fervently, gripping the other man's hand.

A look of great relief crossed Robert Trenwith's face. He had not enjoyed claiming Trewarne Manor which had meant so much to the family living there but the news that an old enemy of Sir Geoffrey had done so had forced him to act.

"You may live there," he told Bart now, gazing steadily at his nephew's incredulous face. "I cannot give Trewarne back to you – I would not be allowed to do so – but otherwise I can do as I wish with it and it will need to be cared for and the land worked as it was before. I leave it in your safekeeping, Bart. Perhaps one day it will return to your children."

He rose to leave and Bart struggled to sit up but he was still too weak and had to lean back against the hard pillow.

"I shall never be able to thank you for all you and Aunt Phillipa have done for us," he told his uncle huskily. "I had no hope of ever again living at Trewarne. I only wish these last terrible months had never happened and all those who died were with us again now."

"It should never have happened," Robert agreed sadly. "Men should be allowed to follow their own path to God without persecution from either side. We have reached a divided way but I pray that we will eventually come to respect one another's views and the right of every man to follow his own conscience. Goodbye, Bart. I hope we shall all meet together again one day either at Penvedn or Trewarne."

"Goodbye, sir," answered Bart, "and again, I thank you."

Robert Trenwith acknowledged his nephew's gratitude with a slight nod of his head and left on the next stage of his journey to Penvedn. He would have little time with his own family before he went to sea once more.

* * *

Bart stayed at the inn for another ten days, impatient with his weak body and the wounds which would not allow him to commence the long ride along rough lanes to the south western tip of Cornwall. He longed to be on his way back home to Kristy and Lady Margaret. With little to do but wait, agonising thoughts of the friends and comrades lost in the past desperate months crowded into his head, their faces blurring into each other until he felt he could bear the terrible memories no longer. It was a relief to be finally declared fit to travel by the landlord and his wife who had obeyed his uncle's instructions to care for the young man faithfully.

He was exhausted, travelling less than fifteen miles each day, frustrated every time he and his companion were forced by Bart's weakness to stay at another inn. Bodmin Moor was shrouded with thick fog for several days, delaying them further, but in late October, Bart found his spirits rising as they rode along the narrow lanes towards Trewarne, the sun shining in a clear blue sky and shafts of sunlight sparkling between rustling golden leaves still dancing on the trees.

The tower of the parish church came into view as they rounded a slight bend. The young priest who had assisted Mister Douglas stared for a moment at the travellers riding towards him before breaking into an eager run across the grass to greet them. Several of the old people from the almshouses looked at Bart in disbelief and he stopped to speak to each one of them before riding the last two miles of the lane which led to the manor.

Kate was crossing the courtyard, her hair under its kerchief much greyer than when the marchers had left Trewarne, but her face lit up as she recognised Bart and her cries of welcome brought Lady Margaret running out to greet her son tearfully as he clasped her with his good arm, carefully avoiding his wounded side. The lines on her still beautiful face had grown a little deeper, her eyes sadder, but she was smiling now, laughing at Bart's eagerness as his eyes searched the courtyard for Kristy while he tried to answer all their greetings and questions. Hugh's freckled face with its still angry looking scar glowed with delight, Alice and the other servants beamed behind him but the most important person was missing and Bart could bear it no longer.

"She said you would know where to find her if she was not here when you arrived," Lady Margaret teased him gently and Bart quickly kissed his mother and Kate before climbing into the saddle again and spurring his horse past the stables, over the wall and onto the open moor beyond. He forgot the pain from his wounds as the mare cantered past the woods, splashing through streams and skirting the large boulders until Bart could see the sparkling green of the sea ahead of him. He guided the animal along the cliff top for some distance before leaving her to graze amongst the bracken whilst he made his way down to the little cove where Kristy sat alone throwing pebbles into the thundering sea.

She turned as a stone clattered down the path under Bart's hurrying feet, hesitating only for a second before her startled expression changed to one of sheer happiness and delight. With a little cry Kristy sprang down from the rock, racing with bare feet across the firm sand towards him, the breeze blowing her soft dark curly hair around her. Bart hurried towards her, bracing himself as she hurtled into his arms, covering her glowing face with kisses as he held her tightly and they clung to each other on the lonely Cornish beach.

* * *

Later as they rode home, Kristy nestling against Bart while the horse picked her way carefully over the moors back to Trewarne, they stopped and dismounted to look down at the beautiful green valley in the fold of the hills where the lonely women worked the land helped by those who had been too young or too old to leave the manor with Sir Geoffrey and Bart four months ago.

"God willing, we shall own all this again one day," vowed Bart, "just as my father and grandfather owned it. We can never forget the past but those of us who are left will begin to raise families and life will come back again to us at the manor and those who work the land. It will take many years but this corner of England will flourish again. It must do for the sake of the thousands of men who died."

Kristy was silent and Bart turned her face towards him, his heart overflowing with love as he looked into her beautiful dark eyes.

"Marry me, Kristy. Marry me soon so that we can recover from this nightmare and begin to live our lives again. I have nothing to offer you now except my heart which loves you and my hands which will work for you until I have a home of our own to offer you once more."

Kristy kissed him tenderly, smiling as he held her closely to him.

"I would rather marry you as you are than marry the rich heir to Trewarne," she answered truthfully. "Now you are like me, you own nothing, but we have each other. That is all that we shall ever need."

The mare became impatient waiting for them and began to amble slowly back across the open moor along the rough track which led down to Trewarne. They did not notice until she was almost out of sight, then laughing together, Bart took Kristy's hand and helped her over the stream. No one could say what the unknown years ahead would bring but for the moment they had love and they had each other. They were content.

HISTORIC NOTE

PENRYN WAS FOUNDED in 1216 by the Bishop of Exeter and in 1265 the Glasney College was built to develop the Church's interest in the far West. It was built at the head of the Penryn river, but after the dissolution of the monasteries by Henry VIII, Glasney was finished and in 1548 Edward VI demolished the building completely. Penryn received its Royal Charter in 1621 in a bid to cure the town of its piracy.

The museum is situated in the middle of the town, under the Town Hall, and is packed with curiosities from throughout the ages, including various bricks and fitted blocks that came from the College. There are two of the old fire tenders from the town, and various pictures of the crews that used them.

In 2014 the museum was very proud to be able to earn its accreditation because of all the hard work from behind the scenes. The museum is free to enter and is open every weekday from 10:00 – 15:30. There is always a very helpful volunteer on hand to greet you.